WE ALL KEEP SECRETS

BOOKS BY SHERYL BROWNE

The Babysitter

The Affair

The Second Wife

The Marriage Trap

The Perfect Sister

The New Girlfriend

Trust Me

My Husband's Girlfriend

The Liar's Child

The Invite

Do I Really Know You?

Her First Child

My Husband's House

WE ALL KEEP SECRETS

SHERYL BROWNE

bookouture

Published by Bookouture in 2023

An imprint of Storyfire Ltd.
Carmelite House
50 Victoria Embankment
London EC4Y 0DZ

www.bookouture.com

Copyright © Sheryl Browne, 2023

Sheryl Browne has asserted her right to be identified as the author of this work.

All rights reserved. No part of this publication may be reproduced, stored in any retrieval system, or transmitted, in any form or by any means, electronic, mechanical, photocopying, recording or otherwise, without the prior written permission of the publishers.

ISBN: 978-1-83790-497-6
eBook ISBN: 978-1-83790-496-9

This book is a work of fiction. Names, characters, businesses, organizations, places and events other than those clearly in the public domain, are either the product of the author's imagination or are used fictitiously. Any resemblance to actual persons, living or dead, events or locales is entirely coincidental.

To my readers, for taking a chance on my first ever book and for your continued support. We write because we are passionate souls. We continue to write because of your passion for reading. Thank you.

First appearance deceives many.

> PHAEDRUS

PROLOGUE

The word *guilty* hits me like a punch to my stomach and I feel myself reel. This isn't supposed to happen. My lawyer said they would either have to convict me of murder or acquit me. He was confident they couldn't return a guilty verdict; that there wasn't enough evidence. My chest constricts painfully. 'I didn't do this.' Bile burns the back of my throat and I choke the words out. Papers are being shuffled, gazes cast down, as if business is over. They're going to take me back down to the cells. My life is over. I would rather it was over than be considered capable of this. Reality hits me as the officers flanking me close claustrophobically in on me. 'This is wrong,' I protest shakily. No one is listening. 'You've got it *wrong*.' My gaze swivels feverishly to the people who've condemned me. Some glance away. Some look uncomfortable. Some shoot daggers of pure hatred right through me.

I don't understand. What just happened? A lurch of terror clutches my insides and I look desperately at the man who assured me I would walk away. His face ashen, he averts his eyes, and hope dies inside me. *Tell them.* I gulp back the stone clogging my throat. He has to do something. The judge accepted the verdict but I don't believe they proved it was me. They don't *know*. Anything. At first they said she'd died of asphyxia due to an asthma attack. Then they said her airways hadn't been narrowed or inflamed and concluded it was a subdural haematoma that had caused an underlying injury and pressure on the brain. The prosecution said the bleed had been caused by her being violently shaken. The forensic neuropathologist said he didn't believe that she could have died from violent shaking. He said there was no spinal cord or neck damage, no bruising to her back or ribs to show she'd been grabbed. In his opinion, her brain injury could have been sustained by a blow to the head, but that could have occurred weeks before. The key word was *could*. They hadn't *known*. It was the testimony of the person I'd trusted most in the world that had condemned me. He'd said he *saw* me bang her head on the side of her cot. How could he have? How could he have done that, given evidence against me as if I meant nothing to him? He knows me, knows that I could never be capable of such an atrocity.

They asked me if I had shaken her. I had to tell the truth, but surely, I reasoned, they would see that it had happened instinctively. 'She'd been crying,' I told them. 'And then she went quiet. I was scared for her. She wasn't moving.' I looked desperately around for understanding and found none. 'I wasn't sure she was even *breathing*. I shook her to try to wake her. She was in my *arms*,' I added quickly as the jurors all breathed in sharply as one. 'Her head was in the crook of my arm. I was trying to *help* her.' My attempts to make them see fell on deaf ears. I even demonstrated how I'd held her that one time I had shaken her, glancing down at the ghost of her nestled close to me. As I looked up to see appalled faces, I knew that the jury was becoming hostile, a term my lawyer had used. I wish I hadn't gone to the nursery so incensed. Wish to God I hadn't drunk so much wine. The jury knew I had. Witness testimony confirmed I had. Soon the police were digging into my history, unearthing my past, my secrets and my lies. I had lied – I'd had no choice. I didn't lie about this, though. *I didn't.*

ONE

SIX MONTHS EARLIER

Ellie

I get the distinct feeling Kat isn't listening as I vent about my broken storage heater. I look up from the computer peripherals we're cataloguing to see her practically drooling. Following her gaze across the shop floor, I guess why. Obscenely good-looking and with just enough beard to exude sheer masculinity, Jake Harington is the stuff fantasies are made of. Well, Kat's anyway. By all accounts he's also charming and affable, making sure to talk to his employees rather than down to them. Not that he's ever spoken to me. The store manager hired me and, having secrets I'd rather stay secret, I've made sure to keep a low profile since I started.

'You're staring.' I give her a nudge.

'Can you blame me?' She fans her face. 'I tell you what, I would with him any time.'

I roll my eyes. 'He's married,' I remind her.

'I know.' She sighs longingly. 'Such a waste when he could have me. Oh crap, he's coming over.' She wets her lips with her tongue and flicks out her hair as our boss strolls in our direction.

'Morning, Kat. How's things?' He smiles and looks her over. He has nice eyes, I notice, striking pale blue, incongruous with his dark hair, and quite mesmerising.

'Good.' Kat nods enthusiastically. 'We're stock-checking. Keyboards and joysticks and, um...'

'Peripherals.' I rescue her as her face reddens considerably.

'Ah. All in order?' he asks, his amused gaze flicking to me and then back to Kat.

'Yes, seems to be. Everything accounted for.' She beams him a smile.

'Excellent.' He nods approvingly. 'Well done, Kat. Keep up the good work.' She almost melts at the compliment. I note the soft cadence of his voice and I have to admit I can see why she would go weak at the knees.

His gaze comes back to me, his eyes straying to my name tag, and I immediately feel my own cheeks heating up. 'Hi, Ellie. We haven't had a chance to meet properly yet, have we? I'm Jake. Lovely to finally make your acquaintance.'

Holding my gaze, he extends his hand, and I feel suddenly ridiculously tongue-tied. 'Likewise,' I manage.

He holds on to my hand for a moment. 'Paul tells me you're doing well,' he says, scanning my eyes. Feeling suddenly exposed somehow, I resist an urge to look away. 'I assume you have previous experience in computer retail?' he asks.

I shake my head and manage to articulate the word 'No.' *Get a grip, Ellie.* 'I worked in childcare previously,' I supply, 'but I saw the advert and fancied a change, so...'

'Here you are,' he finishes. I note the smile playing at his mouth and try to relax. It's just conversation. He's not going to think I'm much of an asset to his company if I can't even communicate. 'I hope you're enjoying working here, Ellie. Any problems, my door's always open,' he adds, finally releasing my sweaty palm.

'Right.' I nod, and cough, and then almost die as my phone

rings on the shop counter. My gaze skitters to the screen and I see it's my landlord, an obnoxious money-grabbing slob who rarely rings back. I know I have to take it. 'Sorry,' I mumble, snatching the phone up and heading quickly to the back of the shop.

After a frustrating call – my landlord assuring me that the storage heater has been serviced and that I would be liable for any repair costs, which I've no hope of meeting – I go back to the desk.

'He's married,' Kat says with a smirk as I join her. Clearly she noted how flustered I was when Jake spoke to me.

'Ha ha,' I reply drily.

'He is a bit gorgeous, though, isn't he?' She emits another expansive sigh.

'Can't say I noticed.' I shrug indifferently and fix my attention on my PC.

'Right.' Kat laughs. 'He's just rung through. He wants to see you,' she says, nodding towards the office.

Hell. What for? Nerves knot my stomach. He's probably about to reprimand me for taking calls at work. I can't afford to mess up and lose the first proper job I've had in years.

A minute later, my breakfast dangerously close to making a reappearance, I tap on his open door, then force myself through it as he looks up from his phone and gestures me in.

'One sec,' he mouths, holding up a hand and going back to his call. 'I said I'll sort it, Megan.' Closing his eyes, he kneads his forehead with his free hand. 'Not yet, no, but—' He stops. Whoever this Megan is, she's talking over him, and from the volume of her voice and his weary expression, I guess she's giving him grief. 'I will. I've said I will.' He glances at me apologetically. 'Look, I have someone here. I'm going to have to call you back.'

'Sorry,' I blurt as he places his phone on the desk and stares at it mutely. 'About taking personal calls,' I hurry on. 'It won't happen again.'

He looks up confusedly. 'Ah, right,' he says. 'It was urgent, I take it?'

'My landlord,' I explain. 'My storage heater's packed up. I didn't think he'd call back and I certainly didn't think he would get it fixed. I was right about the latter.' I shrug disconsolately.

'Sounds like a prick,' he sympathises.

My mouth twitches into a surprised smile. 'He is.'

'Where do you live?' He stands to walk around the desk, perching himself on the edge of it.

'Solihull,' I provide. 'The not quite so good side. A bedsit. Well, more a shoebox, with a stunning view of the dustbin area and mildew decorating the walls. I told my landlord about that too. He told me it was rented as seen.'

He shakes his head. 'Definitely a prick. I'd tell him where to stuff his shoebox if I were you.'

'I'd like to.' I sigh. 'I don't have anywhere else to go, though.'

He nods and twists to pick up a file from his desk. 'You've been here for about six months now, haven't you?' he asks, flicking through it.

'About that.' I chew the inside of my lip, wondering where this is leading. I haven't coughed up to the fact that I was out of work for two and a half years before that, taking cash-in-hand cleaning or babysitting jobs wherever I could.

He nods again thoughtfully. 'I've been looking at your work experience,' he announces, and my stomach turns over. He's obviously wondering about my qualifications, since I admitted to having none. He will also have discovered I didn't provide a previous employer reference. If he ever speaks to my old boss, he'll fire me for sure.

'I see you were employed at a nursery.' He eyes me searchingly.

'That's right,' I manage past the hard lump in my throat. I'm positive now he's going to ask what I've been doing since and where my references are. If I end up losing this job, I'll be homeless. With my history, there's no way I'll easily secure another position.

'Sorry, I'm keeping you.' He smiles, his expression preoccupied. 'I should let you get back to work. I just wondered...' He hesitates, glances down and then back to me. 'I need to ask you something.'

My stomach plummets to the pit of my belly.

'Please don't feel you have to say yes because I'm your boss. And obviously if you already have plans for tonight, it's not a problem.'

Now I'm mystified. He's not about to ask me on a clandestine date, unless he's into inarticulate plain Janes.

'I need a babysitter urgently,' he says finally. 'My wife and I have managed to double-book. She has an important client meeting this evening. Unfortunately, I do too. One of my biggest clients, actually. We have a six-year-old boy and a three-month-old baby and our au pair took off to work abroad. Her timing was abysmal. Megan, my wife, was pregnant, still working, and also trying to make sure the building works to our house were completed. Needless to say, life was stressful enough without the woman we were relying on for childcare leaving us in the lurch. Ollie, my little boy, was quite attached to her, which makes the whole situation worse.'

My heart falters as my mind shoots to my brother. I see his eyes, flecked with fear and uncertainty yet full of trust for me, his big sister, and for a second it feels as if the walls of the office are closing in on me. I take a breath. Try to shut it down. 'That's awful.' Finding my voice, I offer Jake a sympathetic smile. 'I can't believe she was so unprofessional.'

'Me neither,' he says with a heavy sigh. 'Megan thinks I should cancel my meeting – she reckons her appointment was first in the diary. If I do, I'm stuffed. The guy's only over from the States for a few days. But if I don't, she loses a potential client and I'm in the doghouse for the foreseeable.' He pauses, his expression one of quiet desperation. 'I'll pay you generously, obviously, as it's short notice. What do you think?'

I think I could kiss him. This means I can fix my heater. 'Consider me hired.' I smile, delighted. 'I'm happy to help out and I could certainly use the money. Thanks, Mr Harington.'

'Jake.' He smiles. 'And thank *you*, Ellie. I don't fancy another night in the doghouse. It gets a bit draughty in there.'

He has a nice smile. Genuine. 'No problem,' I assure him. 'I'd better get back.' I indicate the shop floor. 'I've left Kat on her own.'

'Great. I'll come and find you later.' He nods to me. 'Oh, Ellie.' He stops me as I turn for the door. 'Sorry, I'm assuming you have, but I should check anyway. You do have childcare qualifications, don't you?'

I freeze. 'Yes,' I assure him, a swarm of frantic butterflies taking off in my tummy. 'If you work in early education, they're very strict about that nowadays.'

'Perfect.' He looks relieved. 'Just out of interest, why did you leave the nursery?'

'I, um...' As the floodgates to my past inch further open and the memories come crashing in, I flail around for an answer. 'It closed,' I lie.

TWO

I'm like a nervous teenager, dithering about my outfit as I wait for Jake to pick me up. I don't want to be wearing anything that shouts *look at me* when I meet his wife, and anything too casual is obviously out. I want something neutral yet professional, but also practical. After diving through my wardrobe and coming up with nothing, I decide I'll just stay in my black work trousers and flat black shoes teamed with a white shirt instead of my red work shirt. It looks safe, nanny-ish.

Surveying myself in the mirror, I realise my hair is oily. *Damn.* The last thing I want is for her to think I don't have good hygiene habits. I check my watch and realise I haven't got time to wash it. Deciding I should wear it up, I pile it on top of my head, then look frantically around for my hair clip. Finally, straggly bits secured with grips, I'm reasonably satisfied. It makes me look mature even if it doesn't do much else for me.

Blowing out a breath, I take a look around, then hurry over to the laundry basket to stuff a dangling bra inside. I can't believe I actually agreed to Jake coming here. Why didn't I tell him the parking was bad and that I would meet him on the main road? I take in the black patches on the walls and ceiling, the mould around the window, the view outside of overspilling wheelie bins, and realise it looks utterly depressing. *Keep calm.* I try to quash the anxiety gnawing away at me. He'll need to ring the intercom at the gate at the top of the entry. I'll just meet him there.

I'm grabbing my bag from the bed when a knock on the front door catapults my heart into my mouth. I know it's him. Apart from my boyfriend, Zach, I rarely have visitors. Smoothing my clothes down, I hurry to the front door and pull it open.

'Hi.' Jake sweeps his eyes over me and smiles, and the knot in my stomach unravels a little. Then tightens again as he glances beyond me to the grim interior. 'Christ, it really is a dump, isn't it?' he observes, a deep furrow in his brow. 'We'll have to see if we can organise you a promotion,' he adds, swinging around back to the entry.

'Promotion?' I bang my front door to and hurry after him. 'But what about Kat?' I ask, slipping out behind him as he holds the gate for me. 'She's been at PCs Plus Peripherals way longer than I have.' The only position available is floor manager, and I can't consider that knowing that Kat's about to apply for it.

'Good point,' he concedes thoughtfully as we approach the passenger door of his sporty-looking BMW 8.

'Impressive,' I comment, not sure if I'm referring to the car or him gallantly opening the door for me. Do men still do that sort of thing?

'Glad you approve.' He smiles as I climb in. 'We'll have to think of another way to make sure you can get your storage heaters fixed,' he says, closing the door and going to the driver's side.

'One. Singular,' I correct him.

He shakes his head in despair and starts the engine. 'How the hell do these people get away with it?'

'There's not a lot I can do, and my landlord knows it,' I sigh.

'So what does your wife do?' I ask as we set off, hoping for some common ground between us.

'She has her own business,' he says. 'Serenity Interiors, providing a professional and prompt service dressing homes.'

Oh. 'That's brilliant,' I enthuse, but my heart sinks. We have about as much in common as I would with Kate Middleton. An actual home to dress, for one. Did I detect a little tightness in his tone there, though? 'It must be difficult with both of you running your own business,' I venture.

'It is a juggling act,' he admits. 'We have the odd run-in, as you'll have gathered.'

'I'm not surprised with a new baby in the mix.' Thinking that she must be Superwoman, I'm growing more apprehensive by the second. What's more, a woman who runs her own business will have an eye for detail. *My* details. I'm beginning to regret snapping up Jake's offer. I'm imagining her to be super-organised, sharply intelligent, artistic. Also beautiful, which she's bound to be if she's with someone like Jake. I'll certainly present no competition in her eyes. I suppose that will be one thing in my favour.

'On which subject, I have an idea about how we can bring you in a little more income.' He glances at me. 'It depends on how it goes tonight and whether you're up for it, but...' I wait, curious. 'We're going to need a babysitter on a regular basis,' he goes on. 'Someone reliable and trustworthy.'

I'm uncertain how to answer. He's obviously told his wife about me, but I imagine she'll have something to say if he's hiring me before she's even met me.

'I'll make it worth your while financially.' He glances at me hopefully. 'My children are the most important thing in my life, so money's not an issue. Making sure we get the right person is, obviously. So what do you think?'

I hear the hint of desperation in his voice and feel quite sorry for him. 'I think it might be best if I meet your wife and children first,' I suggest. I can't quite comprehend that he seems to like me, that he thinks I'm trustworthy. I don't often feel great about myself, but I do right now.

'Probably a good idea,' he agrees with a wry smile. 'We're here.' He nods towards my window.

I turn to follow his gaze and my eyes almost pop out. It's a glass house. From the pinnacle of its sloping rooftop right down to the ground, the front appears to be made of floor-to-ceiling shimmering glass. It completely takes my breath away.

'Do you like it?'

'*Wow!* It must be worth a bomb.' The words are out of my mouth before I have a chance to engage my brain.

He laughs. 'I hope so. The initial outlay was costly, but with Megan providing the design and overseeing the planning and building works, we managed to keep the price reasonable.'

Reasonable? They must have sunk a small fortune into it. I gaze at the chrome four-tier cascading water feature in front of the house, the lush greenery of the surrounding foliage reflected in its windows, and guess that Jake Harington must be a very wealthy man. And his wife is clearly extremely talented. I can't quite get my head around how she managed to accomplish such a feat while carrying a baby *and* having a little boy to care for. She must be a multitasker extraordinaire. But then she has Jake's support, I suppose. She's a lucky woman being married to someone who nurtures her talent. I recall with a sinking feeling how Zach rolled his eyes when, just before I got the job at PCs Plus, I told him I was thinking about going back to uni as a mature student. 'We're supposed to be saving to get a place of our own, babe,' he moaned. 'We can't do that if you're not working, and building up a student debt into the bargain.' As if we could save anyway with me paying extortionate rent on a dump and him spending all his spare cash out drinking with his mates or on the latest games console. I can't help feeling the tiniest bit jealous of Megan Harington.

'Shall we?' Jake cuts through my thoughts.

'Oh. Right, yes.' Realising we've parked, I fumble to release my seat belt, my stomach churning like a washing machine at the thought of meeting her.

'Just one thing.' He stops me as I reach for the door handle. 'I'm going to tell her you've been working for me for a year or so. Do you think you could back me up?' He clearly notices my confused expression. 'She's likely to be a bit wary if I tell her you've only been at PCs Plus for a few months. She's bound to ask if I've run a background check and... Well, I thought it would save any hassle.'

My anxiety ratchets up to a whole new level as I consider that he might actually do a background check, and I realise I'm going to have to play this very carefully. 'No problem,' I assure him. 'They did a Disclosure and Barring Service check at the nursery, obviously, but it's probably a good idea if she thinks you've done one too. It will stop her worrying, which she's bound to otherwise. That's only natural.'

'Great. Thanks for being so understanding, Ellie.' He smiles, looking hugely relieved, and climbs out of the car.

Approaching the front door a minute later, I take a fortifying breath and try to still my nerves.

Jake glances behind him as he opens it. 'She's seeing a new client, so she might be a bit stressed, but don't worry, she doesn't bite. Well, not people she hasn't met anyway,' he jokes.

It's an attempt to reassure me, I assume. It doesn't. About to step over the threshold of a house I couldn't even aspire to in my dreams, I don't feel very reassured at all.

THREE

Following Jake inside, I gaze around in awe. The inside is Instagram perfect: open-plan with black and white polished marble furnishings and high vaulted ceilings. The hall is huge. My bedsit would fit into it four times at least.

'Meg?' Seeing no signs of life, Jake calls out to his wife. 'She might be putting Fern down. Do you want to hang on here, Ellie, and I'll go and—'

'Up here,' a woman's voice shouts back. 'You're cutting it fine, Jake.'

Hearing the agitation in her tone, I glance at Jake, who smiles awkwardly. 'I'll just...' He nods towards the stairs. 'Won't be a sec.'

He skirts around a circular marble table, atop which sits a gorgeous white rose and lily flower display, the sort you might see at a church wedding, then heads up the grand central staircase, also marble. A combination of nerves and nausea churns inside me as I watch him walk along the landing. The balustrades are see-through glass, I note, as are the walls of the hall, beyond which I spy huge soft-grey plush sofas and strategically placed colour-keyed sculptures. Tasteful abstract canvases adorn the walls that aren't made of glass. The place is beautiful, palatial. The sort of house a celebrity might live in. In my supermarket-brand clothes, I suddenly feel gauche and out of place.

As I wait, I try not to eavesdrop, but I can't avoid overhearing. Jake's talking to his son, I gather. 'Hey, little man, how are you doing?' he asks him. 'Did you have a good day at school?'

'Uh-huh. I have a best friend. His name's Ezra,' Ollie replies. Noting that he sounds not quite as exuberant as I imagine he should, a prickle of apprehension runs through me.

'A best friend? Well, that's good, isn't it? Why so glum?' Jake sounds concerned.

Ollie hesitates. 'He's invited me to tea tomorrow, but Mummy says I can't go.' His voice is small, cautious, and my radar goes on red alert. It's probably just me. My little brother is always with me: his insecurity, his caution as he tried hopelessly to negotiate our parents' moods.

'I didn't say you couldn't go, Ollie,' Megan intervenes. 'I said Mummy has an online meeting and that you could go if Daddy picks you up, didn't I?'

Ollie is silent for a moment. Then, 'Can you, Daddy?' he asks uncertainly.

'I, er… I think I can swing it, yes,' Jake responds, and I guess he's going to have to move his schedule around. But that's fair enough, isn't it? His wife shouldn't take the brunt of the parenting.

'You won't make a promise and then let him down, though, Jake, *will* you?' Megan retorts pointedly. 'Come on, Ollie. Into bed.' She addresses her son brusquely, without allowing Jake time to answer. 'Mummy has an appointment. Remember? I told you.'

I hear her footsteps clacking along above me – I assume she's shepherding him to his room – and I can't help thinking she's a prickly cow.

A minute later, I hear her walk back again, and a door overhead closing. I can hear Jake's muted voice but I can't make out what he's saying. Megan, though, I do hear, loud and clear. 'For God's *sake*, Jake! Why are you doing this?'

She marches a few steps and I take a step back towards the front door as the door above is yanked open again.

'Doing *what*?' Jake asks. 'I'm trying my best here, Megan,' he says defensively. 'I've organised a babysitter. She's—'

'A *babysitter*? Are you out of your mind?' She's clearly incredulous. 'Aside from the obvious problems I might have with that, do you honestly think I'm going to leave my children with a complete *stranger*?'

'She's not a stranger.' Jake's tone now is almost defeated, and I really feel for him. 'She's an employee. I know her.'

There follows a heavy pause. Then, 'Oh yes, and how *well* do you know her?' It might have been a perfectly reasonable question, had it not been loaded with obvious implication.

FOUR

I hear her heels on the floor before she appears, stalking along the landing towards the stairs, and I wish the ground would open up and swallow me. As well as feeling slightly terrified, I'm taken aback when I see her. She's beautiful, definitely that, but not the bohemian, arty sort I imagined her to be. Her serious grey business suit and straight-backed demeanour give off an air of someone who's buttoned up and edgy. As she descends the stairs, I note that her hair – chestnut brown with soft balayage blonde highlights – is cut into a severe poker-straight bob. I can't help thinking a messy style would make her look a little less formidable.

She stops halfway down, her face registering surprise. Clearly she didn't expect to find me standing here. She falters for a second and then carries on. 'I'm sorry about that.' She smiles shortly when she reaches me, her eyes quietly appraising me. 'Jake has a habit of doing this.'

I'm not sure what she's referring to, but from her acerbic comment upstairs, I'm wondering whether he has done something more upsetting than letting her down regarding the child-minding arrangements.

'Come through to the lounge area,' she says, gesturing me that way.

I'm debating whether to make my excuses and leave when I notice Jake coming down the stairs. His gaze flicks towards me, but only fleetingly. 'Do you need me to do anything?' he asks his wife.

She shoots him a caustic look over her shoulder. 'Would there be any point me asking if I did?'

'Right.' He kneads his forehead with his thumb. 'I'll get off then. I shouldn't be too late.'

'Don't rush on my account. I'm sure you have more important things to do,' Megan throws sarcastically back.

Jake breathes out a sigh of despondency and turns towards where I'm still standing by the front door. 'Sorry,' he mouths – and what I see in his eyes shocks me. He looks embarrassed, he's bound to be that, but there's something else there: deep, palpable sadness.

'It's okay.' I offer him a sympathetic smile.

He smiles faintly in return, then shrugs dejectedly, pulls the front door open and walks out.

Uncertain what to do, I look back to where Megan stands in the lounge area. As I do, a movement above me snags my eye. I gaze upwards to see a beautiful little boy, a miniature replica of his father, looking down at me. He has his palms pressed against the glass, and his expression is almost pleading. My breath catches, memories of my little brother wearing that very same look flooding excruciatingly back. *Ollie is not Theo.* I shake myself. He's obviously a lucky child who has everything materially his small heart could desire. Emotionally, though, he appears starved, and as much as I now feel inclined to run, I realise I can't. Jake is clearly unhappy. It's obvious that this little boy is too. I don't feel I can walk out and let Jake down. I can't let his son down either. My conscience simply won't let me.

FIVE

My gaze swivels to Megan, who's busy keying in a text – to her client, I assume, guessing she's running late. Quickly I glance back to Ollie and flash him a warm smile. He studies me silently for a second, and then, as if he's made up his mind about me, a timid smile curves his mouth and he gives me a wave. That almost breaks me. I'm sure I can feel the loneliness emanating from him. I have no idea what's going on between Jake and his wife, but their problems are obviously affecting their son. But then it might just be a blip. All relationships have them. And little Ollie might just be shy. Telling myself that my parents' toxic relationship is probably colouring my thinking, I quash my concerns, brace myself and head for the lounge area, where Megan waits, her arms folded, her fingers impatiently drumming her forearms.

She narrows her eyes as I approach her. 'What was that all about?' She nods towards the hall.

Did she see me smile up at Ollie? Panicking as I wonder whether I've landed him in trouble for being out of bed, I decide my best bet is to look clueless.

'The little interchange between you and my husband as he left,' she clarifies.

Realising it's Jake I appear to have landed in trouble by acknowledging him – or rather that Jake appears to have landed himself in trouble for acknowledging *me* – I frown, feigning confusion. 'Jake saying goodbye, do you mean?'

She studies me for a long, searching moment and then turns away. 'Please sit,' she says, indicating one of the expensive sofas. I do as I'm told, sitting carefully lest I crush the plush velvet.

She walks to the other end of the sofa and perches herself on the edge. 'Please forgive me if I seem a little abrupt,' she says with a ghost of a smile. 'As I'm sure you've gathered, Jake has rather sprung this on me.'

Uncertain what to say, I smile understandingly.

'He tends to do that sometimes,' she goes on. 'You'll find he's full of surprises,' she adds cryptically.

'I hadn't realised you weren't expecting me,' I respond, thinking that siding with her is probably my best move. 'It was a bit remiss of Jake not to call you and let you know.'

'It was.' She fiddles distractedly with her wedding ring, twisting it repeatedly around her finger, and then appears to shake herself. 'Hence the heated exchange upstairs.' She smiles apologetically, briefly. 'I'm afraid things get a little fraught around here sometimes.'

'I'm not surprised,' I offer. I note a flash of irritation in her eyes and suspect I might have said the wrong thing. 'I'm in absolute awe of you,' I add quickly, glancing around the luxurious open plan living space. 'I've no idea how you do it all. You're clearly an expert multitasker and extremely talented.'

She seems to relax a little. 'With difficulty,' she admits. 'Anyway, thank you for stepping in at such short notice. You've obviously come straight from work and haven't had time to freshen up.'

I decide not to tell her that Jake let me go early and that what she sees is me at my best.

'And now, thanks to my thoughtless husband, I appear to be running late.' She sighs expansively. 'My client's on a tight schedule,' she explains, checking her watch.

'You'll need to get off then.' I'm about to ask her to give me a quick tour and assure her that the children will be safe in my hands, but I don't get the chance.

'*Obviously*,' she snaps. 'But I'm hardly going to leave my children with someone I know nothing about, am I?'

'No. No, of course not,' I stammer, taken aback by the sudden mood swing.

'So tell me a little about yourself.' She musters another short smile. It doesn't reach her eyes, slate grey in colour and currently as icy as the Arctic.

I sit up straighter, attempting to look professional. 'Well, I work at Jake's Solihull store, as you might know.'

'How long have you been there?' she asks.

'A little over a year,' I reply, recalling what Jake asked me to say.

'And before that?'

'I was out of work for a short while, and before that I worked at a nursery. It closed, unfortunately,' I provide, nerves tightening my stomach.

'And did the nursery run a Disclosure and Barring Service check?' she asks, searching my eyes carefully.

I hold her gaze. 'Absolutely. Ofsted has made DBS checks for nursery staff a role requirement.' I'm not lying about that. At the time, I passed with flying colours.

She nods thoughtfully. 'And you have qualifications, presumably?'

'NVQ Childcare Level 2,' I reel off without batting an eyelid.

Again she nods. She's plainly assessing everything I say,

everything about me. She's currently staring at my hair, and noting her sleek, glossy locks, I wish I'd made time to wash it.

'Where do you live?' Her eyes stray back to my face.

I feel myself flush. 'Solihull,' I reply truthfully.

'With your parents?' Her expression tells me she's assuming I do.

I shake my head. If I never see my parents again it will be too soon. 'I have a small flat. My parents moved to Devon, but I stayed because of my job.' Not wanting any cross-questioning, I flat-out lie about that.

She arches her eyebrows. 'And you're how old?'

'Twenty-one,' I supply.

'Young then,' she says, a look I can't quite interpret crossing her features.

'I think age is relative to experience,' I venture.

She glances away, an inscrutable smile curving her mouth. 'Do you have a boyfriend?'

I'm feeling this is getting a bit too personal but supply the information anyway. 'Yes. We've been together for about a year and a half now.'

'Good,' she says. 'As long as you're not intending to call him and invite him here when I leave?' she adds, eyeing me with suspicion.

And now I'm pissed off. Very. Does she realise what she's communicating here? Apart from the fact that she doesn't trust me, she obviously thinks I'm sluttish. 'I take childcare duties very seriously, Mrs Harington. And I really have no need to try to impress my boyfriend,' I inform her coolly.

Again she registers surprise. Probably because she's gathered that I too have teeth. I'm actually at the stage now where I'm beginning not to care what she thinks. I mean, I need the money, but is it worth it? My thoughts go to little Ollie, his solemn expression as he looked down at me, and I realise I actually do care.

'Good.' She looks placated. 'We women need to be independent.'

I note the almost wishful look in her eye and I'm curious. Does she mean independent financially, or independent as in not reliant on anyone? If it's the latter, perhaps she shouldn't be so reliant on Jake to support her, which he appears to be to be doing.

'Well, that all seems fine,' she says, standing abruptly. 'I'll show you where everything is, shall I?' Once again bemused by her sudden change of direction, I get to my feet, assuming she expects me to follow her.

'The children are in bed,' she informs me confidently as she marches towards the hall. 'Fern had her last feed at seven, so she'll need another one at ten. You'll find everything made up in the fridge,' she adds. 'You might have to nurse her for a while and she loves to be sung a lullaby, but once she goes off, she's a good sleeper.'

I trail after her to the kitchen area, which I soon realise is opulence in abundance. It has a piano in it. An actual grand piano, ffs. I hope I'm not expected to *play* Fern a lullaby.

After showing me where everything is, including the bottle warmer, she takes me up to check on the children. Ollie is tucked under his duvet and appears to be asleep – pretending, I suspect. Little Fern is wide awake, cooing and gurgling, kicking her legs and making grabbing gestures with her hands at her moon and stars musical mobile. Her eyes follow me as I walk around her cot to have a closer peek at her, gorgeous wide blue eyes that mirror her daddy's.

'She's beautiful.' I smile at Megan, who's standing by the door, looking impatient to be off. I know she's running late, but still it strikes me as odd that she doesn't so much as glance at her baby daughter.

'Right, that's everything, I think.' A small furrow creasing her brow, she looks at her watch as we head back down to the hall. 'I won't give you the security codes, as I'm sure you won't need to leave the house. My contact numbers are on the kitchen island. But obviously I'd rather you didn't call me unless it's urgent. I'm assuming you have Jake's number, although I'm sure he'll be *far* too busy to be bothered by mundane things like childcare.'

The acerbic edge is back, I notice, as I follow her to the door.

'Back at about ten thirty.' She gives me a final sweeping glance, collects up her case and bag from the long table by the front door and strides onwards. 'Oh.' She stops at the door and turns back. 'I meant to say, could you lose the hairpins, Ellie, please?'

I blink at her in confusion.

'They're dangerous, don't you think, while nursing a baby? Also, I can always tell when someone has been snooping around, moving things or helping themselves to anything. Just so you know.' And with that, she smiles flatly and turns to sail on out, leaving me gobsmacked.

SIX

I stare after her, stupefied, as she heads towards her spotless white SUV. Clearly, as I can't afford to dress in designer clothes, she thinks I'm dishonest, *and* that I'm about to jump into bed with her husband. Swallowing back a huge lump of humiliation, I close the front door. The woman's a bully. She clearly intimidates Jake. Does she have no feelings? What a full-of-herself cow.

Finding my hairpins, which I quite fancy poking her judgemental eyes out with, I tug them out and pull off the clip. Since I won't be coming back here, I might just avail myself of one of the bathrooms, I decide, of which there are five, one for each bedroom and a guest bathroom. I'm sure that whatever hair products she uses will be extortionately expensive. Kicking off my shoes in the hall, I head for the grand staircase, raking my fingernails through my hair and hoping I don't leave a fleck of dandruff as I go, I'm halfway up when my phone rings. Seeing it's Jake, I answer it, although somewhat reluctantly. I really do feel sorry for him, but I don't think I can do this on a regular basis. My confidence just can't take it.

'Ellie, hi, I just wanted to make sure you were okay,' he says, which surprises me. It's a bit soon for there to have been any problems.

'Yes, all good,' I answer. 'With the children anyhow.'

'Ah.' He obviously reads between the lines. 'I should apologise,' he says awkwardly. 'You must be wondering what you walked into. Megan didn't realise you were downstairs. My fault. I didn't handle it very well.'

I'm taken aback. The woman was horrible to him and he's apologising for her? 'It's fine,' I assure him, softening a little. He could do without me being horrible to him as well.

He sighs. 'It's actually not. I can only imagine how you must have felt caught in the middle like that. You must have wanted to drop through the floor.'

I smile at his intuition. 'It's marble,' I remind him.

'Calacatta. Available from only one quarry in the world, located in Carrara, Italy.' There's a hint of amusement in his voice. 'It was imported specially.'

'Expensive, then?' I guess.

'Nothing but the best.' He sighs heavily again, and my heart squeezes for him. Plainly his best isn't good enough.

'Are you sure you're okay?' he checks, obviously aware that Megan would have been as prickly to handle as a porcupine.

'Honestly, I'm fine,' I reassure him. 'People argue. It's not a big deal.'

'We didn't exactly come across as the perfect couple, did we?' he concedes. 'We're not always like that,' he adds, a wistful edge to his voice now. 'We can actually make it work sometimes.'

'You're having some problems, I take it?' I probe carefully.

'That obvious, was it?' he asks with a rueful laugh.

'Um, a bit,' I answer hesitantly.

'I'll be straight with you, Ellie,' he says. 'I owe you that. We are having some problems right now, yes. We're trying to work through them. I know Megan must have seemed like an ogre, but try not to judge her too harshly. She's not long had a baby and she's under a lot of pressure. She can't bear not to be organised, which is understandable.'

'You don't have to explain, Jake,' I tell him. I'm intrigued but I don't want him to feel obliged to tell me anything he's not comfortable with. 'My turning up was obviously just bad timing.'

He blows out yet another sigh. 'I'm not sure any time is good timing nowadays,' he confides. 'Megan doesn't mean to be the way she is. She just gets a little frustrated sometimes. With herself mostly.'

I'm agog at that. It seems to me that it's Jake she's frustrated with, despite the fact that he seems to be doing everything he can to be there for her.

'She suffered from postnatal depression after having Fern,' he goes on, a worried edge to his voice. 'After Ollie too, to a degree, but this time around it was bad. Her way of dealing with it is to throw herself into her work, which is why I make sure to support her. Try to, anyway. I mess up sometimes, as you may have gathered.'

'But you worked it out,' I offer. The poor man sounds more disillusioned with himself than with his marriage. 'I mean, you didn't let her down tonight, did you?'

'Thanks to you,' he says appreciatively.

I feel my cheeks heat up. I'm not often appreciated. It feels good. Special.

'Sorry,' he adds. 'I shouldn't be burdening you with all of this. I'm not exactly selling you the job, am I?'

I'm not aware I've officially been offered a job. If I have, then despite the rocky start with Megan, I'm thinking that maybe I could put up with her to support Jake. There's also the children; they might yet turn out to be awful, spoiled and demanding, but something inside me tells me they need someone around them who doesn't put work first. 'I love working with children,' I reply, hoping he'll glean that I'm not put off.

'I think mine might need you,' he says. 'Please don't tell Meg I told you, but...' He stops and draws in a tight breath. 'Those problems we spoke about, there was very nearly a tragedy. Ollie had an accident. Megan wasn't home at the time and... Well, it almost broke us. She's been a bit obsessed since, determined that one or other of us should always be there for the kids, which isn't really feasible given our respective workloads. She's just desperate to keep things together. Sorry you got caught in the crossfire.'

'I understand,' I tell him, guessing he needs me to. 'What happened?' I ask cautiously. 'With Ollie?'

'He had a fall.' Jake's voice tightens. 'Down the stairs.'

His words hit me like a physical punch and I reel inwardly as my mind shoots to Theo, his small body lying crumpled and broken at the foot of the stairs, those huge eyes that only seconds before had looked so pleadingly up at me empty.

SEVEN

At the end of the call, Jake asked me again whether I would babysit for them in future. I said I'd think about it. I don't want to let him down, but if I'm going to be here, I think I'm going to have to tread carefully around his wife, who clearly likes to keep hold of the reins.

Carrying on to the landing, I head for Ollie's room, where I find his door open a fraction. 'Are you sleeping?' I whisper, going in quietly. 'Or just pretending?'

He lies perfectly still for a second, and then wriggles out from under his duvet. 'You won't tell Mum, will you?' he whispers back.

His voice is tinged with worry, and I suspect this little man is as wary of Megan's moods as his father is. I try not to blame her – she's obviously struggling to keep all the balls in the air – but a kernel of anger has taken root inside me nevertheless. No child should be fearful of their own family. An image of Theo sitting petrified on the stairs flashes through my mind, and my heart constricts. 'I won't breathe a word,' I promise, swallowing back my emotion, and cross my chest.

He smiles, clearly happier.

'Are you not tired?' I ask, going across to him.

He shakes his head, drops his gaze and begins fiddling with the edge of his duvet. I guess his mum and dad arguing has left him fretful and wide awake.

'I like your duvet cover.' I nod towards it. 'Are those Pokémon badges I see?'

'Uh-huh.' He brings his gaze shyly back to me. 'Dad bought it for me. Mum doesn't like it, though.' His face clouds over. 'She says Pokémon is too violent, but Dad told her it isn't. And that's true, because Pokémon never die.'

'It's a good point.' I nod in agreement. I'm boggling inwardly, though. Does Megan disapprove of everything Jake tries to do? 'I've never played Pokémon, but I quite fancy it. Do you think you could teach me sometime?'

Ollie looks delighted. 'I'm really good at it,' he informs me proudly. 'Dad is, too. He's quite clever.'

I smile at that. 'Is he indeed?'

'Uh-huh. He runs his own business,' he provides importantly. 'Mum does too. They're both really busy.' He deflates a little. 'It means they can buy me lots of nice things, though,' he adds.

I follow his gaze around the room. It appears he does have everything a small boy's heart could desire. An abundance of books and games line his shelves. Boxes bulge with toys. Even so, I can't help feeling he would rather have the one thing money can't buy: his parents' attention. 'You'll have to show me all your toys one day,' I suggest. 'Maybe we could play lots of things together. Would you like that?'

He nods excitedly and I guess my first instinct was right. He is lonely.

'Do you mind if I sit down?' I indicate his bed, and he immediately shuffles over to make a space for me. 'I haven't introduced myself properly, have I?' Lowering myself to the edge of the bed, I extend my hand. 'I'm Ellie.'

'I'm Oliver Harington,' he says, shaking my hand and sounding very grown up. 'But you can call me Ollie.'

'Pleased to meet you, Ollie.' I can't help but smile at his earnest expression. 'I'm going to be looking after you while your mum and dad are working in the evenings. I think we'll get along really well, but I wanted to check you're okay with it.'

He studies me carefully, and for a heartstopping moment I think he might not be very happy about it. 'Are you going to be living here like my second mum did?' he asks tentatively after a pause, his eyes wary and hopeful all at once.

His second mum? I study him, puzzled. What a peculiar phrase. Is he talking about the au pair? 'Who's your second mum, Ollie?' I ask curiously.

'Phoebe,' he provides. 'She said she loved me as much as my mum did and that she would like to be a second mum to me, but then she went away.' His forehead creases into a frown. 'I think it was because I was bad.'

I remember Megan asking how well Jake and I knew each other, and my breath catches. Was Jake involved with Phoebe? No, he wasn't like that. He was just too nice, too caring. I try to dismiss it but can't quite. Something is off kilter. A childminder who'd built up such a close relationship with a child surely wouldn't just take off like that, would she? Wasn't it more likely she was dismissed and Jake was too embarrassed to tell me?

Ollie is gauging me carefully as I ponder, I notice. 'It wasn't because of anything you did, sweetheart.' Wondering who would have made him believe it was, I pull myself up and give him a hug. 'Why on earth would you think that?'

He looks downcast. 'She didn't say goodbye,' he murmurs, and my heart jumps in my chest. Something doesn't add up. 'She probably had some kind of emergency,' I try to reassure him. 'You know, like someone in her family being poorly, so she had to dash off to be with them.'

Ollie nods slowly, but the furrow in his brow tells me he's

not convinced. 'Her mummy was sad she'd gone,' he says, his eyes searching mine uncertainly, as if trying to communicate something he can't articulate.

I swallow. 'How do you know she was sad, Ollie?'

He hesitates. 'She came here. She was talking to my mummy and she was crying. My mummy gave her a hug.'

'Did she?' I force a smile. My chest flutters manically.

'Uh-huh.' A small nod this time. 'Mummy said we missed her too, and that she wished she'd never met him.'

'Met who, Ollie?' I coax him. 'Did she mean a boyfriend?'

'I think so.' He doesn't look too sure, and I guess that might be beyond his understanding.

'Did Phoebe live here?' I ask him. I'm thinking she would have if she'd been their au pair, and that it would have meant that the hole she'd left in Ollie's life would have been so much bigger. Reluctantly, I'm also thinking that she and Jake would have had plenty of opportunity to conduct an affair.

'Her bedroom was the spare room,' Ollie confirms. 'She let me snuggle up with her sometimes, when I had bad dreams. Mummy didn't like it, though. She didn't like anyone going into Phoebe's bedroom.'

Anyone as in who? My heart skitters against my ribcage. It sounds to me as if it wasn't just Ollie she didn't like going in there. Was it the boyfriend she didn't want in Phoebe's bedroom? Or Jake?

EIGHT

After assuring Ollie that he can call me if he needs me, I help him snuggle down in his bed and then go to check on Fern. As I approach the nursery, I'm pondering again why Megan wouldn't even have glanced at her before she left. Perhaps because if she had, Fern would have fretted after her, I tell myself. I'm not sure I'm convinced, though.

Finding Fern sleeping, I tiptoe out again, admiring the beautiful decor as I go. There are none of the baby motifs one might expect to see in a nursery, but the cosy textures Megan has chosen for the chair and rug, along with warm neutrals on the walls, make it inviting, the kind of room a child won't outgrow. The glass wall, which I assume is sun-proof, will afford Fern spectacular views and also flood the room with tons of natural light during the day. Having been brought up on a social housing estate and then living in a dingy bedsit, I imagine how amazing that would be. She even has a rocking horse, the kind of vintage smoky-grey that little girls' dreams are made of. Well, mine were anyway. She's definitely a lucky little girl, assuming that, like Ollie, she isn't starved of the one vital thing a child needs to thrive.

Going back to Ollie's room, I peer around his door. Noting that he's settled down, I decide to have a wander around. I head first to the main bedroom, which Megan pointed out but didn't show me. Because it's a personal space, I remind myself, one I probably shouldn't be invading. Remembering what she said about being able to tell if someone had been snooping, I hesitate at the double doors, but then curiosity gets the better of me and, promising myself to leave everything exactly as I found it, I press the handles down and push the doors open.

I stop and gawp. I expected luxury, but this room is sumptuous. It's located at the corner of the house, with floor-to-ceiling windows and sliding doors leading to a balcony. The early-morning view from here must be stunning. There's a flat-screen TV the size of one of my bedsit walls mounted high on the wall opposite the bed. The bed itself could sleep four people comfortably and is covered in a soft gold satin bedspread with matching pillows. It would allow them plenty of space between each other, I suppose. Acknowledging a stab of jealousy as my mind conjures up an image of Jake sleeping with Megan – in every sense of the word – I stamp it down quickly.

There's a matching chaise longue in one corner, adding to the overall sense of opulence, and the wardrobes running the length of the wall under the TV are huge. Padding across the vast fur rug adorning the floor, I slide open one of the mirror-fronted doors. This is Megan's side, clearly. It houses enough clothes to fill my bedsit – all labels, I guess. Trailing my hand along the hangers, I pause at a black cashmere jacket and bring it out. It's divine. The label inside it says *Joseph* and the price tag, I suspect, would say *in your dreams*. I try it on anyway, pulling it tightly around me. Twirling around, I survey myself in the mirror and my heart drops. I look like exactly what I am: a poor, mousy little girl playing dress-up.

Sliding the jacket off with a sigh, I place it back and go to the other side of the wardrobe. An array of men's shirts, all colour-coordinated and pressed, hang there. There's a lingering smell of aftershave, I notice, an earthy, woody smell with just the right level of sweet. A frisson of sexual excitement shoots through me and I breathe in sharply. What am I *doing*? Jake needs me, but he's never likely to need me in *that* way. If I am going to be here, I need to curb any ridiculous schoolgirl fantasies and focus on the children.

I close the doors and go to the bathroom. As I guessed, it's all grey marble, with vast windows. People on the outside won't be able to see in, I suppose, but still I'm not sure I would be comfortable getting naked in here. Peering in the cabinets, I find a whole range of luxury hair products. Again I hesitate, but my scalp is itching at the very sight of them, and she's hardly going to notice if I use a teeny drop. I settle on a Kérastase Elixir product, mostly because it's the only name I recognise, and set about pampering myself, finishing off with the oil-infused conditioner.

Once I'm done, trying not to drip on the floor, I grab the thick white towel I spy on the towel rail, squeeze as much moisture from my hair as I can, then dab lightly at it. Thanking my lucky stars it's a heated rail, I put the towel back, arranging it the way I found it, and head back to the bedroom in search of a hairdryer.

Having found one in the dressing table drawer, a Dyson, no less, I'm blasting my definitely more glossy locks when I think I hear Fern crying. Quickly I switch the dryer off. It's definitely her. And she sounds distressed. *Shit.* Downing the dryer, I race out of the door and along the landing.

As I reach the nursery, I realise the crying has stopped. But why has it stopped so suddenly? Panic blooms inside me, and I thrust the door open and fly across to the crib. She looks up at me, her huge eyes glassy with tears, her little fists clenched. 'What is it, sweetheart?' I lean to pick her up, and my blood freezes. She's wheezing. Her chest is *rattling*.

NINE

Fear crashing through me, I lift Fern from her crib and hold her to me, massaging her back and trying to recall my childcare training above my spiralling panic. *Babies have narrow airways. Even the slightest bit of mucus can cause rattling or wheezing.* An image of Finley, the toddler who was injured at the nursery because of me, emblazons itself on my mind and a knot of dread tightens my stomach. I have to do something. 'It's okay, little one, I have you. I'll help you.' I shush and soothe her, hold her against me with one arm as I fumble my phone from my trouser pocket with my other hand. My blood pumping, I'm about to press 999 when she snuffles and makes a coughing sound. Shakily I ease her away from me and glance down at my shoulder. Relief floods every vein in my body. It's milk. Just milk clogging her throat.

A strangled sob escapes me, and Fern jumps with surprise. I laugh half hysterically as her beautiful blue eyes grow wide. 'Sorry, sweetheart.' I smile through my tears. 'Did I frighten you? Silly Ellie.' I shake my head, hug her gently back to me and carry her to the chair. With my legs like butter beneath me, I sink into it and lower her to the crook of my arm. 'We gave each other a scare, didn't we, angel, hey?'

Pressing a soft kiss to her forehead, I gaze at her in wonder. Her eyes are filled with such absolute trust, it both petrifies and thrills me. I'm scared of the responsibility of having this tiny human being entrusted to me, but a new determination grows inside me. I feel in my heart that it's some kind of sign, communicating to me that this little girl needs someone to care for her, to watch over her.

Standing, I carry her to the window. The stars are out, twinkling against the ink-black sky high above us. I recall looking through my bedroom window as a small child, tracking a shooting star and wishing my mum and dad could love me. What drives some parents to be so cruel to their children? I wonder, my thoughts going to my little brother. He's never far away, his bruised face, the unbridled fear in his eyes as he looked up at me for the last time seared indelibly on my mind. 'We'll never know, will we, sweetheart?' Blinking away my tears, I smile down at little Fern, who I'm sure smiles back at me.

Hell, the time. I realise with a sinking heart that she's overdue for her feed. 'We need to warm your bottle, little one, don't we?' I chat to her as I turn away from the window. 'And I think a certain little lady could do with a nappy change, don't you?'

She gurgles and laughs and flails a tiny hand towards my face, and I feel a surge of love for her. She's gorgeous, special. I hope Megan appreciates how special.

I'm on my way back across the room after changing her when I see headlights sweeping the drive. Hoping it's Jake, I go to the window, but my anticipation dwindles as I realise it's Megan. With Fern still in my arms, I head to the landing, then think better of taking her down and go back to pop her in her crib. This is a wonderful house, unique and luxurious, but it doesn't feel to me like a child-friendly one. The central staircase might be grand, but even without what Jake told me about Ollie's fall, it appears to me to be a death trap. Going down hands-free with a baby would definitely be a bad idea.

Megan comes through the front door as I reach the hall, and I immediately feel guilty as she looks me over, her gaze coming to rest on my hair. Suspecting it might still be damp, I resist reaching to check. 'Hi,' she says, glancing away to park her case and her bag on the table. 'How did it go?'

'Fine,' I assure her. 'Ollie's fast asleep.'

'I should think so at this time,' she replies tersely. 'And Fern?'

'I was just about to feed her.' My guilt quadruples as she arches an eyebrow and checks her watch. Should I tell her about Fern's wheeze? Worry twists inside me. I feel Megan will judge me, but I can't not mention it. I'm sure it was just the milk clogging her throat, but it's possible she might have an infection. 'She had a bit of a wheeze, which is why I'm late with her feed,' I say hesitantly. 'She seems fine now, though.'

Megan's gaze snaps back to me. 'Did you use her inhaler?'

Did I do what? I look at her askance. 'No.' My stomach churns. 'I didn't know she had an inhaler.'

'She has asthma.' She eyeballs me with a mixture of irritation and disbelief. 'I told you.'

Oh no you did not. I stare at her, staggered. She definitely didn't tell me. I would *never* have forgotten something as important as that.

'Have you been smoking?' she demands.

'No, I don't smoke,' I stammer. I realise that Jake is standing in the doorway; he obviously arrived just after Megan 'I would never smoke around children in any case, and I honestly don't remember you mentioning—'

'Vaping?' She eyes me accusingly. 'Blowing that noxious stuff all about the place?'

'*No.*' I shake my head hard. 'You didn't *tell* me about the asthma.'

'I most certainly did,' she insists. 'I told you you would find everything you need in the cupboard under her changing mat.'

'But you didn't mention her having *asthma.*' I glance at Jake in desperation.

'What's going on?' He steps forward, his troubled gaze swivelling from me to Megan.

'Fern's had an asthma attack and this idiot girl didn't give her her medication,' she snaps.

'But you didn't *tell* me about the inhaler.' I whirl around as Jake races past me to the stairs, cursing under his breath. 'She *didn't!*' I call after him as he charges up them.

Why isn't *she* racing up there? If she's concerned about Fern, why is she just standing there glaring at me? I search her face in confusion, and a cold chill of apprehension runs through me. There's a challenge in her eyes, I swear. What the hell is going on here?

TEN

I have no idea what to do, what to think as Megan strides past me, a glint of triumph in her eyes. It's almost as if she has something to prove. What? She doesn't have to prove I'm incapable. If she doesn't like me, she can just dispense with me – like she dispensed with Phoebe? A confusion of emotions churning inside me, I wait in the hall. I want to leave, run away, but I won't do that. I didn't do anything wrong. She's *lying*. I need Jake to know she is. I need to keep my day job, which I've a feeling I won't if she poisons his mind against me. Whatever is wrong with this woman – and she plainly has some major issues – I'm not going to allow her to rob me of that, of my home, no matter how shitty it is.

'She's fine.' I hear Jake's voice. 'She's dry and content. Ellie's obviously been looking after—'

'She's been in our room! Going through my things!' Megan screams over him, causing Fern to emit a raucous, shocked cry. 'She's been using my *bathroom*.'

There's a pause before Jake replies. 'Did you expect her *not* to need to use the bathroom, Megan?' he asks.

'I didn't expect her to wash her *hair* in there while my daughter was struggling with an asthma attack,' she hisses.

Jake says nothing. I'm guessing he has no idea what *to* say. She must have gone straight to her room and checked everything, I realise with a mixture of disbelief and guilt. It's then that I remember I left the hairdryer out, and suppose I can't blame her. Still, is washing my hair really a criminal offence? Isn't the bigger crime prioritising checking your bathroom over checking your daughter?

A loaded silence follows, then, 'Get her out of here,' she seethes.

'For pity's sake, Megan, calm down, will you? You'll wake Ollie,' Jake tries. 'There's obviously been some misunderstanding. You were in a rush, maybe you—'

'She's used my towel! Her hair is all over it!' she shrieks. 'Get her *out* of my house! *Now!*'

Seconds later, Jake appears at the top of the stairs, his expression both apologetic and guilty. 'I'm sorry,' he starts. 'She's—'

'And check whether she's stolen anything!' Megan shouts after him.

'Jesus.' He closes his eyes.

'She wouldn't be the first one who had, *would* she, Jake?'

I'm out of the door at that.

'Ellie!' I hear Jake behind me as I fly down the drive. 'Ellie, come back. I'll drive you.'

'I'm fine,' I shout back tearfully.

It doesn't take him long to catch up with me. 'You're obviously not fine. Look, we're in the middle of the countryside, it's pitch black – and you've got no shoes on. Please, come back to the car. I can't let you go off like this. I would never forgive myself if anything happened to you.'

I drop my gaze. There's no way I'm going back to that

house, shoes or no shoes. The woman hates me. It seems to me that she hated me before she'd even set eyes on me.

Jake senses my reluctance. 'Will you wait here then?' he asks, placing a hand on my arm and squeezing it gently.

That only makes me feel worse. I nod quickly. Keep my gaze fixed down.

'I won't be long,' he promises, and turns to race back to the house.

Minutes later, he slows his car next to me and thrusts open the passenger door. I scramble in quickly in case the witch is watching through her all seeing windows.

'I brought your shoes,' he says, indicating the footwell.

I nod, my throat too thick to speak, and push my feet into them.

'I'm sorry,' he repeats, his voice full of remorse.

Tears streaming down my face, I keep my gaze on the side window, and Jake falls quiet, driving me back to the grim reality of my bedsit in silence.

After parking outside my building, he turns the engine off. 'Are you going to be okay?' he asks softly.

I nod and wipe my eyes with my shirtsleeve. I sense him looking at me, but I can't face him.

He hesitates. 'I'll walk you to your door,' he offers, but he doesn't move.

'It's not true,' I say after a second. 'What she said about the inhaler. She didn't tell me about Fern's asthma. I swear she didn't.' My tone is flat, hopeless. He's not going to believe me over his wife. Why would he?

When he answers, he takes me completely by surprise. 'I know,' he says quietly.

I turn to him, bewildered.

'I really am sorry, Ellie,' he says, taking my hand and squeezing it gently. 'Megan gets defensive sometimes.' He pauses. 'She also gets a bit neurotic about her things being moved. I think it's all to do with her feeling so down and out of control after having Fern.' He drops his gaze. 'I'm guessing you'll run a mile now, and I wouldn't blame you.'

When he brings his gaze back to mine, I'm shocked by the vulnerability I see in his eyes. Why is she doing this? It's clear he's trying hard to support her, but it seems to me she simply doesn't appreciate him.

'I want you to know that I'm grateful, though,' he goes on, 'for helping me out at short notice. It meant I was able to secure a deal that will secure the growth of the company. And for lending me a shoulder. Christ knows, sometimes I need one.' He smiles, such a heartbreakingly sad smile my heart bleeds for him.

I'm touched by his honesty. Mesmerised by the thumb he trails lightly over my palm. 'I won't. Run a mile, I mean,' I say, feeling clumsy and incoherent suddenly. 'And I'm happy to lend a shoulder. We all need one occasionally.'

'Do we?' He searches my eyes curiously.

I look away. With no idea why, I have an urge to confide in him, to tell him my history, who I am and why Megan would have every right to be wary of me. These feelings both frighten and enthral me. I've never disclosed my past to anyone. Not even Zach knows all there is to know about me. What is it about this man that makes me want to open up to him?

'You can cry on mine any time,' he offers. 'I have two. They're quite broad.'

I laugh self-consciously. I had noticed but think it better not to disclose that particular observation.

'Don't take what Megan said too much to heart,' he urges me after a second. 'She made a mistake. She'll struggle to admit it, but I have no doubt she'll probably be feeling as guilty as hell.'

I nod, though I'm not convinced. 'I didn't steal anything.' I glance guardedly at him. 'I would never do that.'

He sighs and runs his fingers through his hair. 'I know,' he says again. 'She accused our au pair of stealing too. I think that was one of the reasons she left.'

I glance at him curiously. I still have my doubts that I have the whole story regarding Phoebe's departure.

He breathes deeply. 'Truthfully, I guess Megan has always been hard to please,' he admits.

I scan his face, see the despair and conflict there. 'How do you cope?' I ask. *Why do you bother?* is what I really want to ask.

'She's the mother of my children,' he says with a tired shrug.

I can't help but regard him with awe. I expected him to say he loved her, but he didn't. I feel a little surge of hope inside me, ridiculously. Jake Harington really is a rare combination: good-looking, extremely caring, wealthy. He could have his pick of women. He would never be interested in someone like me. I'm about to tell him I think Megan is a lucky woman when I notice Zach ambling towards my building, a slight weave to his walk. I feel a flash of irritation that he thinks he can just turn up despite not having even so much as texted me. For all he cares, I might have been murdered fleeing Jake's house in the dead of night. I'm being harsh, I realise. Zach does care. He loves me, he tells me so. But not often. And there's no escaping the fact that I've been stood up more than once for Grand Theft Auto or whatever the latest hot game is.

'I should go.' I glance at Jake again and feel a flutter deep in the pit of my tummy. Even looking exhausted and dishevelled, he's incredibly handsome.

'Of course. Sorry, I'm keeping you.' He smiles, but his gaze is on Zach, I notice, who's now leaning against his car, an old PT Cruiser badly in need of a paint job that he insists is a 'collectible'. He obviously left it out front earlier with a view to coming back here.

'Looks as if he's had a few pints. Do you know him?' Jake asks, concern crossing his features as Zach heads for the entrance, pressing the buzzer and then shaking his head and pulling out his phone. He keys something into it and my own phone dings a telling text.

Where are you? I read, and my heart sinks a little. Not the right reaction to your boyfriend texting you, I acknowledge. 'We're seeing each other,' I reply vaguely.

Jake nods contemplatively. 'He's a lucky guy,' he says, squeezing my hand before finally letting go of it.

ELEVEN

Zach narrows his eyes as I head towards him. 'Who's that?' He nods towards Jake's car as it pulls away.

I walk past him to key the code into the gate. 'My boss.'

'Right.' He pauses. 'Overtime, was it?'

'I've been babysitting for him.' I glance back at Zach as he follows me down the entry. 'I left a message on your phone. He gave me a lift because he didn't want me coming home on my own.'

'Ah, right.' Zach knits his brow. He's obviously been too busy gaming and boozing to check his messages. I can smell the beer on him. I have a keen nose for it, a legacy of my bleak childhood. 'Flash bugger, isn't he?' he comments, following me into my bedsit.

What would he do, I wonder, if I said I was just too tired tonight and sent him away? I'm beginning to think he's taking me a little too much for granted. He's always doing this, turning up late at night and expecting to stay over – because my bedsit is nearer to his mate's flat than his parents' house. 'You're referring to his car, I assume.' I dump my bag and go straight to the kettle. I'm in the mood for hot chocolate and sleep. I hope Zach isn't in the mood for more.

'Well, you have to admit it's a bloody great status symbol. Why else would the bloke drive a Beamer 8 other than to flaunt the fact that he's loaded?'

'He runs his own company. Several branches, actually.' I realise I sound as if I'm lording Jake up, but I can't help it. Zach suddenly becoming proprietorial when up until now he didn't particularly care where I was tonight has rubbed me up the wrong way.

'He's married, then, is he?'

I turn to face him, amazed by that comment and the insinuation behind it. 'He has children,' I point out. 'That's why I was babysitting for him.'

Zach shrugs. 'Doesn't mean he's not single, though, does it?'

'You're *jealous*.' I stare at him, incredulous. 'I suppose I should be flattered, but actually, Zach, I'm not, because I'm wondering what this says about your opinion of me.'

He squints in confusion. 'I'm not following.'

'You're clearly implying that because he's loaded, I'm bound to fancy him,' I enlighten him, dismissing a pang of guilt. I like Jake a lot, it's true. Not because he's loaded, but because of who he is. He's nice, a decent man. He actually makes me feel good about myself. There haven't been many men in my life who have done that.

'Don't be daft.' Zach rolls his eyes and walks across to wrap his arms around me. 'I am a bit jealous, I admit it. It's a man thing, I guess. But I know you're not going to be impressed by some bloke just because he drives a flashy car.' He hesitates. 'I'm concerned, that's all. Worried he might be taking advantage of you.'

I laugh in semi-amusement. 'It's you who's being daft,' I tell him. 'Jake's not like that. He's nice. All his employees say so.'

Zach doesn't look impressed. 'Yeah, well, I'm sure he is when it suits him.'

'Which means what?' I look at him, equally underwhelmed.

'Meaning he puts it on when he's after something. Let's face it, blokes like him are usually full-of-themselves arrogant pricks who go for what they want and tend to get it, aren't they?'

'I wouldn't know, Zach.' I'm getting irritated with the conversation now. I'm tired. Plus, if there's one thing I know Jake isn't, it's arrogant. He's been nothing but considerate, of me and of his wife. 'I'm going to get ready for bed.' Extracting myself from his embrace, I head for the other end of the room.

Zach follows. I wish he wouldn't. I really don't feel like getting undressed in front of him right now.

'So how many kids does he have?' Sitting on the bed, he unlaces his trainers.

'What is this, Zach? Twenty questions?' Sighing, I collect my pyjamas from the hook next to the bathroom door, intending to grab a little privacy in there.

'I'm just interested, that's all,' he replies, sounding hurt.

My guilt ramps up a level. I'm being awful to him, feeling tetchy after all that's gone on tonight. None of that is his fault. 'Two,' I provide. 'A baby girl aged three months and a little boy aged six.'

Zach glances up, surprised. 'And you're okay with that, are you?'

'Yes.' I look away uncomfortably. 'Why wouldn't I be?'

'Your little brother was the same age as the boy,' he points out.

'So?' I pretend indifference.

He's quiet for a moment. Then, 'You have nightmares about him, Ellie,' he reminds me softly.

TWELVE

As I wait on the shop floor for the first customers to arrive, I suppress a yawn. I'm exhausted from lack of sleep and the nightmares I inevitably had, probably because Zach had reminded me about Theo. The dreams alternated between him and Finley, the toddler at the nursery, two little boys who had suffered because of me. As an image of Ollie floated through my mind, his small body bloodied and bruised, I woke with a jerk, sweat saturating my body and wetting the sheets beneath me. Neither Zach nor I got much sleep after that. Zach has a job installing a safe out in Ludlow this morning. Quashing my guilt, I close my eyes and pray that he will drive safely.

'Late night?' Jake enquires, jarring me as he approaches the desk behind me. 'You look as if you're asleep on your feet.'

'No, I, um...' I glance quickly down as he walks around in front of me. 'Sorry, I didn't sleep too well.'

'No need to apologise.' He smiles as I look up at him. 'I'd be bored too, standing around waiting for customers to show up.'

'It's early yet.' A flutter of nerves takes off in my stomach as he studies me. He's too close, the earthy, woody smell of his aftershave permeating my senses and making me more disorientated than I already am. 'We usually get a trickle of customers around this time and then a steady flow at about ten, leading up to a mad rush at lunchtime,' I gabble, while I try to get a rein on my emotions.

'I'm relieved to hear it.' He nods approvingly. 'I'll make sure I'm around to help lighten the load.'

'We can always use an extra pair of hands,' I assure him with a smile.

He runs his eyes over me, his forehead furrowing into a thoughtful frown. 'Could I have a quick word?' he asks, gesturing towards his office.

'Um, yes, of course.' I feel a prickle of apprehension. I'm guessing that Megan's mood last night wouldn't have been improved by his driving me home. I hope to God she hasn't convinced him I stole something. Taking a breath, I follow him as he walks off ahead of me. I don't miss Kat's eagle eyes across the shop floor following us both.

Once we're in his office, Jake closes the door. 'About last night,' he starts. His expression is cautious, I notice, and my stomach turns over, 'I wanted to apologise for my inappropriate behaviour.'

I blink at him in surprise.

'I was a little overfamiliar,' he explains awkwardly.

I'm too astonished to speak for a second. Then, 'It's fine,' I say quickly, assuming he means taking hold of my hand. 'I mean, I didn't feel you were being overfamiliar, honestly.'

He breathes out a sigh of relief. 'Good,' he says. 'I'd hate it if you thought I might have been. I just wanted you to know that I'm here if you ever need to talk. To be honest, I found it refreshing to have someone I could open up to.'

Rather than argue with, I finish mentally, feeling for him. 'Me too.' I smile.

'Glad to be of service.' He smiles back, his mesmerising blue eyes holding mine. 'I'd better let you get back to the shop.'

'Right. Yes.' I snap my gaze away from him.

'Ellie,' he stops me as I turn to the door, 'please don't think I'm making judgements. I'm not. It's just...'

My heart skitters against my chest as he pauses. *Just what?* I pray he isn't going to say that my working here will be problematical after the disaster last night.

'I couldn't help noticing the scars,' he says softly.

I freeze with my hand on the door handle and a tumult of emotion crashes through me. I work to keep the scars hidden, always wearing long sleeves, bracelets and bangles in the summer. I haven't even confided in Zach about how low I was after what happened to Theo. I'm not sure why. Because I'm ashamed, I suppose.

'It's none of my business,' Jake adds, his voice full of sympathy. 'I only mention it because...' I glance at him as he hesitates. 'You asked me how I coped, last night when we spoke. I said she was the mother of my children, which might have made it sound as if that was the only reason I stay. It's true to a degree, I would never do anything to harm my kids, but...' Again he pauses, taking a breath and pressing a thumb against his forehead. 'The truth is, Megan has been there, in that same dark place you must once have been. I care about her, Ellie. I can't not.'

I see the anguish in his eyes as he looks back at me, and my heart constricts painfully. If ever a woman was looking for one of the good guys, I realise he's here, standing right in front of me. Does Megan see that when she looks at him? If she doesn't, she really needs her eyes opening up to the fact. 'I meant what I said,' he goes on. 'If you ever do need a shoulder, please feel free to come to me.'

'I meant what I said too,' I assure him, and with no idea what else to say, I turn away and slip out of the office. A hard lump clogs my throat as I walk back to the shop floor. Strangely, I don't feel embarrassed that Jake noticed the scars. I feel elated.

He shared what he did because he cares. About me. Zach is so wrong about him.

As I head towards the desk, Kat stops me. 'You two seemed cosy,' she says, arching her eyebrow curiously.

I can't quite meet her gaze. 'It was just a work thing.'

'Hmm?' Her response tells me she's dubious. 'If you say so. Whatever, I'm not sure his wife was very pleased when she saw you going into his office.' She nods towards the customer service desk – and I almost die as I meet Megan's impassive gaze.

THIRTEEN

My nerves tie themselves in knots as I approach her. 'Hi, Megan. Is there something I can help you with?' I ask warily. 'If it's Jake you've come to see, he's—'

'No.' She talks over me. 'It's you I've come to see.'

I close my eyes, praying she isn't about to humiliate me in front of everyone.

'Is there somewhere we can talk?' she asks.

I try to read her expression. She doesn't look hostile. She actually looks quite pleasant, which throws me.

'A coffee shop nearby perhaps?' She smiles.

I frown in confusion. Is this the lull before the storm? I'm sure she's here to accuse me of stealing the silverware, or worse. 'There's a Costa on the high street,' I suggest cautiously, 'but I'm not on my break for another hour. I really shouldn't leave the shop floor without permission.'

'Oh, don't worry about that. I'll square it with Jake. He won't mind.' She spins around and heads for the door leaving me staring uncertainly after her.

'I think you've been summoned,' Kat whispers, coming to

my side. 'Go on, I'll cover for you. But you'd better give me all the goss when you get back.'

Ten minutes later, Megan and I are in Costa Coffee, where she treats me to a latte and insists I indulge in some carrot and walnut cake with her. 'I think I'll have to have an extra workout in the gym after this. It's probably horrifically calorific.' She smiles conspiratorially at me as she picks up her fork and starts tucking in.

My appetite nil, I smile wanly back and glance down at my plate.

'I had the gym installed in hopes of working off the baby fat,' she goes on in between mouthfuls. 'I'm not strict enough with myself, though. Jake uses it most mornings, but then he has more time.' She glances at my untouched cake. 'Are you not eating yours?'

'Um, yes.' I nod quickly and have a nibble.

'Do you work out?' she asks, almost chummily.

'No.' I daresay I might if I had a home gym, I don't add. 'I walk to work, but that's about it.'

'Really?' She looks surprised. 'Yet you're so slim. You have a gorgeous figure.'

I almost choke. 'Thank you,' I splutter. My figure is far from gorgeous. Mind you, it's hard being confident about your looks when your boyfriend's head swivels in the direction of any woman who's blessed in the boob department.

'About Fern.' She puts her fork down and finally gets to the point.

Thinking she's about to accuse me of neglecting or hurting her daughter in some way, my nerves tighten like a slip knot.

She picks up a napkin and dabs at her mouth. 'She's a good baby,' she goes on after an agonisingly long pause. 'I love her *so* much, but...' She falters, and drops her gaze, picking up her napkin and twisting it between her forefingers and thumbs.

I gather she's struggling and I'm unsure how to respond. I

guess her mind must be on what Jake mentioned to me, but I can hardly tell her I know.

She looks up after a moment, a fleeting smile crossing her face. 'I had some problems after the birth, unfortunately. I'm afraid I haven't bonded very well with her, as you may have gathered. Jake says I will. He's says I'm too tense around her. It doesn't help that he tells me I tense up when I'm holding her, but...' Again she falters. Then, 'He's very good with her,' she goes on, a faraway, almost plaintive look in her eyes.

I can't help but feel sorry for her. 'Sometimes it takes time,' I reply, trying to be helpful. 'Not all babies are textbook babies.'

She nods and glances away again.

'It must be difficult for you,' I add in the ensuing silence.

'It's devastating.' She breathes deeply. 'Also confusing, since Fern was a much-wanted baby.' Her eyes are glassy with tears, which shakes me. She appears entirely different to the hard, competent woman I encountered last night. Vulnerable.

'I can only apologise for the way I treated you. I must have seemed like the bitch mother from hell.' She laughs self-deprecatingly. 'You probably felt like walking straight out of the door as soon as you arrived.'

I feel awkward, bad for her, bad also that I *did* consider she was the bitch mother from hell. 'It's okay,' I start clumsily. 'Jake did spring it—'

'Why didn't you?' she asks over me. 'I'm not sure I would have stuck around if I were you.'

I hesitate. 'Because I didn't want to let you down,' I answer uncomfortably.

She arches an eyebrow. 'You mean you didn't want to let Jake down?'

'He *is* my boss,' I say after a second. Then, sure that my cheeks must look like a set of brake lights, I glance away. 'Actually, it was Ollie mostly. He was on the landing and...' I falter as I look back at her. Telling her he looked lost and lonely won't make her feel any better about her mothering skills. 'He smiled at me. He seemed such a pleasant little boy and I decided I would stay and look after him.'

'That's very commendable.' She studies me carefully. 'You should be on your guard. He has winning ways, just like his father.'

I feel a jolt of apprehension. Is it Jake she's saying I should be on my guard against?

'Assuming you'll consider offering your services again, that is,' she adds, taking me completely by surprise.

She obviously notes my astonished expression. 'I'm struggling to juggle all the balls, Ellie, which is possibly why I treated you so badly when I came home. If I'm perfectly honest, I think I wanted to show you up to make myself look a little less incompetent. It's terribly difficult when being a mother doesn't come naturally. It's all had a knock-on effect on my marriage, and… Well, to get to the point, I need help. I'm hoping you can forgive my monstrous behaviour and consider childminding for me, looking after Fern, taking Ollie to school and collecting him, getting his tea. That sort of thing.'

I stare at her, gobsmacked, quite literally.

'You're obviously a huge hit with Ollie.' She smiles hopefully. 'I realise it's a big ask after last night, but I'm prepared to pay you more than your current salary. Do you drive?'

'I… Yes.' I shake my head and try to keep up.

'That's perfect. I'll organise you a little runaround. A Mini, perhaps. How does that sound?'

I simply stare at her. I thought the woman hated me on sight. I thought she thought *I* was incompetent.

'You would have the use of the house and the facilities, of course, whenever you're there. Although you would have to be careful not to allow Ollie access to the pool on his own. But I'm sure you would be aware of that.' She pauses, smiling tentatively. 'What do you think?'

I'm thinking that, as Zach appeared to be jealous of Jake, he might have something to say about my leaving PCs Plus to work in his house, which is what it appears Megan wants me to do. I'm also thinking that given her moods, which appear to swing like a pendulum, it might be sensible to turn the job down. But what about Ollie, who I sensed needed someone he could confide in? And baby Fern? Then there's Jake. 'Is Jake okay with it?' I ask.

'I'm sure he will be,' she assures me. 'As he pointed out when he got back, you did alert us to Fern's asthma attack, and you looked after both of the children well. Truthfully, I suspect he'll be immensely relieved to have someone we can trust to take care of them.'

I take a breath. 'Okay. If you're sure he's all right with it, then yes.' I can at least give it a chance now she's being more honest with me, though I can't quite ignore the niggling little voice in my head that wonders why she would have such a sudden change of heart.

FOURTEEN

A week later, Megan gives me a more thorough tour of the property, starting with the outside and the swimming pool, which is breathtaking, surrounded by lush tropical-looking plants. Gazing around, I note that the pool area has its own bar and a built in-brick barbecue. It's pure luxury. 'This is fabulous,' I tell her, my mouth probably gaping in awe. 'You've done an amazing job. It's like one of those holiday villas in Spain.'

'I'm glad you think so. I was trying for the remote holiday villa vibe.' She smiles, clearly pleased. 'It wasn't finished when we moved in. I was pregnant with Fern, and Jake was really busy, so it was all a bit of nightmare, but we got there. It works, I think.'

'It does. Definitely.' I nod as I follow her back towards the patio doors, noticing the decked seating area as we go. I'm looking forward to sunning myself on it, as long as there's no one around when I reveal my pasty, sun-deprived body.

'Good,' she says, heading towards the hall. 'The gym is through the kitchen area.' She waves a hand in that direction. 'We had a basement room installed especially. As I mentioned, Jake uses it most mornings and some evenings, so if you hear any strange groans and moans coming from that direction, rest assured, it's only him.

I smile, but the hairs on my skin rise at the thought of moans and groans coming from the basement.

'There's a TV in every room.' She indicates the large flat-screen mounted on the far wall of the lounge. 'Although I don't imagine you'll have much time to be lounging around watching TV.'

'Oh. Right, no.' Frowning uncertainly, I follow her as she heads for the stairs.

'We'll be getting a cleaner, but you're okay with a few household tasks until we do, aren't you?' She glances questioningly back at me.

'Yes, absolutely,' I assure her. 'I assumed you would want me to help out around the house, so that's no problem.'

'Good. The right people are always so hard to find.' She heads up the stairs. 'You've seen our room, of course.' I feel a pang of guilt as she walks past it, which was possibly her intention.

She pauses at Fern's room, her hand resting on the handle, her ear pressed to the door. 'She's still sleeping,' she whispers, walking quietly away. 'I was going to show you where her inhaler is so you'll be sure to find it should you need it, but we'll do that later.

Leading the way into Ollie's room, she goes across to the wardrobe. 'His school clothes are on this side.' She opens the door and indicates his small white shirts, which hang as regimentally as Jake's. 'Can you make sure he always has a clean shirt available? I like him to go in a fresh one every day, and socks and underwear, obviously.' She shows me where those are, neatly folded in his dressing table drawers. 'His trousers I tend to rotate every two days.'

'Right.' I nod and digest and follow her as she sails out

again. She really does like everything in its place, doesn't she? I can't help thinking it's a bit OCD.

'This is the spare bedroom. It was our au pair's room.' She pushes open the door at the end of the landing, beyond Fern's room. She doesn't step in, so I stop and peer at it from the doorway. It's a beautiful room, the kind of room you might expect to find in a luxury hotel; all soft, textured neutrals, with a sumptuous fur rug covering most of the floor and wall-to-wall windows looking out over the swimming pool. My thoughts go to Phoebe.

I hesitate, and then decide to broach the subject. 'Why did she leave so suddenly?' I ask. 'Jake said she left you in the lurch so I'm assuming she didn't give you much notice.'

Megan looks me over thoughtfully. 'She did give notice, but not as per her contractual requirements,' she answers. 'There was a man involved. Isn't there always when a woman turns her life upside down?' she goes on with a despairing sigh. 'He was married, I gather, though I only met him once, briefly, when he picked her up. I'm afraid I took an instant dislike to him, unsurprisingly, given that he was cheating on his wife. Also treating Phoebe badly, I suspect. They started arguing as soon as she climbed into the car – because she was late, I think. The relationship was...' she pauses, 'let's say volatile. I think Phoebe thought it was passionate. I heard her talking to him on the phone once, quite by accident. I gleaned he'd decided to leave his wife. I can only assume it was him she went off with so suddenly.'

'Did the police not pursue it?' I frown in confusion. If Phoebe's mother hadn't known where she was, surely they would have investigated.

Megan glances sharply in my direction.

'Ollie mentioned her mother came here and that she was upset. I presumed it was because she hadn't been in touch with her,' I mumble an explanation and pray I haven't betrayed Ollie's confidence.

Megan nods slowly. 'She did report her missing. The police contacted me but I'm afraid I couldn't give them much information other than the man's Christian name. Sean.' She sighs again, regretfully. 'He was a seedy-looking character, involved in criminal activities, I suspect. It wasn't much to go on.'

I nod. 'I suppose not.' Poor Phoebe. I can't help feeling for her, being so taken in by a man she would turn her back on her life and her family for him.

'I'm assuming that as you have a boyfriend you won't want to live in. Should we be unduly late for any reason, however, we might have a need for you to stay over.' Megan brings the subject back to the bedroom. 'There's clean linen on the bed, of course, and the room has its own bathroom. The wardrobe won't open, unfortunately.' She nods towards it. 'Phoebe insisted on having a lock, and we found it broken when she left.'

That seems a bit odd. Why not get it mended? But then I suppose they have loads of other wardrobe space, so they wouldn't be in any particular hurry. 'Would you like me to get my boyfriend to look at it?' I offer as she closes the bedroom door and strides off again. 'He works for a lock and safe company. I'm sure he could fix it.'

'No need to trouble him.' She glances back. 'We have a handyman. He'll get around to it.'

'Is Jake not very handy around the house then?' I ask.

She stops and turns. 'No, Jake is most certainly *not* handy,' she says with a scornful laugh. 'He's always far too busy to take on household tasks.'

'Of course,' I mumble, wishing I'd never asked. 'I just wondered.' My thoughts go to my father with a shudder. He never lifted a finger in the house. But then my mother didn't either. Theo and I had to pretty much fend for ourselves. My little brother's face springs into my mind once more, the fear and desperation in his eyes that dreadful day. He was so frightened, his face tear-stained and covered in livid blue bruising. It was the worst day of my life. The last day of Theo's.

'He has his little hobbies and projects,' Megan goes on, and I shake myself and try to concentrate. 'He likes to nurture people.'

I nod at that. He's certainly very people-oriented at PCs Plus, clearly keen to relate to his staff and get the best out of them.

'People who are...' She pauses, her eyes scanning mine. 'Let's say, less fortunate. He obviously gets great satisfaction from it.' She smiles enigmatically and then walks on, her pace picking up as she heads for the stairs.

I stare after her in bewildered confusion. Does she mean me?

FIFTEEN

Kat thinks I'm making a huge mistake swapping a job with future prospects for one which has none but she accepts that I need the extra money. I was nervous myself at first with Megan seeming so unpredictable, but we soon settle into a routine. One evening, two weeks after I start working at the house, rather than go away and come back, Megan has suggested I stay and play with Ollie after his tea until it's time for her to leave to go to her appointment. I'm happy to, but I do wish she'd given me a bit more notice, as I've had to cancel meeting Zach for a coffee, about which he wasn't pleased.

I'm emptying the dishwasher when Jake gets home. Coming into the kitchen area, he glances at me, but averts his gaze as Megan comes clacking towards us. She's in her work clothes, ready to go off to her meeting. I notice her killer heels, and wonder how she can walk in them.

'You're late,' she says to him.

He smiles wryly. 'Evening,' he answers pointedly.

She ignores him. 'Did you bring the printer cartridges?' she asks as he walks across to flick the kettle on.

He glances back at her, confused. 'What printer cartridges?'

'I mentioned it when I rang you. I told you I have some plans I need to print off for my meeting this evening.'

He knits his brow. 'Right. Well, I don't remember you mentioning it, but—'

'No, because you clearly didn't think it was important, did you?' she snaps. 'Because you consider my job is insignificant compared to yours.'

'Don't be ridiculous, Meg.' Jake sighs. 'I don't think that at all.'

'Just remember which side your bread is buttered, Jake,' she mutters.

Watching the interchange, perplexed, I glance at Jake. He shrugs, clearly also perplexed, then kneads his forehead with his thumb. 'I'll go back out,' he offers. 'PC World will still be open. I'll fetch some from there.'

'Don't bother. It's too late now,' Megan replies shortly. 'I'll email him the plans. We can print them there.'

'Him?' Jake's jaw visibly clenches as he watches her head to the hall.

'Miguel,' she provides.

'Right.' He draws in a breath. 'Give him my regards.'

'I'll make sure to,' she responds flatly.

I'm beginning to sense an underlying current here and I'm not quite sure what to do. 'I could go and fetch the cartridges,' I offer. 'I have Fern to feed, but it shouldn't take me too long to get there and back.'

Megan doesn't answer, and Jake shakes his head in despair. 'Thanks.' He gives me a small smile. 'I wouldn't worry about it, though. She's obviously keen to get off to *Miguel*.'

He enunciates the man's name scornfully, and I wonder why. Uncertain what to say, I smile back sympathetically.

'I'll go and check on the kids,' he says, his expression hurt as he glances again after Megan and then heads despondently for the hall.

I'm perplexed. Why has she turned on him, for no apparent reason that I can see? Yes, he forgot her cartridges, but he tried to put it right. And what was that charged interchange regarding Miguel all about?

'Shall I bring your coffee when I come up to feed Fern?' I call after him, thinking he could probably use one before going out for his evening appointment.

'Cheers, Ellie,' he answers gratefully. 'I'd forgotten about that.'

Megan leaves minutes later, instructing me to make sure that Jake isn't encouraging his son to spend too much time glued to his screen before bedtime. She means playing Pokémon, presumably, which is the game Ollie is usually glued to.

Assuring her I will, I roll my eyes as the front door closes sharply behind her, then grab Fern's bottle and Jake's coffee and head up the stairs after him.

I find him lying on Ollie's bed, his tie pulled loose and his arm around his son's shoulders as he reads to him from his *Pokémon Adventures* book. I carry his coffee across to him.

'Thanks, Ellie.' He smiles appreciatively, but there's a deep sadness in his eyes, dark half-moons under them. He clearly doesn't sleep well, and no wonder when things between him and Megan are so obviously strained.

Leaving him to have a quiet father-and-son moment, I pull the door to and hurry to feed Fern, who's beginning to fret. She's been quite fractious compared to when I first babysat, which is possibly due the change in her routine. I tried everything bar playing the piano to settle her earlier. I hope she drops off more easily this evening. I so want to talk to Jake before he leaves.

Having fed her, shushed and soothed her while she tested her lungs, I'm walking around the room with her in frustration, desperate for her to go to sleep. I breathe out a sigh of relief as I see her eyelids grow heavy. I'm carrying her to her cot when I hear the front door open and close. Thinking Jake must be leaving, I hurry to put her down, and my stomach lurches when I almost catch her head on the cot frame as I lower her into it.

'Shit,' I curse, and she jerks awake. Feeling guilty and sick to my soul at what might have happened, I hug her to me. 'Sorry, sweetheart,' I murmur. 'Silly Ellie.' *Get a grip, for God's sake.* I try to slow the rapid beat of my heart and then to quash my irritation as she begins to whimper again. It's not her fault. I've obviously startled her. I can't help feeling disappointed, though, that I've missed the opportunity to grab some time with Jake alone.

It's a good half an hour before she's sleepy. Carefully I lower her into her cot once again and tiptoe to the nursery door, closing it softly behind me. Theo was such a good baby, and not having much experience of babies at this age during my childcare training, I didn't realise how stressful nursing such a little one can be. At least I didn't actually bang her head. I dread to think what Megan's reaction would be if I had to admit to that.

SIXTEEN

I'm heading along the landing when I notice that the main bedroom door is open. Jake must have forgotten to shut it. Megan insists on that door staying closed, probably to deter me from snooping. I'm about to close it when I spot her make-up bag on the dressing table. Having watched her get ready for her meeting this evening while she gave me a list of instructions for tomorrow – reminding me to collect Fern's asthma prescription, to make sure I'm here to let the pool man in, to be an angel and put the washing on – I can't help being curious about the products she uses. My mother used to cake her make-up on, probably still does, and only ever looked tarty, which my loving father frequently pointed out. Megan, though, applies hers with the meticulousness of an artist, serving to enhance her already beautiful features.

Sighing as I survey my own mousy features in the mirror, I have a little rummage in the bag. It's all quality stuff, unsurprisingly. Yves Saint Laurent lipsticks and eyeliners, Giorgio Armani Luminous Silk Foundation. The Nars Multiple Orgasm Cream Blush makes my eyes boggle. I doubt it will actually make me orgasmic, but the colour is gorgeous and it can't fail to improve my pallid complexion. Zach says he likes my natural look, but then he's more likely to get orgasmic over his gaming than he is over me.

I hesitate, and then decide to try just a tiny amount of the various products. Emulating Megan's careful application, I finish with a final sweep of lash-lengthening mascara and am amazed at the transformation. If it wasn't for my mad tangle of hair, I might actually look attractive. Gathering the hair up on top of my head, I survey myself in the mirror. I might get it cut, I decide. Go wild and get some highlights too.

I'm making sure everything is as I found it when I hear someone coming through the front door. My stomach does a little flip. Quickly I slip out of the bedroom and head back along the landing. I start as I see Jake in the hall.

'Hey.' Looking up, he smiles. 'The guy cancelled,' he says with a sigh.

'Oh no,' I commiserate. He might have let Jake know before he set off.

'Can't be helped. His kid's sick, apparently. He's rearranged, so it's not a problem.' He furrows his brow as he studies me, then tips his head to one side. 'You look different.'

I feel myself blush so profusely I'm thinking I really didn't need the orgasmic stuff. 'I've been experimenting with my make-up,' I tell him, a little white lie.

He nods. 'It's nice.'

A thrill of excitement runs through me. I can't deny I'm pleased he's noticed. He's a genuinely nice person. He really doesn't deserve to be sniped at the whole time. I give him a warm smile back. 'I didn't realise you'd left.'

'Sorry. I should have said. Care to join me for a drink?' He extracts a bottle from the bag he's carrying. 'Liquid sustenance. I stopped by the off-licence,' he adds.

My chest constricts as I realise it's whisky. But he hasn't

eaten. There's no way I can let him drink that on an empty stomach.

He walks through the lounge area towards the patio doors, heading for the seating area by the pool, and I hurry down the stairs.

Five minutes later, after rustling him up a ham and salad sandwich, I go tentatively out to him. I note he's working his way through a large measure of whisky, which he obviously feels he needs, and I worry for him. I know the damage alcohol can do and pray this isn't a habit. 'I made you a sandwich,' I say as he glances up at me. 'You should eat something,'

He looks surprised, and then smiles appreciatively. 'You're a good person, Ellie. Whoever made you feel bad enough to want to harm yourself could never measure up to you in a million years.'

I stare at him, stunned. No one thinks I'm good. After what happened to Finley at the nursery, the people there didn't think so. Nor did the police. I don't think I'm good either.

'Sit.' Jake indicates the seat next to him. 'We'll hear her on the baby monitor in the lounge,' he assures me, guessing why I would be hesitant as I glance back to the house. 'It's a nice night. I can't promise you scintillating conversation, but I could use some company.'

I'm not sure Megan will like it if she finds out, but how can I refuse? He looks so lonely sitting out here on his own, probably contemplating his unhappy marriage.

'Drink?' he asks, about to rise to go to the pool bar for a glass.

'No.' I shake my head. 'I don't. I, um... My parents drank. A lot. I prefer not to.'

He studies me, a pensive frown forming in his brow. 'I understand.' He nods. 'Don't worry, I don't do this regularly.'

'Good.' I smile, relieved. 'It doesn't help fix your problems. If anything, it just makes them worse.'

'I know,' he concedes, 'but at least I'll sleep tonight.'

My heart wrenches for him, but I don't comment. I'm not sure what to say that won't make me seem like I'm prying or passing judgement.

'Was it the bloke I saw outside your building who made you feel like life wasn't worth living?' he asks after a pause, catching me completely off guard.

I have no idea how to answer. He asked directly, but kindly. He could have shied away from it, as most people would, but he didn't, because he cares, because that's the kind of person he is. 'No,' I reply eventually, glancing away. 'It wasn't Zach.'

As I look back at him, Jake scrutinises me carefully. 'You don't want to talk about it, I get it.' He nods. 'Just remember I have a shoulder, should you ever feel you need one.'

'I know.' I smile. 'Likewise.'

We don't talk much about anything too consequential after that, preferring small talk, less painful talk, or else to sit in companionable silence watching the wind whisper across the water.

'I should go,' I say reluctantly after a while. 'It took me ages to get Fern down, but she'll be due her next feed soon and I have to make up some bottles.'

'Thanks, Ellie. For everything.' Jake catches my hand as I stand. 'About Megan,' he says, 'try not to judge her. She doesn't mean to be the way she is. She's just... over-organised, I guess you'd call it.'

I think that might be a slight understatement. The woman seems obsessive to me, and way too possessive of Jake.

'I suppose it's her way of coping,' he adds. 'Probably a better way than hitting the bottle.' He glances wryly down at his glass. 'Like I said, we're having a bit of a rough patch. I'm sure we'll get through it.'

'I hope so,' I say, giving his hand a squeeze. I feel for Megan after all she's been through, but I can't help thinking that Jake deserves better, someone who's capable of caring about him. 'I should get on.'

Giving him a reassuring smile, I reclaim my hand and head back through the patio doors. Hearing a noise on the landing as I pass through the hall, I look up, and my heart jars.

'Fern's awake,' Megan says, her face inscrutable as she descends the stairs.

Shit. I squeeze my eyes closed. 'Sorry, I was going to get her feed ready. I'll go up and fetch her.'

Megan surveys me through narrowed eyes as she reaches the hall. 'Have you been in my room?' she asks, and my heart almost stops beating.

'I, um... Yes, I—'

'Using my make-up?'

I drop my gaze. It will be as obvious as the products on my face if I lie.

I feel her eyes burning into me for a long, unbearable moment. Then, 'Suits you. You might do better to remember less is more, though,' she says, and walks past me.

SEVENTEEN

As I'm going straight to meet Zach from here this evening, Megan has graciously given me the use of the spare room to get changed in. I'm feeling guilty after splurging a good chunk of my first month's wages on high-end make-up, but having taken my time to apply it as meticulously as Megan would, I'm thinking it was worth it. I can afford the odd luxury in my life now. After securing my hair in an updo, I'm inserting the little diamanté studs I've also treated myself to in my earlobes when I hear raised voices downstairs.

'You're never *here*, so why would you care if *I'm* not?' Megan's agitated tones reach me and I feel desperately sorry for Jake. She's being so unfair to him. He made a real effort to get back early tonight and spend some time with Ollie. He took him to play footie in the park and then encouraged him out of his room to play non-computer-based games in the lounge. Admittedly, they ended up playing the Pokémon card game, at Ollie's insistence, but at least he wasn't glued to his screen. And Jake clearly dotes on his daughter. I found him in the nursery the other evening with Fern fast asleep in his arms. He was simply staring at her, as if drinking in every detail.

'Look, just forget it. I can't go on like this, Megan. Do what you want.' Jake sounds exasperated, which takes me by surprise. I imagine it would take a lot to rile him.

Hearing his footsteps on the stairs, I guess he's coming up, and I grab my bag and hurry to the landing.

'I will!' Megan shouts after him, sounding tearful.

I wonder what on earth's going on, since their argument seems to have come right out of the blue. 'Everything okay?' I ask Jake hesitantly.

'As okay as it ever is,' he grates, his eyes full of angry frustration. 'Sorry,' he apologises immediately. 'I didn't mean to snap at you. It's just... stuff. You know?'

Pausing on the landing, he studies me for a moment. 'You look nice,' he comments.

A flutter of butterflies takes off in my tummy. 'Thank you.' I drop my gaze.

'Like the perfume,' he adds. 'Going somewhere special?'

I shake my head. He's just a foot away from me, watching me so intently I feel goosebumps rise on my skin. 'Just to meet Zach.' I give him a small smile. I'm actually not overly excited about seeing Zach, since he's been sulking, demanding to know why he doesn't see more of me.

'Ah, the boyfriend.' Jake smiles, but there's something behind his eyes I can't quite read. It's not jealousy. Would that it were. Sadness, I guess, because he's living such a loveless existence. I so wish I could be the one to fix that for him. 'Enjoy,' he says.

'I'll try,' I answer with a sigh.

'Try?' He frowns, a troubled look now in his eyes, and I realise he's reading something into my half-hearted response.

'Zach's a bit moody because he hasn't seen much of me lately, although I can't think why when he prefers gaming with his friends to being with me,' I explain, and then feel bad. It's true I've been fed up with Zach appearing to take me for granted, showing up when he wanted to, going on about making plans for us to get a place of our own together and then making no effort to do anything about it. I'm not sure I want that now, but Zach's not a bad person. He's just young and self-centred. Unlike Jake.

Jake studies me for a second longer, then takes me completely aback. 'Don't settle for second best, Ellie,' he says softly, moving towards me and reaching to brush a straggle of hair from my face. 'You're worth more than that. You just don't believe you are.'

I'm mesmerised by the concern in his eyes, the fondness. Yes, definitely that. No one has ever looked at me like that before, not even Zach.

I'm about to tell him I won't, but the words die in my throat when I see Megan glaring at me from where she stands below in the hall. Clearly noting my alarm, Jake glances back at her and she shoots him a look a pure venom. 'I know what you're doing, Jake Harington,' she cries. 'I know *why*. It won't work, do you hear me? It won't!'

'Shit!' Jake exclaims as she flies up the stairs, her eyes pivoting between us as she reaches the landing.

'You're so transparent it's laughable,' she hisses, her gaze contemptuous as it settles back on Jake. She doesn't wait for him to answer, but storms on to their bedroom, banging the door closed behind her.

He's about to follow her when Ollie appears from his room. 'Daddy, why are you and Mummy arguing?' he asks worriedly. 'Is it because of me?'

Jake sucks in a breath and hurries towards him. 'No.' Crouching down, he holds the little boy's gaze. 'We had a falling-out, that's all.'

Ollie considers, a small furrow forming in his brow. He doesn't look convinced.

'Why would you think it's because of you?' Jake asks gently.

Ollie hesitates. 'Because I said I loved Phoebe more than Mummy when she went away,' he confesses, his face etched with guilt. 'Mummy said it was a bad thing to say.'

'Christ,' Jake mutters half under his breath. 'No, it's not because of you, Ollie,' he tells him firmly. 'You said that in the heat of the moment because you were upset. Do you understand?'

'Uh-huh.' Ollie nods uncertainly. 'I think so.'

Jake eases him close and kisses the top of his head. 'We all do it, Ollie. Mummy and I were doing it just now, saying things in the heat of the moment. It happens sometimes when emotions get the better of us. It's not because of you, I promise. Okay?'

Ollie nods into his shoulder. 'Okay,' he says, his voice small.

Jake hugs him hard, and something melts inside me. He really is lovely. Why does Megan insist on hurting him so badly?

'Do you want me to stay?' I ask. Zach will be furious, but I can't bring myself to leave if Jake needs me.

Jake glances at me, then shakes his head and smiles gratefully. 'Come on, little guy.' He turns his attention back to Ollie, standing and taking him by the hand. 'Let's go and fire up that Nintendo.'

'Are we going to play Pokémon?' Ollie's eyes gleam with excitement as he looks up at his father.

'We are,' Jake gives him a conspiratorial wink, 'but whatever you do, don't let on to Mummy or I'll be in big trouble, okay?'

As I watch them walk together to Ollie's room, I can't help feeling wary. Jake's being divisive. Deliberately? I wonder. And does he realise he's also encouraging Ollie to be dishonest?

EIGHTEEN

'You could have called me,' Zach says moodily, even though I've just explained why I was late getting to the pub.

'I tried,' I respond defensively, with no idea why I should be. 'You were on your phone. I was driving. I haven't worked out how to send a hands-free text.'

'This will be in your fancy new car provided by your loaded boss?' Zach mutters.

I don't rise to that. It isn't fancy. It's just a Mini Cooper, and it isn't new. I suspect it was Phoebe's before it came to me. It was filthy outside and full of mess inside: sweet wrappers, crisp packets, empty single measure wine bottles, worryingly. She either liked the odd tipple, or she was driven to it by Megan. That wouldn't surprise me. There was also a birthday card for her twenty-first birthday. It was from Jake, heart-stoppingly. But then I can imagine him sending her one, simply out of kindness.

'I'm responsible for those children, Zach,' I point out. 'I can't just walk out if there's a crisis.'

He shrugs and takes a slurp of his pint. 'If you ask me, there has to be a reason his wife's so pissed off with him. I mean, a good-looking bloke driving a flashy Beamer, he's going to get offers, isn't he?'

I sigh inwardly. What is it with men and status symbols? I don't bother to comment.

'So what about us?' Zach asks.

'What do you mean?' With my mind still on Jake and why Megan would stay with him when she so obviously dislikes him, I frown distractedly.

'You know,' Zach answers with an awkward shrug. 'I miss you.'

I pick up my Coke, an evasive tactic while I try to think what to say to him. The truth is, I have used my childminding duties as an excuse to not see him.

'I love you, Ellie,' he says, reaching for my free hand. 'I know I don't say it very often, but I do.'

Oh no. Guilt blooms inside me and now I have no idea what to say. I'm not being fair to him. My feelings haven't changed suddenly because of Jake – I was beginning to wonder if we had a future anyway when I came second to his mates – but Jake has made me realise I don't love Zach the way I'm supposed to.

'We could go back to yours now,' he suggests hopefully, and I feel more awful by the second. I have to tell him I'm not sure about our relationship. I can't bring myself to, though, when he's just told me he loves me.

'Well?' He looks apprehensive, and I feel like the biggest bitch ever.

'I... I'm not sure,' I mumble. 'Megan has an early start tomorrow and she's asked if I can stay over,' I lie.

'Bloody hell, Ellie.' Zach looks well peeved. 'You're always there.'

'No I'm not.'

'Yes you *are*. You're entitled to time off, you know. Unless you can't tear yourself away from Jake, of course.'

'Don't be ridiculous,' I say, feeling caught out. 'I'm responsible for a baby. Part of my job is to be there at night if they need me to be. I can't just—'

'Why do you have to do nights, though? She's not *your* baby,' he points out angrily.

I don't answer. I don't want to argue with him. It will achieve nothing.

'You wish she was, don't you?' He cocks his head to one side, his eyes narrowed as he studies me. 'Is that why you're so determined to dislike his missus, I wonder? Because you're jealous?'

I feel that like a low blow to my stomach. 'It sounds to me like it's *you* who's jealous, Zach,' I retort shakily.

'And I suppose I have no reason to be, right?' He folds his arms and leans back, his eyes hard as they search mine. 'He's just your boss, isn't he? A good-looking, flashy bastard you have no interest in whatsoever – which is why you're wearing make-up and heels all of a sudden.'

'That's absurd.' My face burns furiously.

'Is it?' He holds my gaze. 'I don't remember you ever dressing up to meet me at the local pub before.'

'I'm leaving.' I scrape my chair back and get to my feet, all eyes at the surrounding tables swivelling towards me as I do.

'He fancies his chances, Ellie. You *know* he does,' Zach shouts after me as I stride towards the exit. 'What happened to the woman who worked there before you, hey? Don't you think her leaving them in the lurch is a big fucking red flag? You want to know why his wife's on his back? Find *her*. Ask her why she left in such a hurry.'

NINETEEN

I can't quite meet Jake's eyes as I come through the front door to find him in the hall. He's been in the gym, I gather, noting his sweatpants and a T-shirt that show off his toned physique. It's pretty obvious why Zach would be jealous. This man is undeniably attractive, more so for being hot and sweaty. I feel a flutter deep in the pit of my belly and quickly avert my gaze.

'You weren't out long,' he comments.

'I, um, have a headache. I just came back to get changed and grab my things.' I smile faintly and head onwards to the stairs.

'Can I get you some paracetamol?' Jake asks behind me.

'No. Thanks. I have some in my bag.' I wave back at him and hurry on. I need space to think. Jake's presence, particularly in his current state of attire, is not going to allow me that.

Once in the spare room, I close the door and lean against it. My heart is still banging from all that Zach said, all that he accused me of. Was he right? I can't deny I do have feelings for Jake. I care about him. I'd be lying if I told myself I didn't fantasise about being with him, but I don't imagine in a million years I ever could be. I'm not *jealous* of Megan. I huff and peel myself from the door, pulling off my hair scrunchie as I march across the room. And what on earth was Zach going on about their previous au pair for? It's *him* who's jealous. He's envious of Jake, of all he's achieved; determined to discredit him in my eyes. I *know* Jake. He's not the sort to take advantage of a situation, to hurt a woman. He clearly doesn't want to hurt Megan, who seems hell-bent on hurting him. Phoebe didn't leave in a hurry because of Jake. She left with her boyfriend, for goodness' sake. Agitatedly, I kick off the shoes I chose because they had heels, rather than the flats I normally wear. Zach was wrong. I wasn't dressing up for Jake.

So who were *you dressing up for?* asks a cynical voice in my head.

Myself. Defiantly I reach to tug off my top and manage to catch it on one of the stud earrings I'd forgotten I was wearing. *Damn.* Irritated with myself, I wrestle the top off the rest of the way and the stud plops to the floor. *Typical.* I toss the top on the bed and peer down. The earring is nowhere to be seen. I pad around the fur rug, half expecting to pierce my foot on it. Finally I drop to my hands and knees to search. I'm running the flat of my hand under the base of the bed when I come across something else. Something small and envelope-shaped, probably dropped and inadvertently kicked out of sight. Pressing my hand over it, I slide it out and straighten up. It's a passport, I realise.

Curious, I open it. The photo inside isn't of Megan or Jake, as I expected, but of an open-faced, beautiful young woman. She must be about my age. My mind takes a moment to register the name on the document. *Phoebe Anderson.*

My stomach lurches. It can't be. Didn't she supposedly go off abroad with her seedy married boyfriend? How could she have done that without her passport? Trepidation prickles the length of my spine and I glance to the wardrobe. Why is it still locked?

TWENTY

Dragging my hair from my face, I plop down on the bed and try to take stock. There's probably nothing in the wardrobe. And Phoebe must have realised she'd misplaced her passport and applied for another one. It's the only thing that makes sense. Jake wouldn't have lied about it. Why would he? Still, though, suspicion gnaws away at me and I have another quick check under the bed. Finding nothing but a single shirt button, I straighten up, frowning as I scrape a speck of dried mud off it with my thumbnail. How did it come to be here? The house was built from scratch. As far as I've gleaned, this room was Phoebe's, which means the button must have been hers. But there's nothing suspicious about that. I own several shirt blouses. In fact, one of my staple items of clothing is an over sized white shirt.

Despite my reassurances to myself, though, my heart beats a manic drumbeat in my chest as I concede that Jake might have had an affair with her. He's only human, after all, and I doubt he and Megan have a very satisfactory sex life. Did he tell Megan that Phoebe had taken off abroad when in reality he had her installed in an apartment somewhere? It's possible. Yes, but if so, why isn't he there with her instead of living in purgatory here? Because of the children? I scramble to make sense of it. He wouldn't get custody of them, would he? It's unlikely, unless he painted Megan in a very bad light. Even with her being so horrible to him, he wouldn't do that to her, take her children away from her.

I'm imagining scenarios, I realise. Phoebe had a boyfriend, Megan said so. A dodgy character, apparently, which I'm sure he must have been if he was cheating on his wife. Even so, I still need answers. I need to get into that wardrobe, if only to establish that there's nothing untoward in there. I won't rest for wondering if I don't.

I recall seeing a small toolbox in one of the kitchen utility cupboards and head out of the room, checking on Fern and Ollie on the way. Finding them both sleeping, I hesitate on the landing and then go quietly down the stairs. I'm relieved when I see no sign of Jake in the lounge area. As I walk past the kitchen island, I nearly leap out of my skin when he pops up from behind it. '*Hell.* You almost gave me heart failure.' I press a hand to my chest and attempt to slow my palpitations.

'That scary, hey?' He laughs. 'Sorry, I didn't mean to make you jump. I was just grabbing some red wine. Care to join me for a drink on the patio.'

'That would be nice.' Thinking it will be a chance to do a little fishing, I accept. 'I'll stick to water, though, if that's okay.'

'Ah, right. Still or fizzy?' He heads for the fridge.

'Still's fine.'

He fetches a bottle of water and I follow him through the lounge to the table on the patio.

He chivalrously pulls a chair out for me and, once I'm seated, sits down opposite me. 'So, how's your boyfriend?' he asks. 'Zach, isn't it?'

'That's right.' I try to sound casual. 'He's fine. He has an early start tomorrow, so he didn't mind that we only had a couple of drinks.'

'Sounds like he might have minded?' Jake eyes me curiously as he passes me my glass.

'No, he wouldn't. He's all right,' I assure him. But Zach's not all right, is he? He's jealous, suspicious of Jake's motives. He's wrong about him, I'm confident of that. He's also suspicious about Phoebe's sudden departure, though, and that has shaken me.

Jake nods, but he doesn't look entirely convinced.

'Can I ask you something, Jake?' I venture, after a pause.

'Certainly.' He smiles. 'I'll do my best to answer.'

'The wardrobe in the spare room,' I start hesitantly, 'I can't open it. It's not a big deal,' I add quickly. 'I was thinking I could store one or two things in there for when I stay over. I just wondered why it was locked.'

He looks surprised. 'I didn't realise it was. Megan said it was faulty, but she didn't say it wouldn't open. I'll get Andy to take a look at it. He does a few odd jobs around the house for us.'

'Great.' I smile, relieved. Jake clearly doesn't know anything about it. I'm not sure there's anything *to* know, but I'm glad he appears oblivious to it, which suggests he didn't often go into that room. 'Megan did say she would get the handyman to take a look,' I add, in case he asks her about it, 'but I didn't want to bother her with it.'

'She probably forgot,' he says pensively. 'She gets distracted with her work and one thing and another, as you might have gathered.'

Preoccupied with petty detail, I mentally correct him. I nod understandingly, then take a breath. 'She seems very angry with you,' I venture tentatively.

He looks surprised, then smiles ruefully. 'She does, doesn't she? Although I'm not sure it's me she's angry with.'

I frown in confusion. *Who then?*

He glances at me cautiously. 'She, er...' He stops and draws in a tight breath. 'There's someone else.'

What? I squint at him in utter astonishment. Is he saying what I think he is?

He kneads his forehead with his thumb. When he looks back at me, it's with a mixture of deep embarrassment and hurt, and my heart bleeds for him. 'I'm sorry. I shouldn't have said anything. It puts you in an impossible situation. I'm sure we'll work things out.'

'It's okay,' I assure him quickly, uncertain what else to say. I'm reeling inside. Never in my wildest dreams would I have imagined Megan was treating him like dirt because *she* was having an affair. Why on earth does he stand for it? *How* could he?

'You won't mention that I said anything, will you?' he asks, a flicker of panic in his eyes.

'Of course not. I would never repeat anything you—'

'Well, well,' Megan says behind us, causing me to almost choke, 'don't you two look cosy?'

TWENTY-ONE

I arrive early the next morning, hoping to catch Jake. I'm worried about him. More so because last night Megan didn't launch into him as I'd expected she might. She simply looked at him, a long, searching look, and then walked back inside.

'*Jesus*,' Jake murmured, squeezing his eyes closed. 'I should...' He glanced after her. His expression was one of wary apprehension as he looked back at me, and then he pushed his chair back and followed her.

Going in after him, I watched Megan walk across the hall and mount the stairs. She didn't look at him. She didn't say a single word until their bedroom door closed. Muted, heated conversation. I feel so sorry for Jake. I wish I could pluck up the courage to tell her to stop being such a bitch to him. But I suppose that won't help him if he's living in hope that her affair will blow over. The man must have the patience of a saint.

As I cross the hall, I realise that Jake is already up. He pauses in his coffee-making and smiles at me in that heartbreakingly sad way he has. 'Early start?' I ask, giving him a warm smile back. He looks dreadful, exhaustion etched into his features, dark bruises under his eyes. He clearly hasn't slept a wink. I wish I'd realised that Megan hadn't gone to her appointment last night. I would never have gone out to the patio with him if I'd known she was here.

He glances at me as I go to the worktop to check the bottle steriliser. His ice-blue irises are flecked with such anguish I feel my heart catch. 'I have a buyer to see at the Bristol branch,' he says. 'I could do without it today, to be honest, but I've already postponed once, so...' He shrugs and turns back to the coffee filter.

I watch as he rolls his shoulders, clearly attempting to relieve some of the tension there, and I worry that he won't be safe driving. 'Be careful on the motorway, won't you?' I eye him with trepidation.

'The caffeine will keep me awake,' he says, with another reassuring smile. 'Give Ollie a hug for me and tell him I'll get back as early as I can, will you?'

'I will,' I promise, and turn to the sink to busy myself washing up the glasses we used last night. Why is she doing this? Does she *want* him to crash his bloody car? A knot of anger tightens inside me, and I find myself blurting the words out before I can stop them. 'Why is she so awful to you, Jake?' I turn to him. 'Why do you put up with it? Why don't you leave her?'

He looks shocked at my outburst, and I immediately want to reel the words back in, It's absolutely none of my business. It's beyond comprehension, though, why he would stay with her. He's scared for her after her attempt on her life, I get that, but she treats him with so much contempt.

He nods slowly, as if considering, then heaves in a breath. It takes an eternity for him to breathe out. 'Because I care about her,' he says, repeating what he said once before.

'I know, but...' I stop with an exasperated sigh. *How can you care so much about her when she's so unutterably cruel to you?* I want to ask.

'I know it's difficult to understand,' he adds after a second.

'Can I tell you something?' he goes on. 'About my background. I think it might put things into perspective a little.'

I nod. The look in his eyes is one of uncertainty, as if he's wondering whether he can trust me. I hope he knows that he can.

'I haven't always had such a luxurious lifestyle,' he continues hesitantly. 'I had no money growing up, and it was tough. I come from a broken home.' He pauses, glancing awkwardly down and back. 'Extremely broken. I don't want that for my kids. Whatever's happening between us, Megan's their mother. I'm their father. We owe it to them to try to work things out and be there for them. Both of us.'

I stare at him with a mixture of wonder and confusion. How does that woman sleeping upstairs in the lap of luxury fail to realise how lucky she is to have him? I wonder. I also wonder if Jake realises that staying together for the sake of his children might cause them more psychological trauma than separating would. He looks so vulnerable, though, I decide that now isn't a good time to impart my thoughts.

'I suppose I'm waiting for a miracle,' he adds with a half-hearted smile.

I want to tell him he's waiting in vain, that she never looks at him with anything but disdain in her eyes; that he deserves to be with someone who cares for him. *Someone like me.* The thought creeps into my head involuntarily. 'I understand, sort of.' I offer him a smile back, though my stomach churns with anger and a longing I hardly dare acknowledge. 'I have a similar background,' I confess, feeling safe to disclose at least that much now that Jake has confided in me. 'I get your need not to put your children through a messy break-up. You're a special man, though, Jake Harington. Just so you know.'

'Yeah.' He shrugs sadly 'Would that Megan thought so.'

'Do you mind if I ask you something?' I study him carefully, wondering what his reaction will be. He'll probably tell me to mind my own business. I wouldn't blame him, but I hope he realises I'm only asking out of concern for him.

He tips his head to one side. 'Go ahead.' He looks me over curiously. 'I don't bare my soul often. You might as well go for it while I am.'

'Did you have a prenuptial agreement?' I ask quickly. 'You and Megan. Did she...' I stop as his face again registers shock.

'I, er...' He furrows his brow. 'We did, yes.' He nods uncomfortably. 'I'm not even sure why now, except... There was a blip, when we were engaged, and... Well, we decided it might be best.'

As I see the humiliation in his eyes, I suspect that she might have cheated on him then too. But why attempt to take her own life if she didn't love him? It was a ploy to keep him, clearly. She's treating him like a cash cow. And yet he still cares for her. If I were Jake, I'd feel like killing her.

TWENTY-TWO

Megan surprises me as I'm about to leave for the school run. 'Would you like some coffee?' she calls as I cross the hall. I stop, mystified as to why she would be asking when I have Fern in her car seat and Ollie holding my hand with his coat on.

She turns to face me, her expression perplexed for a second. Then, 'Good Lord, is that the time?' She glances at the kitchen clock and then back to me. 'I must have overslept.'

Clearly, and no doubt blissfully. I work to hide my disdain.

'I'll leave the filter on and you can grab some when you get back,' she offers.

'Thanks.' I force a smile.

'No problem.' She smiles back, and now I'm growing wary. I've been girding myself this morning, fully expecting her to be short with me after finding me with Jake on the patio last night, and here she is being nice to me. What's the catch?

I wait as she walks across to us. I'm thinking she might offer to look after Fern as she's here, though I'd rather she didn't. Fern is fast asleep, but she's been really fretful up until now. Hearing her small chest wheezing earlier, I had to use her inhaler, and she fought me trying to put her face mask on. I'd much rather Megan didn't unsettle her.

I needn't have worried. Her expression pensive, Megan simply strokes her daughter's cheek with the back of her hand and then turns her attention to Ollie.

Her gaze travels to the Pokémon battle figure he's holding, and I swear I feel the tension through his hand as he waits for her to tell him he shouldn't be taking it to school, even though it's Toy Friday. Again, though, she surprises me, looking at him with a smile instead. 'Haven't we forgotten something?' she asks him.

Ollie glances up at me, confusion in his eyes, and I feel for Megan. Judging by her expectant expression and the finger she has pressed to her cheek, she's hoping for a goodbye kiss. Ollie, though, doesn't get the drift. But then she can hardly blame him, since she's not around most mornings when we leave.

Sighing good-naturedly, she eyes the ceiling and then crouches down. 'Bye. Have a good day,' she murmurs, pulling him into a hug.

As she eases away, Ollie smiles, looking pleased. And a touch relieved, I note, that he isn't in trouble. 'You too. Bye, Mummy,' he says politely.

'Thank you. I will.' Megan stands and ruffles his hair. 'Oh, Ellie.' She stops me as I carry on to the door. 'Don't worry about collecting him. I have something on later this morning – I'm seeing Miguel at his city pied à terre before he goes back to Portugal. He has a house he'd like me to look at with a view to possible renovation. I don't have much on later this afternoon, though, so I thought I would pick Ollie up from school and take him to the park. Would you like that, Ollie?'

'Uh-huh.' He nods.

Glancing down at him, I note that he also looks surprised.

'Good,' she says, oblivious, and wanders back to the kitchen.

I assume as she hasn't mentioned Fern that her daughter

isn't included in the family outing. I would like to point out that she isn't likely to hurry the bonding process if she has so little interaction with her, but hold my tongue. 'Bye,' I call instead, and hurry on out.

Half an hour later, having seen Ollie into school, I decide that today is probably as good a day as any to get my hair done. There's a walk-in salon in Worcester. I could go straight there now.

On my way back to the car, I'm about to ring the salon to check how busy they are when I receive a text from Megan: *I think you were the last one in after your chat with Jake by the pool last night. You forgot to lock the patio doors. Can you make absolutely sure you do so in future. I think I mentioned that Ollie's not a strong swimmer. We don't want him wandering out there, do we?*

I stare at it, baffled. I *did* lock the patio doors. After she and Jake had disappeared upstairs, I locked everything up, set the alarm and turned off the lights. At least I think I locked the patio doors. Perhaps Jake went out there this morning?

Whatever, I'll make sure they're locked in future.

TWENTY THREE

Once I'm back, I go straight upstairs and scrutinise my reflection in the large ornamental mirror on the landing wall. I hardly recognise myself. My straggle of mousy hair has been transformed into a gorgeous messy bob with subtle balayage blonde highlights and copper undertones. The overall effect is not dissimilar to Megan's in colour. I've kept mine longer, though, just past shoulder length. I could never be as stunning as Megan but I'm feeling more confident about myself lately. I think it has a lot to do with Jake having confidence in me.

I glance down at Fern nestled in my arms as she looks curiously up at me. 'It's gorgeous, isn't it, sweetheart? Do you think I'll turn heads?' I give her a wide smile and then laugh as she chuckles gleefully and reaches to try to grasp my newly styled locks. 'That's cheered you up, hasn't it, hey? It would be a bit drastic having to have my hair done every day to bring a smile to your face, though, wouldn't it, hmm?'

Carrying on to the nursery, I decide to have a few minutes' playtime with her on her mat before feeding her. After which, I'm thinking I might avail myself of some of the facilities. With my hair just coloured, I doubt a dip in the pool is a good idea, but as the weather is warming up rapidly, I quite fancy reading on one of the sunbeds for an hour.

Fern is delighted by me clapping my hands and then clapping hers together and pedalling her little legs, all of which will help her mobility. She's wide-eyed with excitement, jiggling about as I play peekaboo with her sensory toys, shaking the elephant with the built-in rattle and rustling her Peter Rabbit's ears.

Relieved that she seems more cheerful, I place her carefully in her cot, set her moon and stars musical mobile in motion and go downstairs to fetch her feed. She takes all of it, also a huge relief, and after I've hummed her a soft lullaby, she drifts miraculously off to sleep. I'm amazed. I should take her to the hairdresser's, where everyone cooed and fussed over her, every day if it has this effect.

Finally, some time for myself. The dishwasher needs unloading and I'll have to get Ollie his tea when he comes home, but I intend to make the most of it. Going quickly to the spare room, I dig out the bikini and denim shorts I've had stowed in my overnight bag should an occasion arise when I can actually use them. Since there's no one here but Fern, I decide to be brave and wear just the bikini. I might not immerse my whole body in the pool, but it would be nice to cool off in there.

Taking a towel down with me, and my bathrobe as a cover-up, I go to the kitchen for a soft drink. I pause at an open bottle of red wine on the worktop. One glass wouldn't hurt, I decide. It's time I stopped worrying about things that might never happen and lived a little. Sneaking a small glass, I head on out to the patio to make myself comfortable on the sunbed. Taking a sip of the wine, I'm surprised at how smooth it is. It's obviously expensive stuff. I've had red wine once before, at Kat's birthday curry bash. It was awful, like vinegar. This, though, I could get used to. I take another mouthful and begin to feel nicely relaxed.

I've just fired up my Kindle when I realise I've left my phone upstairs. Sighing, I place the Kindle down and go to fetch it in case Megan calls. *You're entitled to time off.* Zach's words spring to mind and I feel a stab of guilt as I recall how I walked out and left him in the pub. He's messaged me loads since, apologising, asking to meet. I suppose I should call him, although I have no clue what to say to him. My stomach tightens as I recall what he shouted after me as I left: *What happened to the woman who worked there before you, hey? Don't you think her leaving them in the lurch is a big fucking red flag? You want to know why his wife's on his back? Find her. Ask her why she left in such a hurry.*

He's wrong. I did wonder whether Jake might have had an affair with Phoebe, but after what he told me about Megan's blatant cheating, I now very much doubt it. He looked crushed when we spoke this morning. He clearly found it embarrassing and difficult to disclose what he did, but he was honest with me. He trusted me. He wasn't hiding any deep, dark secrets, which Zach clearly imagines he is. Unlike me. Guilt sweeps through me, almost consuming me whole, as an image of Theo lying at the foot of the stairs crashes into my mind, his limbs twisted at impossible angles, his small body broken. And Finley, the little boy at the nursery, I see him as if he's in front of me, petrifyingly still on the play mat, blood in his hair, blood everywhere. I can almost smell it. Who am I to judge Megan, really?

Quashing the memories that so often haunt me, I locate my phone where I left it on the bed, to find Zach has texted me again: *Please get back to me, Ellie. I'm worried about you.* Feeling even more guilty, if that's possible, I decide to call him now, while there's no one around. I should finish with him. I'm being unfair to him. If all we do is argue, there's no future for us anyway. That's not the whole reason, though. The fact is, although I thought I loved him, I don't think I ever truly did, not in the way a person should love someone they're intending to spend the rest of their life with.

He picks up straight away, as if he's been waiting for my call. 'Finally,' he says irritably. 'What's going on, Ellie?'

'I've no idea what you're talking about, Zach.' I try not to be irked by his belligerent tone. 'There's nothing going on as far as I'm concerned. I called because you've been messaging me.'

'Right. So things between you and the hotshot are just platonic, are they?'

Realising that he's spoiling for an argument, my heart drops. 'For goodness' sake, Zach, grow up, will you? He's my boss.' I sigh. Maybe this wasn't a good idea after all. I'm not sure I can handle another argument just now.

'So why are you tarting yourself up for him?' he asks.

'I'm *not*.' I feel my cheeks heat up, partly with indignation, partly with embarrassment.

He says nothing for a second. Then, 'He's trying to get into your knickers. You *know* he is, giving you sob stories, playing on your heartstrings. It's bloody obvious.'

'This is unbelievable.' I laugh in astonishment. Jake is doing nothing of the sort. The fact that Zach thinks he is says a lot more about *him* than anyone else. 'You're being disgusting, Zach, and totally immature.'

'And you're being an idiot if you imagine he'll give a damn about you once he gets what he wants. Blokes like him don't, Ellie. They don't get where they are giving a shit about people, least of all their employees, trust me.'

'I'm hanging up,' I warn him, anger and humiliation burning inside me. 'I'm not listening to this, Zach. You're just jealous. I can't go out with you if—'

'I've seen him.' He talks across me.

I go to end the call. But as much as I want to, I can't. 'Doing what?' My voice quavers. 'When?'

He pauses before answering. He has my attention and he

knows it. 'The other day,' he goes on, a hint of satisfaction in his tone, 'having a cosy meal out with a woman. One way classier than *you*,' he adds, aiming to hurt.

It works. His words cut through me like a knife. I glance in the dressing table mirror. And now I don't feel confident. I don't feel pretty, as I tried to kid myself I might be. Looking at myself sitting in a bikini from Peacocks, which was a big purchase for me, I feel pathetic. I told myself I was doing all this to bolster my confidence. I was lying, I *am* doing it to get Jake's attention. I know it. Excruciatingly, Zach does too.

'It was probably a client,' I respond, because even if I don't have any belief in myself, I believe in Jake.

'Oh, right.' Zach laughs scornfully. 'So it was just an intimate conversation they were having? So intimate, he was stuffing his tongue down his client's throat?'

'*Liar!*' I shout. 'You're lying, Zach. I've been here every evening this week and he's come straight home from work.' Did he *stay* home, though? The nagging thought occurs.

Zach goes quiet again, infuriatingly. 'You've really got it bad, haven't you?' he comments drolly after a minute. 'I didn't say it was an evening meal, Ellie.'

My heart goes into freefall and I end the call. Tears spring from my eyes and I jump to my feet. It's not true. He's making things up because he feels his fragile masculinity is under threat. Does he not think *that's* bloody obvious? Realising how ridiculous I must look parading about in a bikini, I head to the door to retrieve my things from the patio, my heart thudding. It almost stops dead as I pull the door open and hurry out – straight into Jake.

'Ellie? What is it?' He looks me over worriedly. 'Jesus.' His gaze shoots to the nursery door. 'It's not Fern, is it?'

'No,' I blurt, stopping him as he moves in that direction. 'She's sleeping.'

Relief sweeps his features. 'Okay.' He nods slowly, some of

the colour returning to his face. 'So what's happened?' he asks, a furrow forming in his brow. 'You're clearly upset.'

'It's nothing.' I drop my gaze, now acutely embarrassed. I don't want him seeing me like this, almost naked, my pale body and my vulnerabilities on show.

'If it has you in tears, it's not nothing,' he says softly. 'You can talk to me, you know.' He hesitates, then reaches out, pressing a finger under my chin and bringing my gaze gently back to him.

With nowhere to hide, I squeeze my eyes closed. 'It's Zach,' I admit, and swallow.

'Zach?' He sounds annoyed. 'What the hell has he done to upset you like this?'

'Nothing,' I mumble. 'It's just… We argued. He said some horrible things, and… It's over between us.'

Jake looks devastated for me. 'I'm sorry, Ellie,' he says, and wraps an arm around me. 'He doesn't deserve you.' There's nothing in his eyes but compassion and sincerity.

I know then that Zach's jealousy is justified. I should move away, but I can't. I'm mesmerised as Jake continues to hold my gaze. His lips are a whisper away from mine and I am lost, drawn irresistibly like metal to a magnet. There's a flicker of shock in his eyes as my mouth grazes his.

'Ellie…' He eases back, takes hold of my forearms. 'You're upset, emotional. You don't want this.' His voice is hoarse, his blue irises flecked with uncertainty and such deep intensity it sends a shock of sexual excitement right through me.

'Don't you?' I scan his face. If he rejects me now, I will die of shame.

He sucks in a sharp breath. 'I… We shouldn't,' he murmurs, 'I don't want to hurt—'

I silence him with my lips. His body tenses as I thread my arms around him. And then he breathes deeply and leans into me, and I am powerless to resist the desire that pumps like a drug through my body.

He kisses me back, hesitantly at first, and so gently I feel my insides melt. Then he grows bolder, easing my lips apart, finding my tongue with his and inviting me into his mouth. I *do* want this. I want him. The entire surface of my skin tingles in anticipation of him. He wants *me*. My pelvis dips, exquisite longing clenching my tummy as his kiss grows more urgent.

Again he draws back, and I see the agony now in his eyes as he does battle with his conscience. Also a primal urgency that sends a white-hot spasm right through me. He searches my face, then, finding what he needs there, pulls me towards him. One hand glides down my back, the other winding my hair tight as he tips my head back and crushes his mouth against mine.

TWENTY-FOUR

Wordlessly, lips locked, hands all over each other, we fumble our way through the spare bedroom door. 'Are you sure?' he asks, his magnetic blue eyes filled with the same mixture of fear and yearning I feel, and in that moment, I know that whatever the consequences, I'm one hundred per cent sure. He wants me. He cares about me. I didn't dare hope, but he does.

Megan. Her name whispers through my mind and I stuff my guilt down. *She doesn't deserve him.* I nod, but nervousness squirms inside me. What will he think when he sees all of me? What will he think of me afterwards?

He draws in a deep breath as I slide the straps of my bikini top over my shoulders, tugging it down to reveal my breasts. My heart bangs as he grazes his gaze over me, and then somersaults as he moves swiftly towards me. This time his kiss is deeper, sensual, his tongue plunging into me as if he's making love to my mouth. His hands are in my hair, gliding over my back as he trails his lips down my neck, seeking what I need him to. 'You're beautiful,' he whispers.

I catch a moan in my throat as he bends to suck a nipple into his mouth, circling it with his tongue, savouring the taste of me so gently I'm near to coming from that sensation alone. 'Jake,' I breathe, my voice thick with need.

'Shh,' he urges me, easing me back onto the bed. His eyes rove over me as he straightens up and yanks off his tie, fumbles with his buttons and then tugs his shirt over his head. 'You're beautiful, Ellie. Don't let anyone make you feel you're not.'

Joining me, he makes short work of my bikini bottoms and brings his mouth back to mine. 'Positive?' he asks.

Again I nod, incapable of coherent speech. As he positions himself over me, I watch him watching me as he presses himself slowly inside me. I breathe in sharply, my heart flooding with what I now dare to acknowledge is my love for this man. Is it possible that he might love me; that he sees in me something I can't see?

'Okay?' He checks. I love him for that. I absolutely do.

I swallow back a tight lump in my throat, feel a tear slide from the corner of my eye. I don't feel the need to wipe it away, not with him. That has to mean something, doesn't it? 'Perfect.' I smile.

Closing his own eyes briefly, he smiles back, withdrawing and thrusting slowly into me again. Stroking my hair from my face, he looks deeply into my eyes and increases the pace, deep, sure strokes, plunging into me over and over.

I raise my hips to meet him, matching his tempo, pushing my tongue into his mouth, my fingernails finding his back.

He tenses. 'I, er... Sorry,' he whispers. 'Probably not a good idea to leave scratches.'

'Oh. No. Of course.' I blink up at him, mortified. 'I'm sorry. I wasn't thinking. I—'

'Shh. No harm done,' he says. 'We just have to be careful.'

I smile, but my mind whirls. For how long? I wonder. He will have to tell Megan about us eventually. It will be impossible to hide this burning desire we feel for each other. But he can't just announce it, I reason with the voice of uncertainty. He'll need time. He'll need to make plans.

'For now,' he adds, as if reading my mind. The intensity is back in his eyes as he weaves his hands through my hair, presses his mouth back to mine and kisses me hungrily. 'We shouldn't be doing this,' he almost growls, thrusting harder and deeper until I buck beneath him. 'Tell me when, Ellie,' he urges me. He's holding back, so I can...

'Now!' I cry. A white-hot spasm clenches my muscles around him, followed by another, as he groans throatily and jolts inside me.

'Christ.' Exhaling hard, he sweeps his beautiful, concerned eyes over my face. 'Okay?' he checks. Again.

I nod, feeling ludicrously close to bursting into tears. This has never happened to me before. I don't think I've ever climaxed properly, let alone at the same time as a man who cares whether I do.

'Good.' He brushes my lips with his and then eases away from me. 'No regrets?' he asks.

'None,' I assure him. 'You?'

He doesn't look at me. 'We shouldn't have, Ellie. I shouldn't have,' he answers, and my heart falters. 'It's unfair on—'

He stops as a door bangs downstairs. 'Shit!' Shooting off the bed, he grabs his clothes from the floor and wrestles them on. 'Sorry,' he mumbles. 'You should probably...' He looks back at me from the door, his face full of remorse, then heads out and along the landing.

I should probably *what*? Panic climbs in my chest as I hear Ollie calling excitedly, 'Daddy!'

'Hey, little man?' Jake replies. 'How did school go today?'

'Good,' Ollie answers. 'I got a star for reading out loud. My teacher said my vo-cab-u...' he hesitates, 'vo-cab-u-lary is very good.'

'Oh wow. The boy's a genius.' Jake laughs, and a confusion

of emotion crashes through me. He's acting normally, as if nothing just happened between us. *Was* it nothing? Is that what making love with me means to him? Nausea swills inside me as I recall Zach's taunting comments. *He's trying to get into your knickers... you're being an idiot if you imagine he'll give a damn about you once he gets what he wants. Blokes like him don't...* I clamp my eyes closed, try to block out his voice. What we did together does mean something to Jake. I know it does. It was right there in his eyes. He's acting normally because he has to. What else did I expect him to do?

'You're home early.' I hear Megan addressing him in her usual starched tones as I scramble around for underwear, jeans and top and tug them on.

'My meeting finished early,' Jake replies from the landing. 'The guy had a family crisis he needed to get back to.'

'I'm glad we're not the only ones who have family crises,' Megan responds drily. 'Where's Ellie?' she asks – and I freeze.

'Still in the nursery,' Jake answers. 'She's just got Fern off to sleep. I'll tell her you're looking for her when she comes out, shall I?'

Megan doesn't respond for an excruciating heartbeat. Then, 'Do that,' she says, and clacks off towards the kitchen.'

He's lying to her. Lying easily. A knot of uneasiness tightens inside me. Of course he is. I quash it. Because he has to. *For now.*

TWENTY-FIVE

Sure that guilt must be written all over my face, I'm relieved when Megan doesn't look at me as I walk into the kitchen area. 'I'm making Ollie a sandwich,' she says flatly. 'He's hungry.'

'Oh.' I hover awkwardly behind her. 'I was just going to get his tea. I wasn't sure what time you would be back, though, so—'

'Did Fern not have her feed on time?' She talks across me.

'Yes,' I assure her, willing my face not to give me away as she turns towards me. 'She's taken a while to go down, though. I didn't want to leave her as she's been a bit snuffly.'

She narrows her eyes, scrutinising me carefully. 'Might that be something to do with the obnoxious fumes she inhaled at the hair salon, do you think?'

'I, um...' I feel my cheeks flush furiously. 'I parked her pushchair by the door. They left it open because of the hot weather.' I grapple for a way to make it sound like I haven't been neglectful, which is what she's clearly implying.

She arches her eyebrows, and I realise with a sinking feeling that I've just made things worse. 'I was close enough to keep an eye on her,' I add quickly.

She folds her arms, her gaze going to my hair. 'The colour suits you,' she says after an interminably long pause.

'Thank you.' I shift uncomfortably.

She turns to pick up the sandwich and clacks across the tiles, pausing in front of me. 'Nice perfume,' she comments, her eyes holding mine, making me feel horribly exposed.

'J'Adore.' I supply the name, uncertain what else to say.

'I think you might have overdone it a little. You might want to use it more sparingly next time,' she suggests.

I see a flash of suspicion in her eyes and my heart pounds. She knows. After dressing hurriedly, I drenched myself in perfume to mask the smell of Jake on me, all over me – and she *knows*. Swallowing back a hard knot of guilt, I try not to let my gaze linger on him as he comes into the kitchen.

He glances briefly at me and then back at her as she clicks open the waste bin and drops the sandwich in. 'I thought you were making that for Ollie.' He knits his brow in confusion.

'I was,' she answers without looking at him. 'There's no need now that Ellie's finally deigned to make an appearance to get his tea, is there?' Walking back, she hands me the plate. 'You might need to empty the dishwasher before you put that in,' she says pointedly. The look in her eyes now is hard, her cool grey irises flint-edged and full of accusation. 'And then perhaps you'd like to wash the crystal glasses, once you've fed Ollie, of course. They'll need to be hand-washed, as per my instructions.'

'Instructions?' I squint in bemusement.

'I left you a note on the kitchen island.'

What note? I follow her gaze and my heart drops. There is a note there. But it wasn't there earlier. I would have noticed it.

She eyes me coolly. 'Do you think you could at least attempt some of your chores, and make sure my daughter's needs are seen to in future before lounging about by the pool?'

Shit. I left my things out there. I glance at Jake, flustered by her continued insinuation. I didn't neglect Fern. She was fed on time, give or take half an hour. And I didn't take my eyes off her while I was having my hair done, except when I went to the sink. As for the magically appearing note, that was *not* there earlier. I would swear it wasn't.

Jake's gaze flicks apologetically towards me. 'I take it the best glasses are making an appearance for an occasion?' he asks, looking back to Megan.

'A dinner party,' she provides.

'Right.' He nods tightly. 'And would this dinner party be in honour of anyone in particular?' He sounds irritated, and I wonder why.

'Miguel.' She holds eye contact with him for a moment, and then spins around to head to the lounge.

Jake stares after her. 'I don't bloody well believe this,' he grates. 'You're actually inviting him *here?*'

'I don't see why not.' Megan glances indifferently back at him. 'It is my home, Jake.'

'Jesus.' He eyes the ceiling. 'When?' he shouts, now visibly agitated, which takes me aback.

'At the weekend.' She stops and turns to face him. 'He flies back to Portugal in a few weeks, and he has some prospective clients he'd like to introduce me to before he goes. We decided it would be a good idea to have them over here. He thinks the house says far more about my work than my portfolio could. I think he's right.'

'Yeah, well, he would be, wouldn't he, him being God's gift to the world of design.' Jake's tone is acerbic.

'He would, actually,' she replies. 'This house is based on one of his designs for a modernist villa in Portugal. The property that won an international award, you might recall. The Oscar of design awards, for your information.'

Jake laughs scathingly. 'So when's the red carpet arriving?'

Megan smiles flatly. 'Your jealousy's showing, Jake.' She runs an unimpressed gaze over him.' It's not a good look. It's hardly Miguel's fault you don't have an artistic bone in your body.'

He shakes his head as she walks off. Bewildered by the interchange between them, and aware of my own jealousy squirming inside me – he really does appear to be upset by his wife's open adoration of another man – I have no idea what to do. His look dark, angry, he appears to be miles away. I'm not even sure he knows I'm still standing here.

Hesitantly, I move towards him, but he holds up a hand, stopping me. 'I need to see to Ollie,' he growls. 'He's hungry. Do you think we might postpone washing the bloody crystal glasses in Miguel's honour and get him some food?'

TWENTY-SIX

I fight back tears as I prepare Ollie's tea. Forcing myself to concentrate, I use up the last of the meatballs I made yesterday, a Jamie Oliver recipe of which Megan approves. I'm serving them with French fries and a side salad instead of pasta. I'm not sure Megan will approve of the French fries, but with my mind on Jake and how he pushed me away, I'm past caring. Why they can't bring their own mealtime forward and have Ollie eat with them mystifies me. Well, Megan could, at least. Jake often works late – as he'd have to to keep his wife in the luxury to which she's become accustomed in her Miguel-influenced house made of glass. I was right about it being fragile. The cracks are visible. I have no idea how Jake lives here with *her*.

But he wants to, doesn't he? He's said so. Because he comes from a broken home. Because he doesn't want that for his children. Because he *cares* about her. That much was abundantly obvious just now. Megan was right. His jealousy was on show. It was more than males locking horns over their business prowess, though. How *much* he cares for her is what I need to know. Is this Miguel the 'someone else' he spoke of? I have a feeling he is, and that Jake was hoping she would stop seeing him. If so, with him prepared to suffer the humiliation he does at her hands, that can only mean that he must love her, however unfathomable it is. And where does that leave me?

My heart twisting painfully, I swipe away a tear on my cheek. Sensing Megan wafting into the kitchen to top up her wine glass, I turn swiftly to fetch Ollie's cutlery from the drawer, only to end up clanging the knife to the floor. She's across the room in a flash, crouching down to examine the Italian tiles for chips. Finding none, she straightens up. 'Do be more careful, Ellie,' she says with a despairing sigh. 'And do please try to make less noise. We don't want to wake Fern, do we?'

No, you don't. I glare after her as she goes to fill her glass. *You might have to pretend you're her actual mother for five minutes then, mightn't you?*

I look sharply away as she strolls out again. 'Could you uncork the red wine to go with our steak, Ellie?' she calls back without even bothering to glance in my direction. 'Jake likes to let it breathe.'

My eyes boggle after her. *Why didn't you do it while you were there?*

'Oh, and do remember to wash those glasses, won't you?' she adds. 'They'll need polishing once they're dry.'

'Yes, no problem,' I call back. Seething with anger, I extract two bottles from the many they have in the wine rack, one expensive-looking with a cork, the other with a screw top. Uncorking the expensive one, I leave it on the worktop, as instructed, then take the other upstairs with me as I go to fetch Ollie. I'm not even sure who it is I'm angry with, her, myself, or Jake for allowing me to be humiliated by her. But then didn't Jake humiliate me too, all but ignoring me after we'd been as intimate as it was possible to be together? I know his leaping to my defence might have been a bit of a giveaway, but he didn't have to act as if I didn't exist, did he?

Going to the spare room, I open the wine and take a hefty swig, eyeing the locked wardrobe agitatedly as I do, then stash the bottle in my overnight bag and go to Ollie's room.

Finding Jake in there playing Pokémon, I've a mind to ignore him, but my resolve wanes as soon as he looks at me, smiling sadly and mouthing, 'Sorry.'

'It's okay.' I manage a small smile back, then offer Ollie a wider one as he scrambles off the bed asking eagerly, 'Is it meatballs, Ellie?'

'It is,' I assure him, pleased that he, at least, appreciates my efforts.

'Cool,' he says, skidding past me and out onto the landing.

'Hold your horses.' Jake pulls himself off the bed and races after him. 'Ollie!' There's a hint of panic in his voice as he reaches the landing. 'Slow down on the stairs.'

I was right about that too. This house was clearly only ever meant to be a show home. It's definitely not child-friendly. Hearing Fern beginning to whimper from the nursery, I draw in an agitated breath and head that way, peeved that I can't go down after Jake. I have a feeling that Megan will take the opportunity to point out more of my shortfalls. I haven't washed her glasses yet. I'm so furious with her I feel like grinding one up and sprinkling it over her steak.

Fern's in a mess. It takes me ages to change her, which doesn't improve her mood or mine. With my ears cocked for my name being mentioned downstairs, I don't pay her the attention I should, and she's still fretting when I put her back down. 'Shush, honey.' I stroke her cheek and tickle her tummy. It makes no difference. She's working up to a bawl as I hurry to the door to fetch her water from the kitchen.

Reaching the top of the stairs, I stop as I see Jake and Megan at the foot of them. Jake has his back to me, so I can't make out his expression. I hear his tone, though, one of utter despair.

'What the hell are you talking about, Megan?' he asks.

'I made myself quite clear, Jake,' she replies, her tone agitated. 'She left the patio doors open.'

I did what?

Jake sighs. 'When?'

'After she'd been out there drinking *our* wine and sunning herself, clearly having left Fern unattended. And this is after she decides in her stupidity to take a child with asthma into a hair salon to breathe in obnoxious fumes. There's something wrong with the girl, I swear.' Her jaw set rigidly, she folds her arms and waits for Jake's response.

He kneads his forehead. 'I'll have a word with her.'

'A word?' She stares at him, incredulous. 'You're completely missing the point here. She left the patio doors open. Not just unlocked. *Open.*'

'You said.' He sighs again, exasperatedly.

Megan continues to glare at him. 'Are you being deliberately obtuse?' she asks.

'For pity's *sake.*' Jake eyes the ceiling. 'Can you just stop, Megan? Ollie can hear.'

'Ollie might not be here *to* hear!' she shoots back as he half turns away from her. 'By leaving the patio doors open, she gave him access to the *pool.*'

Jake stops and turns back.

'I told her never to leave them open. I even texted her to remind her that Ollie's not a strong swimmer. The first thing he did when he came home was run out to the patio,' she goes on. Lying. She's *lying.*

I did *not* leave the doors open. I came upstairs to get my phone, but I closed the doors. I'm sure I did. And Ollie didn't go straight to the pool. He called to Jake moments after we heard the front door close. He couldn't have run to the pool in that time. Could he? I swallow back an uncomfortable stone in my throat as I realise that he might have come in ahead of Megan;

that she might have taken a minute or two to collect his school bag and her own things from the car.

Might I have left the doors open? I shake my head in confusion and then shrink back as Jake spins around to the stairs. 'What the hell were you thinking leaving the doors to the pool open, Ellie?' he growls, freezing me to the spot.

'I *didn't*,' I insist. 'At least, I don't think I did. I'm sure I—'

'You should never have hired her,' Megan growls as she struts towards the lounge. 'Drinking wine in the afternoon?' she adds, her tone scornful. 'She clearly has a problem.'

'Right.' Jake blows out a breath. 'Tell me, Megan,' he calls after her, 'is there *anything* I can do right in your eyes?'

She skids to a stop and turns back. 'Are you serious?' She scans his face, then laughs in disbelief. 'You are, aren't you? Because *you* can do no wrong, *can* you, Jake?'

He smiles cynically. 'Like Miguel, you mean?'

'Quite unlike Miguel, actually,' she retorts. 'At least he gives a damn.'

'Does he?' Jake's tone is sceptical. 'Are you sure about that, Megan? Seems to me his caring nature only appears when he wants something.'

She glowers at him. 'What's that supposed to mean?'

'Nothing.' He shrugs. 'I just think you're living in hope, that's all.'

'Drop dead.' She storms on.

'You'd like that, wouldn't you?' he calls after her. 'Sorry, my love, I'm not about to oblige.'

'Me neither,' Megan yells back. 'Whatever you're trying to do here, Jake, you won't win, I promise you that.'

TWENTY-SEVEN

With one ear on their vile exchange, I go quickly down the stairs, aiming to bring Ollie up to his bedroom where he'll be safe. As I cross the hall, I hear Jake from the lounge area, his voice tight with anger. 'So you're inviting him here for what reason exactly? Because if it's solely to humiliate me, you might want to have a rethink. We're in this together. Allowing him to get too close is—'

'No we are *not*,' Megan shouts over him. '*You* made your bed, Jake.' I glance in her direction to see her pointing an accusing finger at him. 'Now you can bloody well lie in it.'

'While you lie in someone else's.' His voice is loaded with disdain.

'What utter rubbish. *You're* the cause of all of this.' She looks him over, her eyes shooting daggers of pure venom. 'You know what you did.'

'Every second of every day,' he replies tightly. 'Do you know what *you* did, though, Megan? Because it seems to me that you have no conscience whatsoever.'

She doesn't respond, turning to stride to the coffee table for her wine instead. I watch her tipping it back and I can't help wishing she would choke on it. She clearly has no qualms about subjecting Ollie to all of this. Does she not realise how much it traumatises a child? Possibly for life. I gulp back a hard knot in my throat as I see my little brother's haunted face, the fear that never left his eyes.

'Do you care, Megan?' Jake goes on. 'About anything? About Ollie? About Fern? Because it seems to me that—'

'For pity's sake!' Her voice shakes with anger. 'Can you just *stop*?'

'Why don't *you* stop drinking that stuff and then maybe we could have a sensible conversation,' he growls.

As I walk on, I hear a loud crash, glass smashing, and I rush back to see him straightening up from where he appears to have ducked, I hesitate, torn between going to him or to Ollie, then fly on towards the kitchen island. I can't leave Ollie in the midst of this mayhem.

I find him sitting with his head bowed and his meal untouched. 'Come on, sweetheart, let's go upstairs,' I whisper as he looks up at me, his big blue eyes a kaleidoscope of bewildered emotion. 'They're just having a silly argument,' I try to reassure him as I encourage him down from his stool. 'Mummies and daddies do that sometimes.'

Ollie, though, looks far from reassured. 'Do your mummy and daddy argue?' he asks, his voice so small and anguished I feel my heart break for him.

'All the time.' I roll my eyes despairingly. I've actually no idea whether my parents have even been in touch with each other since the day I walked away from the courthouse and never looked back. My chest constricts as my mind swings back to my brother, and I have to force myself to expel the air that seems to be trapped in my lungs. 'Your mummy and daddy love you, Ollie,' I assure him. 'They just have some things to sort out. It's nothing to do with anything you've done. Try not to worry.'

He nods and looks down. 'I'm sorry about leaving my meatballs,' he mumbles as I take hold of his hand to lead him to the hall. 'I don't think my tummy's very hungry.'

'Never mind.' I swallow and give his hand a squeeze. 'How about I bring you some milk and biscuits when I get Fern's feed. Just in case your tummy feels hungry later?'

He musters up a smile, but he looks lost and lonely as he trudges along beside me and a chilling sense of déjà vu overwhelms me. This child could almost be Theo. I have to talk to Jake; make him see that no matter how much he cares for Megan, this toxic atmosphere is damaging his son.

As we near the stairs, Jake emerges from the lounge area into the hall, and my heart skids to a stop as I see he's cradling one hand in the other, rich red droplets of blood trickling between his fingers to stain the hall tiles stark crimson. Instinctively I lurch towards him, but Ollie is faster. 'Daddy!' he cries, tearing his hand from mine and charging across to lock his arms around Jake's waist.

'It's okay, Ollie. I'm okay,' Jake attempts to reassure him. 'I dropped a glass, that's all.' Clearly at a loss how to comfort him with his hand dripping blood, he looks helplessly to me. My chest feels as if it might explode with emotion: fear for Jake, absolute fury at Megan. He didn't drop a glass. She *threw* it at him. 'Could you?' He nods towards the stairs.

Understanding, I move to take Ollie gently by the shoulders. 'Your hand,' I murmur, glancing at Jake as I steer him away.

'It's fine.' He looks behind him to where Megan is standing with her back to us, her arms wrapped tightly about herself – as if she's the one who's traumatised by all of this, rather than the cause of it. 'It was just an argument about nothing.' He turns back to me with an unconvincing smile. 'Sorry you had to hear it.'

I stare at him in astonishment. This was *not* 'nothing'. What did he do that Megan seems to think he should suffer this kind of abuse? Does she know about us?

TWENTY-EIGHT

What Jake and I have is different, I try to convince myself as I take Ollie upstairs. It isn't just sex. We have a connection, an emotional bond that drew us together. He cares about me. We care about each other. Megan is clearly incapable of caring for anyone but herself.

Trying to ignore the seed of doubt flowering rapidly in my chest, I lead Ollie into his room and then crouch down to his level. 'Daddy's fine,' I tell him, making sure to hold his gaze. 'He's just had a little accident, but it's not serious, I promise.'

'He's bleeding,' Ollie says, working to hold back his tears.

'I know.' My chest aches for him. 'But it's just a small cut. He'll be okay once he's bathed it and put a plaster on.'

A troubled little V forming in his brow, Ollie searches my face. 'Will he come up and see me when he's bathed it?' he asks, his eyes clouded with worry.

'I'm sure he will.' I hug him to me. 'He always does, doesn't he?'

'Uh-huh.' As I ease back, I see that Ollie looks confident of that, at least.

'Tell you what, how about we play a game?' I suggest. 'I

have to feed Fern when she wakes, but we could play for a little while.'

He answers with a small nod. 'Pokémon?' Scrubbing the tears from his cheeks with the heel of his hand, he looks at me hopefully.

I suspect Megan won't approve, but I don't actually care. 'Pokémon it is.' I smile. 'I can't promise to be as good at it as your dad, though.'

'That's okay. We can play a basic game. It's quite easy,' Ollie says charitably.

'Just as well.' I smile and join him as he scrambles onto his bed.

We've barely got through the instructions when I hear Megan's footsteps clacking urgently along the landing. I'm halfway off the bed as she storms into the room.

'You're playing computer games?' she asks, staring at me in disbelief.

'Just for a while.' I glance at her, uncaring of the challenge she might see in my eyes. 'I thought it would take his mind off things until Jake comes up to—'

'You've left my daughter lying on her stomach and you're playing *computer* games?' she cuts shrilly across me.

What? I shake my head in confusion. 'But... she isn't.' My heart thunders as I try to think back. Fern was fretting when I left her to fetch her water. I heard no sound from the nursery when I reached the landing with Ollie and assumed she'd cried herself to sleep even with raised voices downstairs. I should have checked on her. A knot of apprehension tightens my throat and I swallow hard. 'I d-didn't leave her on her stomach,' I stammer. 'Honestly I didn't. She must have—'

'You stupid, irresponsible... She has asthma!' Megan's slate-grey eyes are beams of pure hatred as she glares at me. 'You know she does! What in God's name is *wrong* with you?'

Spitting fury, she spins around to stalk back to the landing.

Stumbling from Ollie's room, I follow, intending to go to the nursery, but stop short as I see Jake mounting the stairs. 'What the hell's going on *now*?' he asks, his gaze swivelling from Megan to me.

'Ask *her*.' Megan flicks her head in my direction. 'I really have no idea why you ever brought her here,' she mutters, strutting past him. 'She's utterly incompetent.'

Jake's gaze comes cautiously back to me. 'And she's supposed to have done what, exactly?'

Megan skids around at the top of the stairs. 'She left our daughter lying on her *stomach*.' She glowers past him to me.

Panic unfurls inside me. 'I *didn't*,' I appeal to Jake. 'She was lying on her back. I was going to get her water and I found you two—'

'*And* she's encouraging Ollie to spend far too much time playing computer games.' Megan splays a hand towards Ollie's room.

'He wanted to go to his room,' I argue. 'I was just keeping him company.'

'He shouldn't be constantly cooped up there,' Megan counters angrily. 'He should be interacting with people. Anyone would know that, let alone someone who's supposed to be trained in childcare.'

Dragging contemptuous eyes over me, she turns to continue on down the stairs, and I stare after her, staggered. Does she not realise that her son stays in his room because she can't be bothered to spend any time with him? That in actual fact, he probably doesn't want to spend time with *her*, a woman who abuses his father?

Jake sighs agitatedly. 'He likes playing Pokémon,' he points out. 'It's a popular game. All the kids his age play it.'

'Precisely,' Megan growls over her shoulder. 'Which is why children his age are struggling with their social skills.'

Jake looks as mystified as I am by that.

'You wouldn't concern yourself with that, though, would you, Jake?' She turns at the foot of the stairs to cast an accusatory gaze over him. 'You're far too busy with other things, *aren't* you?'

He holds her gaze for a second, then looks away. 'I have no idea what you're talking about, Megan,' he replies, running a thumb over the bloodied bandage on his hand. 'I actually think you're getting things out of proportion.'

'Out of proportion?' Her voice goes up an octave. 'Are you aware that behavioural problems relating to gaming have been classified as a mental health condition? That children are becoming addicted, aggressive? Don't you think you should be limiting his screen time instead of encouraging him? That *she* should?' Another derisory flick of her head in my direction before she strides off.

Jake's expression is now one of weary bemusement. 'Fern's all right, though, I take it,' he says, 'since you're apparently not concerned enough to be in there with her.'

Megan's step falters. 'You need to get rid of her,' she mutters.

'Right.' He pauses. 'And should I do that before or after she's looked after *your* daughter while you hold your dinner party in honour of the great Miguel?'

TWENTY-NINE

Cursing quietly, Jake glances at the ceiling.

'Jake?' Desperate for him to believe me, I move towards him, placing a hand on his arm. 'I didn't leave her on her tummy, I promise you I didn't. She must have rolled over, or else—'

'From her back onto her front? She's not even six months old yet.' His look is somewhere between disappointed and sceptical, and my heart plummets to the pit of my belly.

'But I *didn't*,' I insist. 'Megan must have—'

'I can't do this right now, Ellie.' He sighs. 'I need to see to Fern. We'll talk later.'

I stare at him, my cheeks burning with hurt and humiliation. Why is he doing this? Would it hurt him to whisper something to reassure me that he's not sorry about what happened between us? He is, though, isn't he? Clearly.

I feel my throat closing, tears rising so fast I struggle to hold them back. 'What did she mean?' I blurt as he turns away.

He turns back, a puzzled frown crossing his face.

'When you were arguing downstairs.' I lower my voice, mindful of Megan overhearing. 'She said, "You know what you did". What *did* you do, Jake? What did *she* do that you think she has no conscience about?' I lift my head defiantly. 'Is this something to do with Phoebe?'

'Phoebe?' He looks thunderstruck. 'No. Why would you think that?'

I hold his gaze. He glances away, and my stomach constricts.

'It has nothing to do with our previous au pair,' he says tightly. 'Megan was talking about what happened after Fern was born. She was struggling to cope and I wasn't there for her. Not as much as I should have been, anyway.' I note a flicker of guilt cross his face. 'I'm sorry that things seem so complicated, that you're caught up in the middle of it, but please try to understand. Megan's postnatal depression was severe. So severe she wanted to take her own life. I can't just turn my back on her, or on the children. I have to—'

'Jake!' Megan shouts from downstairs. 'Could you please see to Fern instead of leaving me to do everything. I'm getting her feed!'

He drags a hand over his neck. 'Can we talk later?' he asks, his eyes hopeful.

Guessing that I have no choice, I answer with a small nod. A turmoil of confused emotion churning inside me and a thousand questions flying around in my head, I watch him go to the nursery, then follow him along the landing. As I pass the nursery door, I hear him talking softly to his baby girl. 'Hi, sweetheart. What's all this fuss about, hey? Come on, little munchkin, let's make it all better, shall we?'

I imagine him lifting her from her cot, gazing lovingly down at her, and my chest tightens. Carrying on to the spare room, I close the door and draw in a long breath as I lean against it. I'm not wrong about him. I can't know all of him, I'm not naïve enough to imagine I can, but I do know he's a caring man. Why then is this kernel of doubt growing inside me?

As my gaze falls on the bed, I breathe out, expelling air from my lungs in short gasps as I picture him there, his eyes looking into mine right down to my soul. His body moving in tandem with mine, touching the very core of me. None of this is his fault. He's in a catch-22 situation. Megan is guilting him into staying with her. It's obvious. I should never have allowed myself to become involved with him. He's never going to leave her, not unless she does something so appalling he can't countenance staying. After being on the receiving end of physical abuse from her, does he not realise that she just might? I don't understand any of it. If she doesn't want to lose him, why is she being so cruel to him?

My gaze strays from the bed to the wardrobe. Why is it still locked? Where is the handyman who was supposed to be coming to fix it? I think about the passport I found, which I've taken back to my bedsit. I'm not sure why I did that, but something isn't right. I can feel it. It's not just the mystery of why Jake would stay with a woman who makes him miserable, but the circumstances of Phoebe's departure. Where did she go? *Did* Jake cheat with her? Might *he* have been the married man? No, that's ludicrous. Megan told me about Phoebe's boyfriend. None of this makes sense to me. How is it that a house that's so transparent holds so many secrets?

I need to do a social media search. First, though, I need to know what lies behind those locked doors. I grab the stashed wine from my bag and glug back a hefty swig, then find my nail file. Going to the wardrobe, I insert it between the doors. After sliding it up and down, I make contact with something – the lock, I assume. I wiggle the file around, to no avail, apply pressure to it, attempting to force the doors, but the only thing I succeed in doing is bending the file.

Frustrated, I toss it back in my bag. I down another swig of wine, then grab my phone. Hesitating briefly, I select Zach's number. Guessing that he's seen my name flash up on the screen and decided not to answer, I'm about to end the call when he picks up. 'To what do I owe the pleasure?' he asks, a sarcastic edge to his voice. 'I suppose it's too much to hope that you've seen the light and decided the bloke's a tosser after all?'

'Zach...' I sigh, 'please don't.'

He draws in a breath. 'Okay, I'm sorry,' he says, blowing it out. 'You can't blame me for being a bit pissed off, though, Ellie. I think most men would feel the same being dumped for some flash bloke who sails into your life and steals you away.'

A small smile curves my mouth. 'That was almost poetic.'

'If I'd known you needed poetry...' He sighs disconsolately.

I pause, unsure what to say.

There's an awkward silence for a moment, then, 'I didn't say it often enough, but I do love you, Ellie.' There's a rare vulnerability in his voice that takes me aback.

'Zach...' I swallow a lump in my throat.

'I know, I know, I blew it, coming across as a crass prat,' he goes on, sounding more like himself. 'Just so you know, though, I'm here if you need me. You know, if you ever want to talk or anything.'

Tears spring to my eyes once again, and I have no idea how to answer.

'I might have to work at it, but I can listen sometimes,' he quips.

'Thank you,' I mumble, feeling awful. Part of me wishes I could unravel the last few months of my life and go back. But do I want to? Do I really wish I'd never met Jake Harington, a man who makes me feel good about myself? I don't feel that great about myself now, though, do I?

'So?' Zach asks. 'I take it you called me for a reason?'

'Yes.' I snap my thoughts away from Jake. 'I, um, need a favour.'

'Ah. As in?' he asks warily.

'I was hoping you would be able to open a locked wardrobe for me.'

'You mean there at the house?' He sounds surprised. 'Don't tell me the man's so tight he's refusing to get a locksmith in?'

I ignore that. 'They have a handyman. It's just that it might take a while for him to get round to it, so I hoped you might help me out.'

'Is it urgent, then?'

'I've managed to lock my purse in there,' I lie. 'And my make-up.'

'I can see why the latter would be important,' he responds moodily.

As he goes quiet again, guilt weighs heavily inside me. I'm using him – and he knows it. 'When?' he asks resignedly after a second.

'Later tonight?' I ask hopefully. 'I'll keep an eye out for you and let you in.'

'Under cover of darkness, you mean? It all sounds a bit cloak-and-dagger to me. Why so late?'

'They're at loggerheads here right now,' I confide, which is basically the truth. 'And I really do need my purse.'

'All's not as perfect as it might look then?' Zach comments, his sarcastic tone back.

'Is anything ever? So, will you?' I ask, deflecting the subject.

He emits a heavy sigh. 'What time?'

'About eleven? I'm staying over, as Megan has an early start. Text me when you arrive.'

'Okay,' he agrees reluctantly. 'As long as I don't end up being arrested.'

'You won't,' I assure him. 'I'll make an excuse if anyone sees you.'

'Yeah, that should be interesting. I hope he's not the jealous sort.'

'There's nothing going on between us, Zach,' I repeat, glad that he can't see my scarlet face.

'Right,' he says flatly. 'If you say so.'

'There *isn't*. Look, will you come or not?'

He pauses before answering. 'I'll be there,' he agrees eventually. 'I'm in the middle of something, so I can't promise to be bang on, but I'll do my best.'

'Thanks,' I say gratefully. I give him the address and sign off, breathing a sigh of relief. There's probably nothing in the wardrobe, but with my mind in overdrive, I'll feel better for knowing for sure.

After taking another swig of wine, I push the bottle back into my bag. I'm heading for the door when I hear a clunk right outside it. *Shit.* I take a quick step forward and yank the door open – to find Jake on the landing with Fern in his arms.

'Sorry. Dropped my phone,' he explains, gathering the baby to him. 'Megan's gone out.'

I look at him curiously. 'She didn't mention anything to me.'

'No.' He glances down. 'She, er, had to see someone, apparently.'

When he looks back at me, I note a flicker of something in his eyes. Annoyance? Embarrassment? The 'someone else' then, I gather.

'I just had a call,' he goes on. 'The security guard at the Birmingham shop. He reckons the alarm's been tampered with. I need to go and take a look. Could you...?' He nods down at Fern.

After all that's gone on, I hesitate, but then relent on the basis that he can hardly take her with him. 'Okay.' I sigh and reach for her.

'Thanks, Ellie.' He smiles appreciatively. 'I might be gone a while,' he warns me. 'I expect Megan will, too.' I note his intake of breath, that deep sadness in his eyes I've seen before, and despite everything, my heart aches for him.

He leans in to kiss Fern's cheek, and though my lips are only a fraction away, he doesn't steal the kiss I hoped he would. I've been a complete fool, haven't I? I've fallen in love with this man, but how could I ever have hoped he might love me? For all that she is, for all she does to him, he still loves Megan. The realisation lands like a punch to my stomach.

'Make sure to set the alarm, won't you? We don't want any unwanted visitors.'

I nod. I can't trust myself to speak.

'Back as soon as I can,' he says. His look is distracted as he gives me another small smile and then hurries to the stairs. I watch him go, a prickle of apprehension running through me as I wonder whether he might be following Megan.

THIRTY

The house is quiet. Too quiet. Trailing around upstairs, I have another check on Ollie, who I find still fast asleep, surprisingly. He was upset after Jake left. 'Where's Daddy?' he asked, clearly wondering why he hadn't come to say goodnight to him. When I explained that he'd had to rush off to one of the shops and that Megan had an appointment she'd forgotten about, he nodded disappointedly, the look in his eyes one of resignation. It was too old a look for a boy aged just six. That woman has a lot to answer for.

Heading to the nursery, I push the door quietly open and go across to the cot. Fern is just as I left her, lying on her back. Jake was right – she couldn't have rolled onto her tummy on her own. I have seen her beginning to rock from side to side while reaching excitedly for her musical plush toy when I placed it on a blanket on the floor next to her, but she simply hasn't gained the skills yet to roll over unassisted. Why did Megan lie about it? I assumed it was to discredit me in Jake's eyes, but now I wonder whether it was attention-seeking behaviour.

As I go back across the room, I realise I've somehow set the antique rocking horse in motion. I've no idea how. I didn't go around to that side of the cot, so I couldn't have knocked it. Goosebumps prickle my skin as it creaks eerily from where it stands in front of the rain-lashed window, the ink-black sky a backdrop beyond it. I might have considered it was the floor giving or a draught blowing, but for the fact that the floors are all marble and the windows are tightly sealed.

Shaking off a shudder, I hurry back to the landing, then pause. I shouldn't have snooped that first time I came here – if Megan hadn't been so bloody rude, I might not have. Now something compels me to. Heading for the main bedroom, I slip inside and set about going through wardrobes and drawers.

It doesn't take me long to find something that doesn't belong here. My blood thrumming, I quickly pocket it and hurry back to the spare room to stash it somewhere safe. Glancing around, I stuff it under the fur rug. I have no idea what it means or why I'm doing this, but there's no way now I can ignore the niggling voice in my head telling me something is amiss. After making sure the rug is straight, I check my watch, wondering what I should do about Zach. Eleven has come and gone and he hasn't texted me. He's obviously got caught up in his gaming. Nothing new there. So much for his offering to be there for me.

Nerves churn my stomach as I wait, wondering now where Jake is. Why he hasn't called to let me know what's happening. If there was some kind of break-in at the Birmingham shop and whoever was responsible was still hanging around, anything might have happened.

I'm about to call him when I hear the front door opening and closing. I dash to the stairs. Disappointment and apprehension surge through me as I realise it's Megan. Looking her over, I'm shocked by her appearance. Even under the subdued hall lighting, I can see that her complexion is deathly pale. Normally styled to within an inch of its life, her hair is hanging in damp rat-tails. Her clothes are wet through, and she's shivering violently. No longer a stylish, buttoned-up businesswoman, she looks bedraggled and vulnerable.

'Ellie?' she calls, her voice tremulous.

THIRTY-ONE

Seeing Megan sway as if she might be about to pass out, I quash any anger I feel towards her and hurry down the stairs to help. 'I'm sorry,' she mumbles as I wrap an arm tentatively around her and shepherd her further into the hall, 'for the awful way I've treated you; the dreadful things I've said. I've just felt so lonely and confused lately. I...' She trails off tearfully and presses a hand under her nose.

I can't help but feel for her. Also, a deep sense of shame. She *has* been awful, temperamental, bossy and bitchy, but that's nothing compared to what I've done to her; what Jake and I have done to her. 'It's okay,' I reassure her, because she clearly needs me to. 'You're shaking. You should get out of those wet clothes,' I suggest, steering her gently towards the stairs. She leans on me as I help her up them, which confounds me. This isn't like her at all.

'Are the children all right?' she asks once we reach the landing. Her expression is almost one of alarm as she glances towards the nursery – and now I feel slightly scared. This is a side of her I've never seen before, and I begin to realise why Jake is concerned for her.

'They're sleeping like angels,' I assure her. 'Would you like me to make you a hot drink?'

Nodding, she whispers, 'Thank you,' and turns shakily towards her room.

I watch until she goes in and then head back to the stairs. I'm halfway down when Jake comes through the front door. He glances up as he realises I'm there. 'Her car broke down,' he explains, clearly noting my bewilderment. 'I passed her on the main road.'

That would account for her appearance. 'Lucky you spotted her,' I say, descending the rest of the way. Considering where I suspect he thought she'd been, I'm surprised he didn't drive on by. But that's not Jake, is it? 'She's in the bedroom. I'm just going to make her a hot drink,' I add, not sure what else to say. I can't question him about why he's been treating me so coldly, nor can I mention what I found in one of the bedroom drawers. Not now.

'Thanks, Ellie.' He smiles gratefully. 'I'll be going in a bit later tomorrow. We limped the car to a garage. I'll need to make some calls and then I'll drive her out to fetch it.'

I nod and carry on towards the kitchen.

He stops me. 'Will you stay? Please, despite everything? Let me make it up to you?'

I'm not sure how he intends to do that, but I'm glad he's concerned for me on some level. 'For now,' I answer, preferring not to make a commitment. 'Ollie and Fern need me.'

'Thanks.' He closes his eyes in relief. 'We should talk,' he adds quietly. 'Do you think we could meet up later tomorrow, assuming you have no—' He stops as there's a sharp knock on the front door behind him.

Frowning, he turns to open it.

'Mr Harington?' a female voice asks.

'That's right. Can I help you, Officer?' Jake says, and the hairs rise over my skin.

'DS Jacobs,' the woman says. 'And this is PC Amir. We're trying to locate an Ellie Taylor. Are you able to confirm that you know her?'

He hesitates before answering. 'She's our childminder. Is there a problem?'

'Do you think we might have a word with her?' she goes on.

'I, er...'

'Jake?' I venture towards him, my chest palpitating. Why would they want me? Is it something to do with my parents? If so, I really don't want to know.

'You'd better come in.' He stands aside.

Dread pools in the pit of my stomach as the officers step into the hall. 'What's happened?' I scan their wary faces for some indication of why they're here.

The woman, a plain-clothed officer, produces her identification. 'I'm Detective Sergeant Hannah Jacobs and this is PC Arshi Amir. And you are?'

'Ellie,' I confirm, my mouth suddenly dry. 'Ellie Taylor.'

She smiles sympathetically. 'Is there somewhere we could sit down, Ellie?' she asks.

I stay where I am, my mind conjuring up images of my little brother, every sinew in my body tensing. 'Could you please just tell me why you're here?'

The two officers exchange glances. 'We found this address programmed into Zachary Kendall's satnav,' DS Jacobs informs me. 'It's also listed as a contact address for you. Are you aware that you're named as Mr Kendall's primary contact in case of an emergency?'

My heart lurches. 'Emergency?'

'I'm afraid I have some very bad news,' she goes on, her expression cautious. 'I'm sorry to tell you that Mr Kendall was involved in a fatal road traffic accident late this evening.'

THIRTY-TWO

Fatal. The implication of the word hits me like a sledgehammer. 'No!' I push Jake away as he tries to hold me. 'He can't be! I've spoken to him. Tonight. He...' *He was on his way here.* Nausea roils inside me as I stare at them dry-eyed with shock and ice-cold fear. 'No,' I whisper, every fibre of my being screaming for it not to be true. 'Please no.'

'Ellie?' As the strength drains from my body, Jake reaches for me again, circling his arms around me and easing me to him. 'It's okay,' he murmurs, pressing my head to his shoulder and stroking my hair softly. 'It's okay.'

But it *isn't*. A sob chokes my throat and I snatch my gaze up to look at him in bewildered disbelief. This is *my* fault. I gulp back the guilt and the terror soaring inside me. Zach was coming here. He knew I was using him and still he was coming, because he loved me. 'How?' I squeeze the word past the constriction in my throat.

DS Jacobs hesitates. 'A post-mortem examination will need to be completed to establish probable cause of death, but we believe he suffered traumatic brain and spinal cord injury.

These types of injuries usually occur due to the vehicle rolling over.'

'How did he come to roll over?' Jake asks as my mind tries to digest what my heart refuses to believe. 'Was there another vehicle involved?'

'As far as we can ascertain at present, no,' the other officer replies. 'It appears to be due to driver negligence. The deceased...' She pauses, her gaze flicking apologetically to me as I flinch. 'Mr Kendall was travelling at speed and careered off the road at a particularly hazardous hairpin bend. His vehicle is several years old. It's possible it wasn't regularly serviced.'

'Jesus.' Jake blows out a breath. 'Had he been drinking, do you think?'

I want to scream at him to stop. Zach *does* service his car. It's old, tatty to look at, but he loves it. And he would never drink and drive. He leaves his car outside my bedsit if he intends to have a drink. He's obstinate and hot-headed sometimes, but... *Was.* My heart folds up inside me.

'I'm afraid we won't know that until the post-mortem...'

Her words fade in and out as an image of Zach's body, lying bloodied and broken, flashes through my mind and panic grips me, rising so fast in my chest I feel it might choke me. He was on his way *here*. A jumble of thoughts fight for space in my head and I can't make sense of anything. Can't breathe.

'Ellie?' Jake says urgently. 'You're okay. I've got you.' His voice, thick with emotion, reaches me as if through a long, dark tunnel and I blink hard. I can't make them go away, though, Zach's eyes, rich hazel eyes, always dancing with amusement, so angry when I last saw him, now flat and opaque. My little brother's eyes, child's eyes, their innocence stolen. Lifeless. My fault. *All* of it.

'What's going on? Why are the police here?' Megan's voice, alarmed, permeates the fear that's suffocating me. I hear the clack, clack of her shoes as she crosses the marble floor, coming to take Jake away from me before I break him too.

'Ellie's boyfriend,' he answers, still holding me. *Please don't let go.* 'He's been involved in...' He stops, attempting to support me as the strength leaves my body.

'He was coming here,' I whisper.

He scoops me into his arms. 'She needs to lie down!'

THIRTY-THREE

FOUR WEEKS AFTER THE ACCIDENT

'Are you sure you're okay?' Megan asks, glancing at me across the kitchen. She's been nothing but kind since the night the police called and my world imploded, insisting I stay here until I was emotionally stronger. She even drove me to the funeral, taking hold of my hand as she sat quietly by my side. She told me to take as much time as I needed, cancelling her appointments, seeing to the children herself. All of which only compounds the guilt I carry around like a stone inside me.

Concentrating my attention on the hummus cucumber cup appetisers she's decided on for her postponed dinner party, I smile and nod. 'I'll be fine,' I assure her. I'm not fine. I don't think I ever will be. I can't stop thinking about Zach. He fills my dreams and every waking moment. How did it happen? There was no trace of alcohol in his system. He didn't deserve for his life to be snatched away so cruelly. He was brash sometimes, immature in many ways, but at his core he was a kind person. That was what first attracted me to him. Tears sting my eyes as I recall how he came to my rescue. I was on the Birmingham to Solihull train after an abysmal job interview when some weirdo decided to harass me, sitting down next to me, making lewd comments and blowing beer breath all over me. 'Excuse me, mate,' Zach said, appearing in the gangway to loom over him, 'I think you'll find that's my seat. And the lady,' he nodded towards me, 'is my girlfriend. Piss off.'

Eyeballing him steadily, he waited while the guy moodily vacated the seat, and then sat down in it. 'Don't worry, I'm not going to hassle you.' He smiled. 'I just thought you'd like to get rid of that jerk.'

Swallowing hard, I swipe a tear from my cheek and try to still the anger that writhes inside me. So many times I've wished I could turn back time, do things differently. It strikes me now that the only thing that would have saved the people around me from being hurt was if I'd never existed.

'How's it going?' Megan asks, and I jump as I realise she's standing right behind me.

'Okay.' I blink hard and try to focus on the garnish I'm preparing.

'Could you chop the parsley a little more finely?' she asks, peering over my shoulder. 'Miguel's a terrific cook,' she goes on, heading towards the cooker. *As well as an award-winning designer*. I sigh inwardly. She's serving traditional Portuguese food in his honour. She obviously hero-worships him. She must have mentioned his name a thousand times in between issuing me instructions on setting the table and cleaning the house, which she obviously wants to show off to her guests in all its shimmering glory. I'm only glad I don't have to polish the glass walls as well as the crystal glasses.

'This is a meal he showed me how to cook while we were collaborating on the house. Portuguese beef stew with vintage port,' she says, plucking off the lid of the cast-iron casserole it *absolutely has to be* cooked in and sniffing the contents. 'The secret to its success is to add the sediment along with the port.'

She picks up the port from the worktop and walks back to me. 'You have to simmer it until the port's evaporated, then add the red wine, turn the heat to low, cover it and leave it to cook until the meat is tender.'

'Right,' I say as she hands me the bottle.

'I'm just off to get changed.' She turns towards the hall. 'Oh, you won't forget Fern's due her feed soon, will you?'

'No. I'm on it,' I assure her, doubling my efforts to concentrate on what I'm supposed to be doing. She'll be up there ages, I imagine, since she so obviously wants to impress Miguel. Still, I'd rather be busy, which at least gives me less time to think.

Once the casserole is cooking, with me praying I've chucked the right amount of red wine in – I never have quite worked out what size a 'cup' is – I pour myself a much-needed glass, glug it back and then run upstairs myself to check on Fern. She's due her feed at seven o'clock, but she's still sleeping when I peek into the nursery. I decide to grab the time for a quick freshen-up, and then go and look in on Ollie.

'Time to snuggle up in bed, Ollie,' I tell him with a smile.

He looks up from where he's parked cross-legged in front of his TV.

'What are you watching?' I ask him, as he nods reluctantly and gets to his feet.

'*Pokémon the Series*,' he answers inevitably, heading for his bed as good as gold. 'I think Ash is going to be a Pokémon Master soon.'

'Exciting.' I smile and tuck him up under his duvet. 'I'll see if I can find time to watch it with you tomorrow and you can bring me up to speed.'

'Cool.' He smiles back, pleased.

'Did you brush your teeth?' I check.

'Uh-huh.' He nods. 'Is Mummy's dinner party starting soon?'

'It is.' I reach to switch on his night light. I treated him to his favourite pizza for tea, and I'm hoping that the smell of the beef stew wafting around the house doesn't make him feel hungry.

'Does that mean Daddy will be back early tonight?' he asks excitedly.

I feel for him. He hasn't seen much of Jake lately. But then Jake has been working hard, meaning I haven't seen a great deal of him either. When he has been here, I make sure not to be too familiar with him, particularly around Megan. I'm stronger than I was, functioning, but I feel as if I'm balancing on a knife edge. I don't think I would cope if Megan went back to being as vitriolic as she can be. Jake has asked me to meet him for lunch next week. I'm apprehensive about it, but at least then we can talk, honestly, and I'll know where I stand. Right now, with Zach gone, I feel such an emptiness inside me, I can't bear the thought of being alone.

'I expect he will be,' I tell Ollie. At least, I'm assuming he will be. It's going to look a bit odd if Megan ends up hosting her dinner party on her own.

'Will he be able to read me a story?' Ollie asks, looking hopefully up at me.

'Ooh, I should think so,' I assure him. Jake always looks in on both Ollie and Fern. I think he's the one constant in their lives. 'I'll make sure to remind him, okay?'

'Okay.' Considerably brightened, Ollie snuggles down.

I feel for him. He seems to be such a lonely child. I make a mental note to invite his friend Ezra to tea one day soon, and lean in to give him a hug. 'Night, night.'

He hugs me back hard, and my heart catches. He reminds me so much of my little brother it hurts. My thoughts are on Theo as I head for the door, his huge brown eyes looking pleadingly up at me, his small body trembling, his fear so palpable I can taste it.

'Ellie!' Megan says sharply, jarring me as she emerges from her room. 'What on earth are you doing? My guests are due any minute.'

I frown in confusion.

'Fern's *crying.*' She looks at me in astonishment.

I'm astonished in turn. She hasn't been crying for that long. But I'm acutely aware that she is. It seems to me that the little girl has become more unsettled and fractious since Megan has been looking after her. I'm struggling, but I daren't admit it. Every time Fern cries and I can't quieten her, I feel like bursting into tears myself. I know what it is, this painful hopelessness I feel inside. I felt the same after Theo. I so wish I could talk to Jake, the one person I think will understand. Or at least I *did* think so. Now, I just don't know. My emotions are so confused.

I think back to how he was short with me when he learned about the dinner party. The fury in his eyes directed at me. The disappointment and scepticism when he questioned whether Fern could have rolled over on her own. He was upset, agitated with Megan. I can't blame him for that. She was so bloody awful to him. That he didn't seem to trust my word over hers regarding the incident with Fern, though, that hurt. Was he really oblivious to how crushed I was by his indifference to my feelings? I just don't know. I've hardly seen him since Zach died.

Is it because of Zach that I'm so filled with uncertainty? I can't help going over the things he said. I picture him in my bedsit that night he saw Jake drop me off. He was moody, typically Zach. He was also sensitive, kindness in his eyes as he realised he'd upset me. Recalling what he said — *I'm concerned, that's all. Worried he might be taking advantage of you* — how he wrapped his arms around me, I swallow back the lump that seems to be permanently wedged in my throat.

'Well?' Megan snaps me back to my lonely present. 'Are you going to see to her?' The doorbell chimes, and without waiting for an answer, she spins around and swishes along the landing. I note her vintage off-the-shoulder feather-hemmed dress and realise she has no intention of dealing with Fern herself. The dress is made of silk and probably cost an arm and a leg.

Tears brimming too close to the surface, I blink them back and head for the nursery. 'What is it, sweetheart, hmm?' My voice shaky, my nerves coming at me because of Megan and what her attitude will be if Fern keeps crying, I go straight across to the cot and lift her out. Her little face is blotchy and I wonder whether she's teething early. Deciding to check her gums once she's changed and fed, I carry her across to the changing mat.

I'm halfway through changing her, smiling and making funny faces to try to distract her, when I realise I've forgotten to warm her bottle. I debate whether to leave her while I run down, and decide not to. She's hiccupping and snuffling, and after the scare around her asthma attack, I don't want to take any risks. Holding her close to my shoulder, I head tentatively along the landing. Aside from the lethal staircase, I have no idea why I should feel wary about taking her down. The fact is, though, I can't help feeling that Megan's children are like little flowers in the attic; that she prefers them out of sight and out of mind, especially if they're crying.

As I reach the stairs, I realise that she's in the hall, talking to whoever's arrived. They're facing the stairs, which means I won't be able to slip past them. 'Oh, Miguel, it's stunning,' she gushes, a hand placed to her breast as she gazes wonderstruck at something propped against the huge hall table. 'What a lovely thing to do.'

This is him, then, the great award-winning Miguel, who's clearly come bearing gifts. He's tall and dark, I notice, like Jake, but he doesn't look Portuguese. The way he's dressed, though, in a collarless linen shirt with tanned pecs on show, and white chinos, he clearly spends loads of time abroad.

'How could I resist capturing something so beautiful in paint?' He beams her a white-toothed smile and I note his arm sliding around her waist as he leans to kiss her cheek. I'm thinking they're a little too demonstrative in their affection for each other.

'Thank you.' She smiles, gazing up at him, clearly enraptured.

'The pleasure was all mine,' he assures her.

She's leaning in to reciprocate his kiss when Fern goes rigid in my arms, her whimpers about to ratchet up to a sob. Megan's peeved gaze swivels in my direction, and I smile in an everything's-in-hand sort of way, even though it's not, and press Fern to my shoulder. I'm about to make the perilous descent of the stairs when the front door opens. Despite my confused feelings about him, I feel a flutter in my tummy as Jake walks in. He falters just inside the door, his gaze travelling between the pair in front of him, who have quickly disengaged. His eyes go back to Megan, his expression inscrutable as he looks her over in all her bare-shouldered glory, and then to the gift propped against the table. His face darkens.

'Jake.' Miguel smiles, extending his hand.

Jake hesitates, then steps forward to shake it, but not overenthusiastically, I notice. 'Michael,' he says, with no hint of a smile. 'Or are we still addressing you as Miguel?'

'The latter.' Miguel's gaze travels over him as he steps back. 'I'm well known by that name now, after all.'

'So I gather. Busy?' Jake asks him, holding his gaze.

'Very. The price of fame,' Miguel replies with a theatrical sigh.

Jake's mouth twitches into a wry smile. 'Not too busy to dabble in your hobby, I see.' His eyes flick back to the gift.

'Well, she does make a rather captivating model,' Miguel replies with a smirk.

A tic spasms in Jake's cheek. He drops his gaze fast.

'Jakey, Jakey.' Sighing expansively, Miguel moves to drape

an arm over his shoulders. 'Relax, little brother. You're so uptight. It's just a painting.'

I gasp in disbelief. She's having an affair with his *brother*? *And* she's bloody well flaunting it. I look between them. The likeness is striking, I realise, apart from the fact that while Miguel is still smiling, Jake's expression is murderous.

THIRTY-FOUR

'I'm going to get changed,' Jake mutters, tearing his gaze away. As he heads for the stairs, I note the look he shoots back at Megan, one of contempt bordering on hatred, and a chill of apprehension runs through me. Tonight is not going to end well. I can feel it.

My heart rate ratchets up as Jake climbs the stairs. How can he bear it? How can he still be with her? It's no wonder he's been so off with me. She's *destroying* him. Why is she doing this? Bringing this Miguel – Michael – who clearly has a massively inflated ego, here, to Jake's house? Is she getting some kick out of seeing Jake suffer, playing one off against the other? She wants to have her cake and eat it, doesn't she? It seems to me that she's determined to take Jake for all she can get, torturing him in the process. She's trying to make him leave, isn't she? And then she'll move his own brother into his bed.

Noticing me as he nears the top of the stairs, Jake falters. 'Ellie, hi. I didn't see you there.' He attempts a smile, but there's such torment in his eyes my heart splinters for him. 'How are you doing?'

'I'm okay,' I assure him, jiggling Fern in my arms as she

starts fretting again. I'm not okay. I'm scared, emotionally depleted and exhausted, but he doesn't need to hear that right now. 'You?'

'I've been better.' He glances back to the hall, where Megan and Miguel are strolling towards the lounge and the open patio doors that overlook the pool. Looking pig-sick, he tears his gaze away.

'Why do you stay with her?' I blurt. I can't help myself. We've been as intimate as it's possible to be. He must know he can confide in me.

He drags a hand tiredly over his neck. 'I have no choice,' he says simply.

Because he doesn't want to leave his children. I understand. I do. But why can't he see that this toxic relationship will be far more psychologically damaging to them in the long term? Why can't he see what she's doing – with his own brother, for God's sake? The woman's a monster. A ruthless, manipulative bitch. She's using him. Bloody well *abusing* him. Utterly humiliating him. Yet still he stays. Does he really think that if he waits it out, she'll choose him over Miguel? What kind of idiot does that make me? I imagined he could love me. It was nothing but a pathetic fantasy.

'Is she okay?' He nods at Fern.

'She's fine,' I assure him, though actually, she's not. I'm sure she's picking up the stressful vibes. 'Jake, I need to ask you something,' I start hesitantly. I *have* to ask. I have to know that what went on between us meant *something*.

'About?' Jake's expression is weary, as if he doesn't want to do this right now, and that alone upsets me.

'What happened between us,' I push on, praying he won't lie to me, 'did it mean anything to you?'

Panic floods his features, and he urges me further along the landing. He's clearly concerned that someone might overhear.

'Well?' I demand, frustration and hurt churning inside me.

'Ellie, I...' He trails off, clearly struggling for a way to tell me what I'm already gathering.

I feel sick suddenly to the depths of my soul. 'Was it a mistake, Jake?' Anger unleashes inside me. 'Something you took because it was on offer? Is that it? Did you use me to relieve your own pent-up frustration?'

'What?' He looks as if I've slapped him. 'No. That's not how it was.' He glances quickly over his shoulder. 'It *did* mean something. Of course it did.'

'But you haven't *mentioned* it.' I choke back my tears, try to placate Fern, who's growing more anxious. 'You haven't said a single word about it since that day. In fact you've barely looked at me.'

He closes his eyes, 'Because it shouldn't have happened,' he says bluntly, driving an icicle straight through my heart.

'I need to get Fern's feed.' Swallowing hard, I attempt to move past him.

'Ellie, wait.' He sidesteps, blocking me. 'I meant I shouldn't have *allowed* it to happen. I knew you would end up getting hurt and I didn't want that. It was the absolute last thing I wanted. And I didn't mean to avoid talking about it. I just didn't know how.'

But I *am* hurt. He must know I am. I scan his eyes. His gaze is earnest, intense, apologetic – and I have no idea what to take from that. 'I need to get Fern's feed,' I repeat, looking away.

'Can we talk?' he asks. 'Later? When this charade downstairs is over?'

'Is there anything to talk *about*?' I ask bitterly. 'I'd hate you to feel—' *Obliged*, I was going to say, but I stop as Megan's voice floats up from the hall below. 'I should go.' I avert my gaze.

'I'll take her.' He reaches for Fern as she wriggles in my arms. 'You go and grab her feed.'

I hesitate. Like me, he probably realises Megan won't want a crying baby to cramp her style while she's trying to entertain her guests. I doubt Fern and Ollie have even crossed her mind – they certainly won't now that she appears to be paying rapt attention to Miguel.

Realising that Fern will be better off up here out of the way, I hand her over. Jake's smile is heartbreakingly sad as he gathers her to him.

I watch him talking softly to her as he carries her to the nursery, and my emotions rage inside me. He is a caring man. I *know* he is. Yet he's crushed me utterly.

Swiping away the tears that plop down my cheeks, I take a tremulous breath and steel myself to face the awful woman who means much more to him than I ever could.

The moment I set foot in the kitchen, she turns and snaps at me. 'I said leave it to cook over a low heat, did you not hear me?' It didn't take her long to revert to type, did it? Zach's death forgotten as if it never happened. What do men see in her? I wonder. Outwardly she might be beautiful, but inside she's ugly. She doesn't deserve to be a mother. She doesn't deserve Jake.

'It is on low.' I extract one of the feeds I made up earlier from the fridge and glance across to her.

'You have to turn the knob the other way, to the lowest setting.' She demonstrates. 'It's not rocket science, Ellie. Surely you've cooked something other than basic fare before?'

I feel my cheeks flush. 'No,' I admit. 'Not really.'

'Lord save us.' She presses the back of her hand to her brow. 'Did you put the wine in?' She glances around, presumably looking for the bottle.

My eyes skitter towards where it stands on the kitchen island. 'Yes,' I reply, and mentally cross my fingers, hoping she doesn't notice there's not much left.

'How much?' She marches across to it.

'Two cups. That's what it says in the—'

'But it's almost empty.' She holds it up, staring at it and then at me as if thunderstruck. 'For God's sake, can you not read a simple recipe?'

'I... I'm not sure what a cup is exactly,' I stammer. 'I guessed it was about—'

'Just go and feed the baby,' she mutters, marching past me. 'You do know how to read ounces, I assume?'

I'm speechless. With tears welling afresh, I'm tempted to tell her where to stuff her bloody wine bottle. I don't. Determined not to cry in front of her, I head quickly back to the stairs. I get a good look at Miguel's painting as I pass it, and I can see immediately what infuriated Jake. The model's head is bent demurely, her hair obscures her face, and one arm, strategically placed, covers her naked breasts, but it is undoubtedly Megan. Is this what she meant when she said she and Miguel had been collaborating? What an absolute cow. Miguel is no better, bringing the painting here. It's beyond comprehension.

Flabbergasted, I hurry back upstairs, desperate to continue my conversation with Jake. There's a small part of me that hopes he meant what he said and that he backed away because he didn't want to hurt me. A bigger part of me hopes he will see the light and throw his vile wife and her conceited lover out.

I find him by the glass wall when I go in. He's cradling Fern in his arms, staring up at the night sky as if looking for answers.

He turns around as I approach. 'She's sleeping with him, isn't she?' he says, his voice choked.

I have no idea what to say. I suspect that anything I offer, whether it be speculation or sympathy, won't help.

'Do you think she looks like me?' he asks quietly after a moment. I note the expression on his face as he stares down at Fern, a mixture of heart-rending, palpable sadness and obviously suppressed anger, and my stomach lurches. He doesn't think the little girl is his.

THIRTY-FIVE

The advantage of working in a house made of glass is that I can see everything. As I clear the table in the raised dining room, I glance down to the lounge area. Just below me, Jake stands apart from the other guests, studying the painting, which has been hung in a prominent position, replacing one of the abstract canvases on the wall just below me. His jaw is tense I notice, and he's swilling back the red wine Megan selected to complement the beef stew.

I take a glug from one of the half-filled crystal glasses left on the table. I'm angry with Jake, but still my heart bleeds for him. He thinks Fern is Miguel's child, her startling blue eyes inherited from his brother rather than him. But how would he ever prove it? I'm not familiar with the intricacies of DNA testing, but would a straightforward paternity test be able to distinguish between brothers as possible fathers? Would Jake even take a test? I think not. I think he's been holding on to the hope that Megan wouldn't have done that to him.

I left him feeding Fern. She was still fretful and he was cradling her in his arms, trying to soothe her. It's clear that he loves her; that he's caring and providing for her while Miguel swans off to Portugal, popping back when he feels inclined to 'collaborate' with Megan. How can they do it? They're both treating him like dirt. Why is *she* doing it? Why doesn't she just choose Miguel? Is it because she fears she might lose Ollie? I can't get my head around any of it. Fuming at her treatment of Jake and of me, I take another glug of wine. I'm aware that my odd glass is turning into too many; that with my family genes I should stop, but I'm so furious right now I don't care.

My eyes pivot to Megan, and I get some small satisfaction as I note the poisonous expression on her face. She's jealous, watching Miguel steadily, her eyes spitting fire as he chats to one of her female guests, Carly Simons, a fashion designer and a woman of some means, I've gleaned, who owns an old country house converted into apartments which she's looking to refurbish. She's gorgeous. Much younger than Megan, and wearing a short tie-waist silk dress, pale green in colour, which is stunning against her dark skin, she looks as if she's stepped off the pages of a glossy magazine. From the lavish attention Miguel is paying her, I gather she's a rival for his affections.

I watch as he regales her with tales of how he made his name building extravagant apartments for the super-rich. 'Mostly footballers, sports personalities and the like; high-net-worth individuals who have firm ideas about what they want,' he says, as Carly looks at him enraptured, more by the good looks he shares with Jake than by his self-important conversation, I suspect. 'My role is never to question, but to make people's dream homes come true,' he goes on, so full of himself it's a wonder he doesn't burst. 'If they want indoor lagoons and glass bridges, that's what they get.'

'Wow.' Carly is clearly impressed. 'I'm not sure a Stratford country house lends itself to an indoor lagoon, but it sounds amazing.'

Miguel nods, accepting the compliment with a self-assured smile. 'I consider myself an artist,' he drones on, expounding his own virtues. 'Properties speak to me. I tend not to go in with a floor plan, rather to design as I go. My influence rubs off on other designers, as you can see.' He gazes around Jake's house, his eyes travelling past Megan without pausing – to her obvious irritation.

'This place is beautiful,' Carly acknowledges, smiling in appreciation as she follows his gaze. 'You're clearly an inspiration.'

As Miguel tries to look modest, Megan casts a murderous glance at the woman whose avid attention is clearly inflating his already massive ego. She smiles apologetically at another guest, whose attempts at conversation with her are falling flat, then walks stiffly across to Jake. 'Do you think you could make an effort?' she hisses, her smile now fixed in place as if glued there. 'I'm supposed to be networking. You standing there looking as if you'd rather be somewhere else doesn't give a good impression.'

Jake's sideways glance is one of acerbic amusement. 'I was just thinking.' His gaze strays back to the painting. 'I was wondering how I would portray you if I had an artistic bone in my body, which I don't, as you've pointed out. I decided that paint wouldn't be the best medium.' Arranging his face into a smile, he picks up a figurative stone sculpture from its plinth next to the painting. A frown crosses his brow as he studies the artist's statement – Megan insists on mounting these next to her exhibits to portray the authenticity of the artwork. '"The figures appear incomplete to describe a condition of emptiness. Hollow humans",' he reads and leans close to her ear. 'It captures you perfectly, don't you think?'

My breath stalls as the figurine slides from his hands, landing with a crash to shoot a thousand slivers of ceramic across the Italian marble tiles.

Megan's eyes harden. '*Bastard,*' she mouths.

As heads angle in their direction, Jake's apologies are convincingly profuse.

Miguel's expression is alarmed as Megan whirls around, her face incandescent with fury. He looks quickly back to Carly. 'I must show you the patio area,' he says. 'Megan borrowed one of my designs. I must say, she's made an extremely good job of it.' No doubt aiming to distract the woman from the impending disaster, he slides an arm around her waist and steers her outside.

Megan looks as if she might implode. Breathing sharply in, she strides across the lounge area to the hall and then sweeps up the stairs, all eyes following her as she goes.

I glance up as she reaches the landing, my own breath stalled as I wait for her next move. I'm guessing Fern's still fretting. I left her unsettled; I had no choice but to while I came down to do Megan's bidding.

I wait and listen. Hearing nothing above the now subdued conversation, I assume she's gone to her room. I breathe a sigh of relief and start to gather up the dishes.

Rushing to pick up the tray I've loaded, I spin around and manage to swipe one of the half-empty wine bottles from the table. *Oh no.* It would have to be red wine. My heart sinks as I realise it's about to bleed into the grouting in the floor tiles. Clanging the tray down, I pluck up an open bottle of white, grab a handful of napkins and soak them with it, then drop to my knees. As I'm crawling around on all fours, trying to limit the damage, I glance up to meet Jake's gaze. His look a combination of weary and helpless, he shrugs and mouths, 'Sorry.'

This time his apology incenses me. What is it he's apologising *for*? For using me? For having deliberately set out to? My fury escalates, bubbling white-hot inside me. Is this what he thinks of me, that I'm a servant? A convenient shag when he feels like it? Is this where he believes I should be, on my hands and knees, mopping up their mess?

With my gaze on Jake, I hear Megan rather than see her, as everyone does. They can't fail to as she shrieks, 'For God's sake, Ellie, will you stop making eyes at my fucking husband and get up here and see to Fern! She's *crying*.'

THIRTY-SIX

'Christ, is she ever going to stop?' Jake eyes the ceiling. 'I'll go,' he says, his jaw clenched as he looks back to me.

Am I supposed to thank him for offering to see to his own child? The child he thinks isn't his, I remind myself with a flicker of guilt. Even so, I don't feel inclined to gush with gratitude. My inclination is to get this lot cleared up and get out of here.

Collecting up the soggy napkins and retrieving the bottle, I pick up the tray again and head to the kitchen. I'm seething as I dump the dishes. Muttering to myself, ignoring the argument upstairs – they can kill each other for all I care – I find the mop bucket, slosh water and detergent into it and lug it back through the lounge and up to the dining area, careless of what people might think. Looking highly uncomfortable, the guests appear to be gravitating towards the hall anyway, ready to leave. I can't say I blame them. If Megan's commissions depended on this little soirée going well, I think it's fair to say she's blown it. Serves her bloody well right.

Having cleaned the tiles and grouting as best I can, I take the paraphernalia back to the kitchen and set about loading up the dishwasher. I'm crashing dishes and crystal glasses in there alike and not giving a damn about what her majesty might think when Jake reappears. 'They've left,' he says, his tone weary. 'Unsurprisingly.'

I draw in a breath. 'Is Fern all right?' I ask tightly. I don't turn around. I'm seething with fury at the way Megan has treated me, the way *he's* treated me. Realising that the wine I've been swigging back has gone to my head, however, meaning I might not be as in control of my emotions as I'd like to be, I decide it might be a good idea not to voice my thoughts right now.

'I think so,' he says, sounding uncertain. 'Megan was with her when I went up.'

'Did she have an attack of the guilts?' I growl. Fuelled by alcohol, the words fall from my mouth unhindered by process of forethought.

Jake doesn't answer for a second. Then, 'I'm not sure she's capable of that particular emotion,' he answers quietly.

I feel for him. My tendency is to wholeheartedly agree with him, but I don't want to get into that conversation. I'm just too angry to be the gullible, sympathetic person I obviously have been.

'Leave that,' he says, moving towards me. 'You've done enough tonight. I'll finish off here.'

'That's very thoughtful of you,' I retort, slamming the dishwasher door and spinning around. 'You might want to check it before you turn it on in case your *wife* doesn't approve.'

As I march past him, determined not to be distracted by his permanently tortured penetrating blue eyes, he catches my arm. 'Ellie, I am sorry,' he says. 'For everything. If things were different—'

'Don't, Jake,' I warn him, a combination of disillusionment and bitter disappointment festering inside me. 'I really don't want to hear any more of your self-pitying bullshit.'

His face pales. He's shaken by my bluntness, clearly. I wait for him to say something. I'm not sure what. I don't want his apologies. I want him to say he'll tell her about us, that he'll leave her. Or else ask me to bear with him. Anything that doesn't confirm that what happened between us was just sex. Still he says nothing, simply drops his gaze.

'I'm going to get my things.' Snatching my arm away, I look him over scathingly and then turn away.

I try to convince myself I don't care as I rush across the hall, ignoring Megan, who's coming down the stairs, glaring at me as she does. But I do care. My heart feels as if it's being ripped from my chest. Feeling devastated, degraded, bitterly ashamed that I could have been so utterly naïve; most of all, unbearably guilty – Zach would still be alive if not for me – I hurry up the stairs.

Flying to the spare room, I shove the door closed, hoping Jake will get the message if he follows me. I'm guessing all of this will leave me jobless as well as broken-hearted, and I don't want to talk to him, not now, if ever. After stuffing my things into my overnight bag, I grab my phone. I'm about to call a taxi when I receive a text. My heart jolts as I read it: *Your employer has been in touch with me. You might do well to call me. It's your mother, by the way. I'm sure you remember me.*

But... *how?* My chest close to exploding, I jab the call button. 'How did you get my number?' I snap as soon as she picks up.

'Hello, Ellie. Lovely to hear from you. I'm fine, thanks for asking,' my mother replies facetiously.

Bile rises like acid inside me as I realise she's slurring her words. 'What do you want?'

'Charming.' I hear her suck in a breath and guess she's taking a draw on her cigarette. I'm so tempted to end the call, but I don't. She's rung for a reason. Whatever it is, it won't be good, but I need to know. 'Your boss supplied your number,' she says at length, shocking me to the core.

'When did she call you?' I try to get my head around what she's saying.

'It wasn't a woman, it was a man. Jake, he said his name was.' She exhales slowly.

My head reels. 'But how did he know where you were?'

'The nursery gave him our address. They wouldn't supply him with any other information, so he came to see me – because he was concerned about you, he said.'

A new wave of panic unfurls inside me. 'What did you tell him?'

'Just the facts,' she says, after another lengthy pause. 'Don't worry, I didn't tell him anything he wouldn't already have found online.'

My mind ticks feverishly. 'When did he come to see you?'

'I can't remember exactly,' she answers blithely. 'A good few weeks back.'

I feel as if the air has been sucked from my lungs. He knew about my history? He said he'd noticed my scars, pretended sympathy. *Why?* If he knew all there was to know about me, why not just say so? I try to rationalise it. But I can't. Because *I* know. He told me that Megan had wanted to end her life. He said that to elicit *my* sympathy, didn't he? With sickening clarity, it occurs to me that he set out to use me. For what? If it was just sex, it doesn't seem like much of a prize. It obviously wasn't, I think bitterly, since his inclination hasn't been for a repeat performance.

Swallowing back my excruciating hurt, I work to compose myself. I won't give my mother the satisfaction of hearing the devastation in my voice. 'So why call me now?' I ask her.

Again she pauses. 'Because, believe it or not, I'm concerned about you too.'

'Ha,' I scoff derisively.

'I got to thinking,' she goes on, ignoring me. 'I wondered why he wouldn't have shared the information with his wife. She also paid me a visit. She didn't appear to know her husband had been.'

Megan. I shake my head in bewilderment.

'She said it had obviously slipped his mind as they were both so *terribly* busy,' my mother continues, adopting a plummy tone. 'Call me cynical, but something about her didn't feel right. I thought to myself, that one's up to no good. I wanted to let you know. I would have called before, but I guessed you wouldn't want—'

'I have to go.' I cut her short and end the call.

They know all about me. My head reels, nausea and panic swirling inside me as I realise that there's absolutely no one in the world I can trust. Not my mother. Not Megan. Certainly not Jake now he's gone behind my back. Why have they done this? It's almost as if they're playing with me. I feel like a pawn in the middle of some twisted, dangerous game, my every move dictated by their moods, each of them using me to score points off the other. I wonder with a lurch of fear what their next move will be.

THIRTY-SEVEN

My stomach twisting in confusion and apprehension, I go out onto the landing. Fern is quiet, finally, but she's been crying for most of the evening, upset and miserable – because her own mother doesn't want her. Babies pick up on these things. Will Jake want her now he's admitted to himself he isn't her father? I recall how he muttered, *Christ, is she ever going to stop?* when Megan screamed down the stairs, accusing me of making eyes at him. He was angry. Wasn't he likely to be, though, at a constantly crying baby who isn't his, especially with the man who *is* the child's father – his own brother – standing just yards away? I felt so sorry for him, scared for him. Now, I'm more scared *of* him.

They're arguing now the guests have gone, inevitably, right there in the hall, neither of them with a thought for Fern or Ollie. Morbid fascination drives me closer to the stairs to eavesdrop. 'Why are you still doing this, Megan?' I hear Jake growl.

'I have no idea what you're talking about,' she replies indifferently.

'For fuck's sake! I *know!*' I watch as he rakes a hand through his hair, his face tight with angry accusation as he glares at her.

'You *know* I do. Do you really expect me to go on with this bloody sham?'

Folding her arms across her chest, Megan looks him over with cynical amusement. 'You don't have any choice, do you, Jake? Thanks to you, we're destined to be together for ever. Best learn to live with it.'

'Doomed, more like.' He eyes her coldly. 'Does *he* know?' he asks.

'About what you did?' She tips her head interestedly to one side.

His expression one of contempt, Jake drags his gaze away. 'You know damn well what I'm talking about.'

Megan sighs and shakes her head. 'I need a drink,' she says, heading across the hall.

'I've had enough of this,' Jake grates behind her as she walks past him to the kitchen.

'So what are you going to do? Leave me?' she asks sarcastically over her shoulder. 'You won't. You know you can't. Oh, and just for your information, I know about *you* too. You just can't help yourself, can you? Does it boost your ego, Jake, having poor unfortunate young women idolising you? I can't quite see the attraction myself. She's improved her look, largely by copying mine, but she's quite a plain little thing, isn't she?'

I step back, my heart pounding. She's talking about me. I recall our conversation when she showed me around the house. Her enigmatic smile when she told me Jake liked to nurture people. People who were less fortunate. Did she know he planned to have sex with me? Is this his modus operandi: befriending vulnerable young women, empathising with them? He told me he came from a broken family. Clearly that was after he'd seen for himself my unfortunate roots. Was it all to gain my trust, my sympathy. Is there any truth in *anything* he's told me?

It's just a game to them, isn't it? He's used me to make her feel jealous. She's using me until it suits her purpose not to. Suddenly they're as transparent as the glass house they live in. They're getting some kind of kick out of ruining people's lives. Did they play the same cruel game with Phoebe?

A turmoil of emotions warring inside me, bewilderment and complete incomprehension, I move back to the stairs. I'm about to go down and confront them when I hear Jake. 'Beauty's only skin deep, though, isn't it, Megan?' he retorts acerbically. 'Standing next to you, pound for pound, she's way more attractive than you could ever be.'

I squint in bemusement before the hurt hits me like a hand grenade. A hard lump expanding in my chest, I go to the nursery and across to the cot, where I stand for a long moment staring down at Fern. She's sleeping, but her face is blotchy, her cheeks red raw with the effort of crying. What kind of future is she going to have with a mother who's incapable of caring for anyone but herself? A father who's just realised she isn't actually his?

Gently I lift her from her cot, place my hand on the back of her head, gather her to my breast and carry her across to the window.

'Sleep contentedly, little one,' I whisper. 'We don't want Daddy to be annoyed, do we?' Pressing a gentle kiss to her hair, I squeeze her closer and begin softly singing, Brahms' 'Lullaby', which I know always soothes her.

> *Lullaby and good night, thy mother's delight.*
> *Bright angels around, my darling, shall guard.*
> *They will guide thee from harm, thou art safe in*
>   *my arms.*
> *They will guide thee from harm, thou art safe in*
>   *my arms.*

Fern is as silent as a lamb as I hum on. There's no sound at all but the gentle plop of rain against the window, like fingernails tapping hauntingly against the glass. As I look out at the night sky beyond it, I imagine Theo up there, looking down at me; see his huge brown eyes, filled with fear. He trusted me. He shouldn't have. This little girl trusts me. I can't leave her here. Standing there, feeling insignificant against the vastness of the universe, I wonder at the impact of my actions on the lives of those around me; what might have been if I hadn't made so many wrong decisions. Theo died because of me. Zach would be alive today if not for me.

Thunder rumbles, clouds clashing deep in the belly of the night, as I continue to stare unseeing out of the window. 'God moving his furniture,' I whisper to Fern, as I used to whisper to Theo. As the heavens open, heavy rain now lashing against the glass, I turn away, press my back to the window and slide to my haunches, letting the tears fall. Fern lies unmoving in my arms. She's beautiful. So quiet now. So peaceful.

Lightning jars me, followed by a clap of thunder so loud, I'm sure the foundations of the house shake. Fear gripping me as I imagine the glass shattering, I grab hold of the rocking horse and attempt to lever myself to my feet. It's the glint in its black eyes as another crack of lightning illuminates the sky that forces the scream from my mouth.

My chest thudding, I wait and listen. Hearing footsteps along the landing, I snap my gaze to the door. They're heavy footsteps, I realise; Jake's, not Megan's. I watch as the handle is pressed down. Quickly I glance back to Fern, jiggle her in my arms. She doesn't stir, doesn't murmur. And now I need her to. I need her to cry. I shouldn't have stayed. I should have slipped away. '*Fern.*' I shake her, will her to open her eyes.

My heart lurches as I realise that Jake is standing in the doorway. 'What are you doing?' he asks, his face frozen in shock and confusion.

'She won't wake up. I can't make her wake *up!*' I gulp back a sob as he takes a stumbling step forward, his eyes travelling from my face to his baby girl lying like a limp rag doll in my arms. In two sudden strides he's in front of me, looming over me, and I shrink back as his incomprehension gives way to deep, visceral anger. Then Megan is there too, behind him on the landing, her face drained of colour, her expression horrified. *I was trying to keep her safe! From her!* I want to scream it, but I don't. He won't believe me. He loves her.

'Give her to me.' His voice is hoarse, a guttural whisper, and I clutch Fern closer, willing the warmth of my body to breathe life back into hers. I hear Ollie coming from his room, see Megan going to him, and I pray he will be all right. 'I said *give* her to me!' Jake yells, jolting my gaze back to him.

His hands trembling, he takes her from me and cradles her tenderly in the crook of his arm. I see the rise and fall of his throat as he studies her lifeless features. '*No.*' His voice cracks, his chest heaving as he turns his gaze to the ceiling. 'What did you do to her?' He snaps his gaze back to me.

'Nothing. I was j-just holding her,' I stammer. 'Megan was in here. Earlier. She—'

'What the *fuck* did you *do* to her? His eyes drill into mine, the ice-blue irises blazing with fury, and I want to run, hide. Curl up in a corner and crawl inside myself. As he sinks to his knees, the cry he emits is like nothing I've ever heard before from a human being; that of a wounded animal.

Suddenly there's a cacophony of noise: Jake's raucous sobs, sirens wailing, blue lights flashing, tyres screeching, voices shouting, footsteps urgent across the marbled tiled floor in the hall.

I'm trying to make them hear, to tell them it wasn't me, as I'm led from the house. As I'm escorted to the waiting police car, my gaze snags on Jake's BMW and my feeble protestations die in my throat. I twist around, straining to see it more clearly.

How did Jake's front bumper get damaged? *When* did it get damaged?

I look back to the house. Jake stands at the open front door. He's watching me carefully, his expression hard. Then he steps back, closing the door, and an icy chill of terror runs through me. I hear Zach's voice. At the time, what he said sounded like jealousy. It wasn't. It was a warning: *You're being an idiot if you imagine he'll give a damn about you once he gets what he wants. Blokes like him don't, Ellie. They don't get where they are giving a shit about people.*

THIRTY-EIGHT

Jake

As our child is taken away, I lean my head against the front door and try to do the simplest thing of all and just breathe. Impossible. I clamp my eyes closed – to no avail. Fern's delicate features are scorched indelibly on my mind. I feel her, the impossible lightness of her as I held her in my arms. She was so still, so beautiful, like a perfect porcelain doll. I would give anything to take back the fury I felt when I finally acknowledged what had been staring me in the face since the day she was born: that she wasn't mine.

'Mr Harington,' I hear someone say behind me. 'Mr Harington.' DS Jacobs' voice is sympathetic. I feel her hand on my arm. The physical touch jolts me.

Swallowing back the hard knot of fear in my throat, I turn to face her. 'What happens now?' I ask hoarsely. I search her face for some clue to her thinking. Her expression gives nothing away.

'As I said earlier, the sudden unexpected death of an infant requires the case to be referred to a coroner. There will be a full investigation to look for unnatural causes as well as possible medical causes, including infectious or genetic diseases. We'll keep you fully informed.'

I nod, wish to God that I could turn back time. I would swap my life in a heartbeat in exchange for Fern's. It isn't an option. My soul is so warped, even the fucking devil would pass. A toxic mixture of raw grief and unbearable guilt at my unforgivable actions this evening swirls inside me.

'Do you think I could have another word with you and your wife?' the detective asks.

Again I nod, guessing the questions will be endless and inevitable. I feel some relief that it's the same detective who delivered the news about Zachary Kendall. She saw the devastating impact her boyfriend's death had on Ellie. She will gather that her state of mind must have been affected. At least I hope she will.

'I realise you've suffered a tragic loss,' she goes on carefully, 'but it would help if you and Mrs Harington could clarify a few points for us.'

Panic twists my gut as I wonder what points, whether the answers we give will tally. Ollie is my main concern, my priority. He needs us to be there for him. I intend to be, whatever it takes.

Megan is sitting on one of the sofas. Her emotions laid bare, raw and exposed, she sobs, hot tears of acrid grief streaming down her cheeks. I go to her. I have to. I pray she won't push me away and risk exposing the wide-open cracks in our marriage.

As I lower myself down next to her and take hold of her hand, I feel the tension through it. She doesn't snatch it away, though, and relief sweeps through me. My worry is that she will break down, lose control, when she could conceivably say or do anything.

DS Jacobs takes a seat on the stool opposite us. 'I know you've given your preliminary statements – thank you for that. I also realise this must be terribly painful for you, but if you could bear with us a little longer.' She smiles compassionately at each of us in turn. 'Could you just clarify, to the best of your recollection, how long Miss Taylor was in the nursery before you heard the scream and realised something was wrong?'

'We can't be sure exactly,' I answer for both of us. 'She'd been upstairs twenty minutes or so.'

'And you say she was acting strangely?'

I nod and close my eyes. 'Her behaviour was unusual, yes,' I clarify. 'She dropped a tray while clearing the table, spilled some wine.' I indicate the dining area and the crimson stain that still decorates the floor. 'It wasn't a big deal, but she seemed distressed; frustrated and angry.'

'And you've no idea why?' the detective asks.

'Not really, no.' I run a hand over my neck, my guilt intensifying under the woman's steady gaze. 'She's been struggling since losing her boyfriend so tragically, understandably.'

'Emotional?' Jacobs asks.

'Drunk,' Megan replies flatly. 'She stole our wine.'

Jacobs makes a note. 'Did she make a habit of drinking while caring for the children?'

Megan answers with a tight nod. 'More so since her boyfriend...' She trails off and wipes a trembling hand across her cheeks.

DS Jacobs nods thoughtfully. 'Just one more thing.' She glances between us. 'You said you'd checked on Fern earlier. Could you just confirm what time that was, approximately, and who it was that checked on her?'

'Jake,' Megan says.

'Megan,' I answer at the exact same time. 'That is,' I squeeze her hand hard, 'I went into the nursery to find Megan in there. She left to go and see our guests off. I checked Fern was settled and then followed her out.'

'Right.' The detective frowns briefly, then gets to her feet. 'I think that's all we need for now. We might have a few more questions, and again apologies for having to ask them at such a sad time. The family liaison officer will keep you up to date with any developments meanwhile.'

I thank her and walk her to the door, my chest feeling as if it's about to explode. Once she and the other investigating officer have left, I head for the stairs to go to our boy, who waits, frightened and alone, in his room. I have to protect him. I have to keep pretending, lying, bleeding steadily inside. Ollie needs me. I have to get him through this. I have to find a way to be there for him. I feel deep remorse for what I've done to Ellie, desperately sorry for her, but there is nothing I can do to help her. I cannot, *will* not, be separated from my son.

THIRTY-NINE

THE DAY ELLIE CAME INTO MY LIFE

Megan

She truly is beautiful. Untarnished by life, the life Jake and I are forced to live in this house made of fragile glass, my little girl lies in her cot, looking up at me, gurgling innocently. As I reach to stroke her warm, peachy cheek, I see a flicker of wariness in her eyes and my heart dips painfully. It's her daddy she wants, not me. When she looks at me, it's as if she knows I'm flawed; as if she can see through the flesh and the blood and the bone right down to the core of me. Jake says she senses my guilt, which only compounds it. He says I'm too tense and that I need to relax with her. I try. I love her *so* much. Yet I feel I don't deserve for her to love me. That if she does, I might damage her. I catch him watching me sometimes when I hold her, his ice-blue irises drilling into mine, filled with such accusation it only makes me feel more inept.

I have to find a way to make it right. I have to be there for my baby daughter. She needs me, emotionally, physically. Smiling to try to reassure her, I reach to lift her gently out, check she's dry, then hold her close. She's not reassured. As she begins to fret, I feel my own tears rising. 'I'm sorry,' I whisper, a deep sense of shame washing through me as I imagine what might have happened to her if Jake hadn't called the ambulance. After the catastrophic consequences of his affair with Phoebe, I convinced myself my little girl would be better off without me, that my little boy would. Jake certainly would have been. I realise that now. It has become more obvious with each passing day since that he wants to be rid of me. Why then didn't he simply leave me to die? I tell myself he had a fit of conscience. I'm not sure I believe it. Rather, I think he panicked, uncertain as he would have been of the contents of my will. Is that just me, though, my cynicism? I'm clearly capable of such awfulness. I just don't know any more.

Would he have continued to be a father to Fern if the hospital hadn't been able to save me? Would he have asked Michael to take her? Jake asked me once if Fern was his. Out of some deep-rooted jealousy, his own insecurity, he made up his mind long ago that I would prefer his brother over him. He was measuring me by his own standards. Michael and I are colleagues, we are close, but we're friends, not lovers. It was Jake I loved, unwaveringly.

I squeeze Fern closer, kiss her soft, downy head and breathe in the sweet smell of her. She nestles into me, and I'm hard pressed not to let the tears fall. What did I do that my husband could treat me with such calculated cruelty? I worked to try to forgive him when he hurt me so badly before our wedding. I tried to believe him when he said it was a moment of madness; that he'd been drinking too much because he was under so much pressure while trying to start up his business. He was bitterly ashamed, cried actual tears, swore he loved me. I tried to understand. To forgive him. I will never forgive myself for what I did on the day he fractured what was left of my heart. I didn't wait for his apologies, his claims that this was another moment of madness. Rage consumed me, swallowed me whole. Then followed the blackness, the deep, dark pit I couldn't climb out of.

As I kiss Fern's temple and ease away from her, she looks at me curiously. I'm sure she does. I might be mistaken, but I sense she sees the tear that spills down my cheek. I swallow the stone inside me and smile for her, smile widely. 'It's okay, sweetheart,' I say. 'Mummy's not sad. Mummy's smiling. See?' Inside, I'm soaring. My baby's not wriggling and tetchy in my arms. She's looking at me and she's not crying. It might not be a big thing to some. To me it's a small miracle. As she flails a hand, I catch it and kiss it, marvel at the smallness of it.

She gurgles, looking at me now in open wonderment, and in that moment, I want to call Michael and cancel our appointment. I want to curl up with my baby girl nestled close to me. Yet I can't. I can't let this commission go. Work is what keeps me sane. Without it I would be at Jake's mercy, and I simply can't be.

'I think it's time to pop you in your cot, little one.' I kiss her temple again. 'Daddy will be here soon.' I try to sound joyous about that as I lower her gently back down. She doesn't fret – another small miracle – but waves her little limbs excitedly instead. 'Night, night, sweetheart.' I kiss my fingers and press them to her cheek, then turn away before the temptation to stay, or even gather my children and run away, becomes overwhelming.

I can't flee, though I dearly wish I could, not with the hold Jake has over me. I would have to change my identity, leave my children. However scared I am, I will never do that. Quashing the notion, I head along the landing, pausing as my phone alerts me to a text. Retrieving the phone from my jacket pocket, I see it's from him: *Just leaving the office. Back soon.* It's short and formal, as most of our conversations are now.

Good. I reply equally shortly. In the absence of any childcare, Jake promised faithfully to reschedule his meeting, and then forgot, as he has done on several occasions. As he's aware of my reluctance to employ a childminder who doesn't meet my exact requirements, and why, I can only conclude that he's doing this deliberately.

Sighing, I head on to my son's room. I find him sitting cross-legged on the floor surrounded by Lego. I'm trying to encourage him away from his computer games. I worry about him becoming addicted, that it might affect his mental health. Most of all, I worry that he seems so isolated sitting on his own glued to his Nintendo. I'm sure it can't be healthy. Jake disagrees with me, of course, saying that all kids are into computer games nowadays and that Ollie would be isolated if he wasn't, which gains his son's favour.

He glances up. He doesn't look delighted to see me as he once did, doesn't jump up and charge at me, or wave his latest creation excitedly for me to see. A small furrow in his brow, he concentrates on his model-making endeavours instead. He began to grow away from me a while back, after Phoebe arrived to worm her way into my life, working to take everything from me, to turn my son against me. Jake tried to convince me differently, telling me I was becoming paranoid, because of the blip in our relationship before we were married. He said he was concerned for me, for my mental health. He wanted me to question my sanity. He still does. Does he realise, I wonder, since the scales were peeled from my eyes, that I'm possibly saner than I've ever been in my life? That I know *exactly* what he's doing?

'What's that you're making?' I ask Ollie, walking across to kneel beside him.

My son's gaze flicks to mine. 'A T. rex,' he answers quietly.

My heart squeezes. I miss him, the closeness there once was between us. 'He has big teeth,' I comment, eyeing the plastic creature's large claws and gaping mouth.

'So he can eat his prey,' Ollie explains, plucking up what appears to be a ribcage.

I watch as he slots it in the dinosaur's mouth and wonder if this is a suitable toy for a six-year-old. Jake would tell me I'm being neurotic. On this occasion, he would probably be right. 'It's a very fine T. rex,' I tell Ollie, dismissing my concerns. 'He looks a little bit tired, though. Do you think it might be past his bedtime?'

'Five more minutes?' He glances hopefully up at me.

'No more minutes.' Despite being desperate to win back his affection, I remain firm. 'Come on, I'll help you clear up, and then once you're tucked in, you can have a few minutes' reading time. Okay?'

'Okay.' Realising there's no wiggle room, Ollie sighs and gets to his feet. 'Is Daddy going to be here soon?' he asks, inevitably.

'Soon,' I promise, quashing the hurt I feel that he so obviously looks forward to seeing his father.

He nods, looking pleased. 'Will he read me my bedtime story?'

'I'm sure he will.' I force a bright smile and help him scramble into bed, then give him a hug and head for the door.

I've barely reached the landing when I hear Jake's car pulling up outside. '*Yes!*' Ollie exclaims behind me, and I guess he's also heard it and is following me.

'Back to bed, Ollie,' I scold him. 'Daddy will come up and see you shortly, but only if you're all tucked up under your duvet. Go on. Mummy has a business meeting, remember?' I urge him gently back to bed and attempt to still the nerves I always feel knowing my husband is about to walk through the door.

'Meg,' Jake calls as he comes into the hall, and I feel myself tense as I realise he's talking to someone. A female. My heart skids against my ribcage as I hear him call her Ellie. Who is she? A member of his staff, presumably, since he texted to say he was coming straight from the office. Trepidation twists inside me. Why has he brought her here?

FORTY

'Up here. You're cutting it fine, Jake,' I call down to him. Then, trying for some level of composure, I wait while he bounds up the stairs. Reaching the landing, he flicks his eyes cursorily over me. A broad smile curves his mouth as he looks past me, and I gather that Ollie has reappeared. 'Hey, little man, how are you doing? Did you have a good day at school?' he asks, sweeping him into his arms, and a conflict of emotion churns inside me. Whatever Jake has done, Ollie has unshakeable belief in him. I don't want to damage that, which would be to damage my son.

I wait while Ollie tells him about his day. I'm taken aback when he says I wouldn't allow him to go to his friend's house for tea. Does he really think I would be so mean? I see from the look Jake shoots me that he's judging me, upsettingly, in front of our son, reinforcing my bad guy image. I know that in Ollie's mind I'm the reason Phoebe, who he adored – largely because she indulged his every whim, spending hours in front of the computer with him – left so suddenly. He overheard the blazing arguments we had about her. After one such argument, when Jake, being the caring soul he is, had picked her up from the village pub, I heard Ollie ask him why I didn't like her. Jake told him I did, that I was just tired, that was all. 'Why is Mummy always tired?' was Ollie's next question. He meant, of course, *Why is Mummy always angry?* That hurt. So much. How did I explain? How did I tell my little boy that mummies couldn't like other women their daddies had sex with?

Remaining calm now, I patiently point out to Ollie that I said he could go as long as Jake was able to pick him up. At which Ollie turns beguilingly to Jake. 'Can you, Daddy?'

Jake agrees, but hesitantly. I suspect he wants Ollie to think I've let him down, but on the other hand, how can he tell him he can't pick him up without also letting him down?

Once I've encouraged Ollie back to bed, I follow Jake into our bedroom, closing the door behind me.

'How's Fern?' He glances back at me as he walks to the wardrobe.

'Fine,' I answer as I wait for him to enlighten me as to who the bloody hell is standing in my hall. 'She was settled when I left her.'

'Really?' He glances at me again, his expression surprised, slightly cynical. 'That's a first, isn't it?' He doesn't say 'a breakthrough' or 'well done', because he wants me to continue to feel bad about myself, to doubt myself. I quash the hurt, again.

'Did you manage to postpone your meeting?' I ask him, working to keep my voice even. He's fetching a clean shirt from the wardrobe, I notice. Why would he be doing that unless he's going out?

'Not exactly, no.' Unbuttoning the shirt he has on, he turns to face me. 'It's an important meeting, Meg. I have to—'

'For God's *sake*, Jake!' I stare at him in disbelief. 'Why are you doing this? Please, just stop, will you?' Turning back to the door before the tears that are threatening spill over, I yank it open.

'Stop doing *what?*' He follows me as I head for the landing.

'I'm doing my best here, Megan. I've organised a babysitter. She's—'

'A *babysitter?*' I whirl around, incredulous. 'Are you out of your mind? After what happened with Phoebe, his cruel lies to try to allay his guilt, the devastation to our lives and our children's lives blighted, he's brought another woman home? It's like déjà vu. He's cranking it up a notch, isn't he? I eye him narrowly. He's trying to drive me back to that dark place I reached once before. I won't let him. 'Aside from the obvious problems I might have with that, Jake,' I say shakily, 'do you honestly think I'm going to leave my children with a complete *stranger?*'

'She's not a stranger.' His tone is agitated – for her benefit, no doubt. His eyes tell a different story. I see the challenge there and it occurs to me that he would quite like me to lose my temper, regardless of the upset to our children. That way he'd have a witness to his wife's unstable behaviour. A willing little witness, no doubt. 'She's an employee. I know her,' he adds, pushing home the knife he's already driven into my heart.

I stare hard at him. Even now, I want to believe he's not doing this. But he is, isn't he? I *won't* let him. 'Oh yes?' My voice is loaded with contempt, and I actually don't care if she hears me. 'And how *well* do you know her, Jake?'

Fury outweighing the fear that's settled like ice inside me, I tear my gaze away and head for the stairs. I have no choice but to play him at his own despicable game. I can't run. I can't leave. If I could, I would, in a heartbeat.

Halfway down, I stop in surprise. I expected to see a Phoebe lookalike, some sexually alluring, worldly creature. What I see before me is a girl barely out of her teens. Far from being bright and bubbly and 'keen to meet me', as Phoebe was, she looks unsure of herself. I'm destabilised for a second. She really doesn't appear brazen enough to turn up here if she is having an affair with my husband. It's possible she has a schoolgirl crush on him, hence her eagerness to please him, but from her lack of attention to her appearance, I don't get the immediate feeling that she's any threat.

I hesitate for a second to collect myself, then continue on down and force a smile. 'I'm sorry about that. Jake has a habit of doing this,' I say, dropping a less than subtle hint that I hope she might get.

After a short exchange with Jake, who's followed me down, offering to help while looking convincingly browbeaten, I beckon the girl to follow me and go through to the lounge area. While she moons sympathetically at my crestfallen 'knight in shining armour', I text Michael to tell him I'll be late. I could have cancelled, but aside from the fact that we need to draw up plans on how best to approach the possible new commission, which is for a famous fashion designer, and which I need, I *have* to talk to him. I have to tell someone of my fears about what Jake is trying to do to me. I need Michael's shoulder, which is always there for me, now more than ever.

When she comes in after me, finally, she looks like a frightened little mouse, one that wishes it were anywhere else. I suspect, though, that she doesn't want to let Jake down. I know how that feels. There was a time when I didn't want to let him down either. I gave him everything: my heart, which I realise was worth nothing; free access to my bank accounts. I even borrowed from my father to help him grow his fledgling business. It wasn't enough. To me, it seems he won't be satisfied until he's stripped me of everything, emotionally as well as materially.

As I look at this girl perched nervously on the edge of my sofa, it occurs to me that he's chosen her precisely because she is unworldly, therefore pliable. She will present no challenge to him. From her gutsy determination to stay, rather than walk away, which I would certainly have done after overhearing what she must have, I glean that she must have feelings for him.

For a second, I want to confide in her and tell her to run, and then I laugh inwardly at my own naïvety. Jake has brought her here to plant suspicion in my mind. It would probably sound insane to anyone who doesn't know what I know. She will think I'm mentally unbalanced. She will feel sorry for him. He will use her to destabilise me. The game has started, the ball is rolling. He will tell me I am insane, imagining things. I'm not.

Instead, I sit up straighter and apologise again to her, citing Jake springing the situation on me as reason for my rudeness. And then I grill her. I'm short with her, blunt to the point of brutal, causing her to alternately shrink back and then bristle at my apparent judgement of her. I'm not sure she isn't lying about her qualifications. She doesn't break eye contact, but her cheeks flush deep crimson. Did Jake do a background check? Given the time he's had to organise this, I think not. I make a mental note to do it myself.

'How old are you?' I ask eventually.

'Twenty-one.' She frowns, clearly assuming I'm questioning her competence.

'Young then,' I comment distractedly. After talking to her, I don't believe she's involved with my husband. Infatuated, possibly – he's a good-looking man – but not involved. Jake hasn't made his move yet, then. He will, though, and with so little experience behind her, she'll be easy prey.

'I think age is relative to experience,' she replies after a beat, surprising me. She obviously does have some backbone then. That's good. She might need it.

I change tack and ask her whether she has a boyfriend, my aim to make her feel as uncomfortable as I can. It works. I note that she looks peeved as she confirms that she has.

'Good,' I murmur without thinking. If she's in a relationship, then my worries might all be baseless. 'As long as you're not intending to call him and invite him here when I leave?' I add, guessing I'm making her positively hate me.

A flicker of annoyance crosses her face as she clearly gathers the implication. 'I take childcare duties very seriously, Mrs Harington,' she informs me indignantly. 'And I really have no need to try to impress my boyfriend.'

I raise an eyebrow. Appearances deceive, it seems. She's obviously quite shrewd. I hope she's shrewd enough to know when she might be being used.

The look on her face is bewildered as I impart my last instruction. I have no doubt, now that I've specifically told her not to, that she will go through my things, which will be reason enough for me to be the bitch wife Jake wants her to believe I am. What choice do I have? For her sake as well as my own, I have to make sure she leaves and won't ever want to come back.

FORTY-ONE

As I drive to Michael's apartment, I feel guilty at my treatment of the girl. She impressed me, holding her own, even though I was awful to her. She was clearly taken with Fern, smiling warmly as she looked down at her. In another world, where Phoebe hadn't happened and my marriage was happy, she might even be the perfect babysitter. But Phoebe did happen, and Jake sealed his own fate. Now he's trying to find a way to change it. Being free of me, the person who could destroy his future, is his only option. I cling to the hope that I'm wrong. That I'll wake up one morning and realise that the nightmare I'm living is just that. I'm a fool. This is my reality. Jake wants to be rid of me. In bringing Ellie to my house, he was communicating that clearly. It's a game to him, one with high stakes. I can't let him win.

Michael will be pleased to see me. I console myself with that thought as I pull up in front of the large Victorian country house owned by the fashion designer Carly Simons. Michael lives in a vast first-floor apartment in the building, and is trying to secure a lucrative commission refurbing the other apartments. He's bringing me in on it, the idea being for me to pick up the work once he goes back to Portugal. I'm grateful to him for that. I need this, not just the work and the kudos that goes with it, but for someone to believe in me.

Once he buzzes me in, I check my appearance in the large gilt-edged mirror that decorates the foyer. I don't look too bad, I decide, despite the sleepless nights and the years creeping up on me. Make-up can hide a multitude of sins, the evidence of too many tears cried.

Michael swings his front door open before I've even pressed the bell. 'Megan!' he exclaims, trailing his gaze over me and leaning in to kiss my cheek. 'Looking gorgeous as ever.'

'Flatterer.' I smile, pleased at the compliment and the warmth I see in his eyes. I can't remember when Jake last looked at me like that.

'Only where it's deserved.' He smiles mischievously back and leads the way into the apartment.

'Wow.' I gaze around in awe at the work he's done since I was last here – before Phoebe and the day I wanted my life to be over. Would I have felt that way if my hormones hadn't been at war? I've asked myself that question over and over in my horror and shame. The answer is, I honestly don't know. I suffered so badly with postnatal depression after Ollie. Jake knew it. When I think about that in context to what he did, it terrifies me. Or at least it did. I'm stronger now – in part thanks to the medication, which helped me initially. I'm in control. The me he sees on the outside is no longer who I am on the inside. My life will be influenced not by the actions of others, but by my own.

'I take it you approve?' Michael asks, relieving me of my jacket as I slip it off.

'I do,' I assure him.

'I decided to keep the nineteenth-century features intact.' He hangs the jacket on the coat stand and nods upwards to the wedding-cake plasterwork cornicing.

'You made the right decision,' I say, impressed. Wandering further in, I note that he's kept the English country house aesthetic throughout, furnishing it with a mixture of antique hand-crafted pieces: consoles and vintage chandeliers alongside comfortable sofas upholstered in cream linen. The vast windows allow the light to flood in, and with his own paintings and carefully chosen abstract wall art as a backdrop, the effect is stunning. 'It's beautiful,' I gasp, worrying that he might be putting a little too much faith in me to carry his work through to the other apartments. I have the template here, but I'm nervous about bringing it together as expertly as he has.

'Do you think I've captured the homely feel?' he asks, tipping his head to one side.

'Definitely.' I nod approvingly and follow him through to the kitchen, where he's installed a huge stainless-steel-topped island that works fabulously with the cornices and chandelier. 'It's truly inspiring,' I tell him, meaning it.

'Excellent.' He looks relieved and reaches to turn the coffee filter on. 'I wanted to get away from the stark, modern look in favour of a warmer, more textured feel.'

'You've achieved that. It's amazing,' I reassure him. 'Honestly. I'd live here in a flash.'

Clearly pleased by my enthusiasm, he smiles as he turns to me, but there's an underlying sadness in his eyes, and I feel bad, recalling how he once asked me to move in with him. He asked me again when I was so low I could barely function. *You need to get away from him. He's no good for you, Megan*, he almost begged. How was I supposed to tell him that although there's nothing left between us but mistrust and blame, I can never leave Jake? I could have an affair, find the comfort I so badly need in Michael's arms. He wants it, I know he does. I wouldn't be doing it for me, though, but for revenge. It would bring me no satisfaction. How could it when the man I would be cheating on doesn't want me? And how fair would it be on Michael? He's my inspiration, my friend and my confidante, but I don't love him. I don't think I'll ever love anyone as much as I once loved Jake. I couldn't stop loving him when he first cheated on me. I loved him even when Phoebe arrived to destroy my life. I sensed the sexual chemistry between the two of them long before I became pregnant with Fern. I'd have had to be blind not to see the furtive glances they exchanged. Could they not see that to an outsider – and that's how I felt in my marriage – it was transparently obvious that something was going on?

'How are you?' Michael breaks through my depressing meanderings.

Hearing the genuine care in his voice, I feel my throat close, emotions I've tried to keep in check bubbling to the surface. 'I'm okay.' I shrug, and glance away. 'Actually, I'm not. Not really. I...' I waver, realising how crazy it might sound, but it comes spilling out anyway. 'I think he's trying to make me do it again. Jake, he... I think he wants me dead.' I breathe in sharply and swallow hard.

Michael clangs down the cup he's picked up and rushes across to me. 'Hey, hey, come here.' He circles his arms around me. 'I'm sure that's not true, Meg. Why on earth would you think—'

'He's brought another girl home,' I go on tearfully. 'Someone from his office. He said he'd asked her to babysit, but...' I trail off. It does sound insane, even to my own ears. Am I getting this horribly wrong? I feel that Jake has been acting strangely of late: watching me carefully, checking on me, asking how I am. He hasn't done that since the early days after Phoebe. Why this repeat performance? Why bring a girl from his office home unless to mess with my mind?

'Does she have babysitting experience?' Michael asks, reasonably.

I nod, and falter. I really do feel as if I might be going mad, anxious and shaky, thoughts pinging scattergun through my mind, nauseous from lack of sleep. Am I overthinking this? The girl does have experience. Jake said she had. She confirmed it. 'She has childcare qualifications apparently, but...' I'm just not sure.

'Well, there you go then,' Michael tries to reassure me. 'He's not that cold and calculating, Meg.'

Isn't he? I think back to Jake's denials, his insistence that there was nothing going on between him and Phoebe and that it was all in my mind. I can't believe those aren't the actions of a cold, calculating man. And the way he seems to want me not to bond with Fern. Is *that* all in my mind?

'You're upset,' Michael goes on, his voice full of sympathy. 'You've not long had a baby. With all that went on around the birth, you're bound to still be feeling emotionally fragile. Jake's probably stuffed full of guilt over his fling with your au pair. It's probably some misguided attempt to try to make it up to you.'

'No. It's more than that.' I scan his face, willing him to believe me, because if this really is all in my mind, I'm going to be questioning my every thought and action. 'He hates me, Michael. I can feel it. He doesn't want to be with me, but he won't leave me, because...' I stop short. Michael doesn't know the secrets I hold, the lies I've told. He knows about 'Jake's fling', as he refers to it. He knows about my suicide attempt. I told him I'd been depressed, but no more. And no matter how desperate I am to confide everything, that's how it has to stay.

He nods thoughtfully. 'Does he still think that we...?'

I lower my gaze. 'I'm not sure. I think so.' I recall the horrendous argument Jake and I had when I arrived home after meeting Michael to discuss the plans for the new house. Nothing had gone on between us, nothing ever has, but still I felt guilty when I found Jake waiting for me as I stepped through the front door. I'm not sure why. Because I could talk to Michael, I suppose, where Jake and I seemed to have lost that connection, one I badly wanted back yet I could never seem to break through his defensiveness.

'Good night?' he asked facetiously, sweeping unimpressed eyes over me.

'I'm surprised you noticed I was out,' I replied, attempting to step around him. I hadn't thought he would miss me. He and Phoebe seemed more like a couple than we were. I tried to convince myself that it was because I was out at work and she was there. Permanently. But I wasn't convinced. I tried to rationalise his jealousy. I had been spending a lot of time with Michael, but truthfully, I felt that Jake didn't want me even then; that his jealousy was simply based on the fact that he didn't want his brother to have me either.

He sidestepped, blocking me. 'Ollie was asking for you,' he informed me. 'He has a tummy upset.'

My heart fluttered at the thought of Ollie being poorly while I wasn't there, and I tried again to move round Jake to go to him. Again he stopped me. 'Phoebe's with him,' he said.

'But why didn't you call me?' I searched his face, anger unfurling inside me. I didn't want Phoebe with my sick boy. But for the fact that Ollie had clearly bonded with her and I would be busy with a current project as well as overseeing the construction of our new house, I wouldn't have had her there at all.

'I tried. You were otherwise engaged.' Jake held my gaze, his own filled with steely accusation.

'Oh don't be so ridiculous,' I snapped. Did he really expect me not to have contact with the man who was opening doors for me? Who was more a friend to me than my own husband was?

'If anyone's being ridiculous here, it's you,' he growled. 'Why are you doing this? Do you really hate me that much?'

'I have no idea what you're talking about.' Averting my gaze, I pushed past him. 'I'm going to shower.'

'Right,' Jake said tersely behind me. 'Tell me something, Megan. Have you considered Ollie in all of this?'

Grinding to a halt, I whirled around. 'Have *you*?' I hissed. 'Have you considered for one second where what *you're* doing will leave him?'

'For fu...' He raked a hand through his hair. 'I'm not doing *anything*,' he insisted, his gaze flint-edged and furious.

Tears stinging my eyes, I dragged myself away and continued on. I wouldn't rise to the bait. He wanted to argue. He wanted justification for his own behaviour, years ago and then. I wouldn't give him that.

Hurrying up the stairs, I hesitated at Ollie's door. When I heard Phoebe beyond it, reading to my son in excited, animated tones, I wanted to go in and throttle her. Realising that I was in danger of losing control, I carried on to the main bedroom instead.

After a while, Jake came up, causing me to stop undressing. Thanks to the graphic images that played through my mind of him making love to a lithe twenty-year-old girl, my self-esteem had plummeted. Also, worryingly, my tummy was beginning to expand and I hadn't yet told him.

'Can we just talk, Megan?' he asked, sighing wearily. 'I mean, this is all completely nuts. Can't we just stop taking chunks out of each other and have a sensible conversation?'

I felt my anger spiking. 'You mean can I stop imagining things?'

He held his hands up in despair. 'I give up,' he said with a shake of his head. 'Think what you like.'

'Are you fucking her yet?' I asked him outright.

He emitted another exasperated sigh and turned for the door.

'Do not do that, Jake. Do *not* ignore me, or I swear to God I'll divorce you,' I warned him, flying across to grab hold of his arm.

He massaged his forehead with his free hand, then turned to look me straight in the eye. 'Do you know what? I don't care. Just do it,' he said coldly, challenging me.

He knew I wouldn't. Aside from the fact that, in an attempt to show him I trusted him, I hadn't made him sign a prenup, I loved him. He knew I did. All I wanted was for him to love *me*. To want to be with me. 'Do you really expect me to just accept your lies, Jake?' I asked him, swallowing back a hard knot of emotion.

'*My* lies?' He held my gaze until, knowing there was no reasoning with him, no way to pursue it without further argument, I turned away – and then he walked calmly out. Humiliation and hurt burn in my chest as I recall his expression, a mixture of incredulity and icy contempt. That was the day I realised I was frightened of him, of his obsessive jealousy, which was unbelievable given his behaviour. More so, though, because he actually seemed to believe his own lies.

As Michael holds me, I cry into his shoulder, deep, gut-wrenching sobs that have been held back for too long.

'Do you still love him?' he asks as he soothes me, stroking my hair as if I'm a child in need of comfort. I am right now. Oh, how I am.

I shake my head. I don't love the man Jake has become. I still care about him. I'm frightened for him, as well as of him. After Phoebe, when we realised we had to stay together, I wondered whether there might be a sliver of hope for us. That was my moment of madness. We're together now because we have no choice, a dark shadow hanging over us like a guillotine. There can be no love between us, no trust. The foundations of our relationship are broken. There's no way to fix things. Even so, Jake is still insanely jealous of Michael. He's always considered that his brother's success came too easily.

I've been seeing more of Michael recently because he brings some normality into my bleak, bizarre life, just for a short while.

Do I want Jake to think there might be something between us where before I denied it? Possibly. Perhaps I have used Michael to plant seeds of doubt in Jake's mind, just as he has in mine. I want him to hurt as much as I am. How naïve is that? How can someone hurt if you take away something they don't want?

FORTY-TWO

Arriving home, I notice Jake's BMW on the drive, and my heart jars as I imagine what he might be doing inside with Ellie. Seeing him still sitting in his car, talking on his mobile, my racing heart slows. Still, I feel sick, disorientated and dizzy. Does he realise the physical and emotional impact all this has on me. Does he care? I think not.

Taking a deep breath, I walk past him. I can feel his eyes trailing after me as I approach the front door and brace myself to go inside. When I do, I walk straight into Ellie in the hall. She seems uncertain, self-conscious, as I pause to look her over. I guess why. Her hair is damp. She clearly picked up on my earlier catty comments and decided she should wash it.

Composing myself, I ask her about the children. When she tells me that Fern has had a wheezy chest, though, my composure flies out of the window. 'Did you use her inhaler?' I snap.

Flustered, clearly, she denies knowing about the inhaler. Of course she would. My blood pumps and my mouth runs dry as I realise I forgot to tell her about it. What in God's name is wrong with me? How could I have *done* that?

Nerves writhe inside me as I hear Jake come through the

door behind me, and I yell at her, accusing her of smoking or vaping, anything rather than see that look in his eyes that tells me I'm incompetent, a bad mother who's incapable of caring for her child. Ellie is obviously distressed. She hasn't done anything. She knows she hasn't, that it's me at fault, not her. Me who'd put my child at risk.

'But you didn't mention her having *asthma*,' she insists, glancing at Jake as if he's her saviour. *He's not!* I want to scream at her. *He's using you! He'll kill you! Can you not see that I'm slowly dying inside?*

'What's going on?' he demands.

'Fern's had an asthma attack and this idiot girl didn't give her her medication.' I've barely got the words out before he's racing past me to bound up the stairs, Ellie calling tearfully after him that I didn't tell her. She looks at me imploringly as I walk past her. My guilt almost chokes me, but I say nothing. How can I? What can I say that will make her see that Jake is pitting us against each other? I can't tell her that I'm in danger. She's not likely to believe it any more than she will believe she's in danger if she continues to be taken in by him. I have to survive. I have to beat Jake at his cruel game to keep my children safe. As much as I resent this vulnerable girl he's brought into my life, I have to find a way to keep her safe too. Yet I have no idea how.

'She's fine,' Jake assures me, coming out of the nursery as I reach the landing. 'She's dry and content.'

My heart rate returning to somewhere near normal, I'm about to go and check on her myself when I notice our bedroom door is open a fraction. Ellie has been in there. I expected she would. I set her up, thinking it the perfect excuse to get rid of her. I didn't think it through. She works with him. Her not being here is not going to stop her being manipulated by him.

Jake follows me as I head quickly in that direction. 'Ellie's obviously been looking after—'

'She's been in our room!' I cut him short, my gaze snapping to the hairdryer, then to the wardrobe door, from which protrudes a telltale piece of clothing. And now I'm growing worried. I didn't envisage her delving into everything. What might she have found? 'Going through my things!'

I go to the wardrobe, yank the doors open and slide my hand across the top shelf. They're not there. My antidepressants, they're gone. I'm not using them other than occasionally to help me sleep, but in truth, I wanted Jake to think I still was. As weak as it now seems, I hoped he would feel guilty, that he would worry I might make another attempt on my life. How stupid was I? In hiding them in plain sight, I gave him the means to do the job for me.

Is this why I've been so forgetful, feeling confused and anxious? Aren't those the very symptoms I had when I started them? No, he wouldn't. My heart pounds. Would he? Promising myself never to accept another drink or meal prepared by him, I whirl around. 'She's been using my bathroom.' I hurry in that direction. I don't think I did, but might I have left the tablets in there?

Jake follows me, watching quietly as I look frantically around, then pull the bathroom cabinet open and search fruitlessly through it. A mixture of confusion and fear churns inside me. *Did* Jake take them?

'Did you expect her *not* to need to use the bathroom, Megan?' he asks after a moment, his voice edged with despair.

'I didn't expect her to wash her *hair* in here while my daughter was struggling with an asthma attack,' I hiss, not wanting Ellie to hear, though I imagine she already has; that she will be judging me, as he is, for worrying about her using my bathroom above concerning myself with my daughter.

My chest heaves, guilt and frustration rising so fast I feel it might choke me. 'Get her out of here,' I snap. I need space. I can't think. Can't *breathe*.

'For pity's sake, Megan, calm down, will you? You'll wake Ollie.' Jake moves towards me. 'There's obviously been some misunderstanding. You were in a rush, maybe you—'

I yank my towel from the rail and spin around to face him. 'She's used my towel! Her hair is all over it!' Tears spring to my eyes and I hate myself for giving in to them in front of him. 'Get her *out* of my house! *Now!*'

His expression inscrutable, Jake studies me for a moment, then walks to the landing with a weary shake of his head.

'And check whether she's stolen anything!' I shout after him. 'She wouldn't be the first one who had, *would* she, Jake?' I guess he'll know I'm referring to Phoebe, who availed herself of my things without asking. I assumed he made her promises he didn't intend to keep, that she thought I would leave and she would take my place. I imagined briefly that he might be riddled with remorse when things ended so catastrophically. He wasn't. I wonder now if he's capable of feeling anything at all.

FORTY-THREE

Our bedroom is in complete disarray. After making sure that Fern was sleeping and checking on Ollie, I went through all the wardrobes and drawers, leaving clothes spilling out. I can't find the tablets anywhere. Frustration and panic spiralling inside me, I drag my hair from my face and rack my brain. Where are they? *Is* this all in my mind?

No. The tablets were there. I know they were. I wouldn't have put them anywhere else. Where might they be hidden? *The bed.* It's the only place I haven't looked. Going across to it, I drop to my knees and slide my hand between the mattress and the base. Finding nothing my side, I glide my hand under the bottom end of the mattress. I'm searching Jake's side when my gaze snaps to the door.

'What the...?' Walking into the room, Jake glances around, noting the mess in astonishment. 'What in God's name are you doing, Megan?' he asks, his voice tight with a combination of anger and despair.

Ignoring the fact that he's been gone far longer than it should have taken to drive the girl home and come straight back, I straighten up to glare at him. 'Where are they?' I demand.

He squints at me as if mystified. 'Where are what exactly?'

'You know damn well what.'

He simply shakes his head in that way he does and turns back to the landing.

'My antidepressants,' I yell after him, then curse myself as Fern stirs. 'They're not here.' I lower my tone. 'You've taken them.'

'Right.' He presses a hand to his forehead and emits a scornful laugh.

'I know, Jake.' My voice quavers. 'I know what you're trying to do.'

He turns slowly to face me. 'What are you insinuating, Megan?' he asks, a deep furrow forming in his brow.

'I know what you're *doing*.' Though I try hard to hold them back, the tears come, cascading hotly down my cheeks. 'You need to *stop*.' I wipe them away. 'You have to give them back to me, or I swear I will call the police.'

He stares at me for a long, searching moment. Then, 'I don't bloody believe this,' he mutters. His face is as dark as thunder as he comes towards me, and I instinctively back away.

He stops. 'You're serious, aren't you?' He looks me over incredulously. 'You actually think that I... Jesus.' Glowering at me for a second, he spins around and storms to the bathroom.

'Can you blame me?' I throw after him. 'The tablets are not *here*, Jake. If *you* were me, what would you—'

I stop as he reappears, eyeing me coldly as he strides to the dressing table. 'Your tablets,' he says, slamming the packet down. 'I put them on top of the bathroom cabinet when I found them right here where you left them. I moved them because it occurred to me that our *son* could get hold of them.' He pauses, looking me over scathingly. 'You're losing it, Megan. I have no idea what all that was about with Ellie, after she'd been kind enough to help us out, but I do know you need to get a grip. Fast. For *both* our sakes.'

Tearing his gaze away from me, he heads to the door. 'I'm going to bed. I'll be in the spare room.'

'Why did you bring her here?' I call shakily after him. 'Without telling me. Why did you do that after everything that happened with Phoebe?'

Jake falters. 'Because we needed someone at short notice, because you had a *business* meeting.' I hear the pointed emphasis. 'We both work, Megan. We need a childminder. Whatever happened in the past – which I wish every second of every day I could undo – if we're going to continue to function, we need someone we can depend on. I happen to think Ellie would have been ideal if you hadn't decided to be a complete bitch to her.'

He turns and walks on. Stops again. 'I'll tell you something, Megan, if ever I needed evidence of how unfit you are to look after the kids, I've witnessed it tonight. Ellie has too.'

My stomach roils as he disappears through the door. *But you won't need evidence to take my children away from me if I'm dead, will you?* I want to shout after him, but I don't. He's bluffing. He can't leave me and take the children away from me. He knows he can't. That's why he's doing all this. My chest bangs. Are he and Ellie working in collusion? The sickening thought strikes me.

Once I'm sure he's downstairs, I go to my online GP app. It doesn't take me long to establish that my repeat prescription is months away. It *was* due in a couple of weeks. Someone has already ordered it. Icy realisation spreads through me. Someone has collected it. Does Jake really think I'm so confused I will imagine it was me?

I need to talk to Ellie, I realise. I need to apologise to her. I'm sure I have her measure. She's pliable. If I'm going to beat Jake at his own game, I need to know how much Ellie knows. I also need to keep her close if I'm to have any hope of stopping him.

FORTY-FOUR

Ellie's a bag of nerves as she approaches me across the shop floor. She mumbles something about not being on her break yet, but once I assure her I'll square it with Jake, she agrees to go for a coffee with me, though somewhat reluctantly, judging by the wary look on her face.

Once in the café, I treat her to coffee and cake and make an effort to chat to her, small talk mostly, admitting I'm battling to lose the baby fat, complimenting her on her figure, at which she almost chokes on her cake. When I think I've won her over a little, I place my fork down and, swallowing my pride, apologise to her, confiding that I had some problems after Fern was born. My throat catches as I tell her that, though I love my daughter, I struggled to bond with her, and I find myself close to tears again. Is it the tablets? I'm not sure. I feel so emotional lately. I ask her why she didn't walk away when she realised what she was getting into, studying her carefully as I wait for her answer.

I guess it's not the whole truth when she says she didn't want to let Ollie down. She does have a crush on Jake – her blushes give her away – but I don't believe she's a willing participant in his manipulations. If I'm to continue to work, which I have to if I'm to save my sanity, I need someone I can trust with my children. And if I can't trust her regarding Jake – love makes people blind, I can attest to that – I will find out in time. I will try to protect her, I have to, but I will play Jake's game. In facilitating him, I might even win.

When I finally get to the point, admitting that I'm struggling to juggle all the balls and asking her to come and work for me, she stares at me in astonishment.

'You're obviously a huge hit with Ollie,' I continue, smiling hopefully. 'I realise it's a big ask after last night, but I'm prepared to pay you more than your current salary. Do you drive?' I tack on quickly, wanting to outweigh the negatives with the incentives.

'I... Yes.' She shakes her head in confusion.

'That's perfect. I'll organise you a little runaround,' I offer. 'A Mini, perhaps. How does that sound?'

The girl continues to stare speechlessly at me.

'You would have the use of the house and the facilities, of course, when you're there. Although you would have to be careful not to allow Ollie access to the pool on his own. But I'm sure you would be aware of that.' I pause and smile hopefully. 'What do you think?'

I watch her carefully as she weighs up the pros and cons. She'll be working in luxurious surroundings. Obviously that's a plus. She'll possibly see more of Jake, who generally works between his various offices. A big plus for her, I think. She'll also be seeing quite a bit of me. A negative, undoubtedly, but I think she will bite.

Once I've paid the bill, I walk her back to the shop, where I leave her still looking slightly stunned and go to Jake's office. Finding him not there, but the door open, which is lax of him, I go in and wander across to his desk. I'm leafing idly through his paperwork when my eyes fall on a file next to his PC. Ellie's file, I realise, my heart leaping. I glance over my shoulder, then pull it quickly towards me. I don't have time to extract much more than her address before I hear footsteps coming along the corridor. Quickly I reposition the file, leaving it exactly where it was, and walk across to the window.

'To what do I owe the pleasure?' Jake asks. From his tone, I gather he's not overly thrilled to see me. It hurts, but I ignore it.

'I came to take Ellie for a coffee,' I say, guessing he will be curious as to why.

He is. I note the furrow in his brow as I turn to face him. 'I gathered,' he replies, closing the door.

He obviously noticed her absence then. Is he perturbed at being out of the loop? Probably. 'I asked her if she would consider coming to work for us,' I add.

Jake looks astounded. But also... relieved, I think.

'I considered what you said, and I realised you were right,' I go on. 'She's ideal for the job and I was a complete bitch to her. I think my memory must be failing me. I've been so confused lately.' I pause, smiling wanly, eyeing him carefully.

Do I see a flash of guilt before he looks away? I think I do.

'I explained to her that I've been struggling, though I didn't tell her everything, obviously – I wouldn't want her to know that I actually felt suicidal.' I see another flicker of guilt as he walks across to his desk. 'Then I begged her forgiveness and offered her the job.'

'Right,' Jake says, gauging me uncertainly as he lowers himself into his chair. 'Good idea. I think she'll be perfect.'

'I'm glad you agree.' I smile pleasantly. 'I've told her she can start immediately. I've also said we'll give her a pay rise. I thought we might go halves on that, if it's okay with you?'

'Er, right, yes. No problem,' he says, his expression now a combination of mystified and guarded. He's no doubt wondering whether he's at a tactical advantage or a disadvantage.

'Great.' I'll go and let her know. I think she was a bit

worried about leaving you in the lurch here. I told her you'd be fine with it, that your family comes first.' I hold his gaze for a moment, and then turn to the door. *You're right to be guarded, Jake*, I think with some small satisfaction. *I'm in the driving seat now.*

FORTY-FIVE

Ellie is clearly thrilled with the facilities available to her. Having driven to her address, where I gathered from the moody young man coming out of her building that it was a run-down bedsit she lived in rather than the flat she'd spoken of, I guessed she would be. She obviously isn't averse to embroidering the truth about her personal circumstances. Did she mention to Jake that she has a boyfriend?

The young man eyed me with suspicion until I mentioned who I was, pretending that I'd come to pick Ellie up and that I'd obviously got my timing wrong. 'Oh, right, so you're her boss's wife then?' he asked.

'I am.' I smiled pleasantly.

'Wow.' He looked taken aback, and then slightly awkward. 'Sorry,' he said, clearly embarrassed by his initial response. 'I'm just relieved, to be honest. To meet you, I mean. I couldn't help wondering why your husband would have employed Ellie so fast. It all seemed a bit rushed, and I, er...'

'He was obviously impressed with her experience,' I rescued him as he glanced down at his trainers, looking as if he would quite like the pavement to swallow him up. 'Lovely to make your acquaintance...?' Extending my hand, I eyed him questioningly.

'Zachary.' He offered me his. 'Likewise. I'd better get going. I'm meeting a mate and I'm running a bit late.'

He was jealous, suspicious of Jake's motives, I realised, watching him walk to his car, an old PT Cruiser that had seen better days, indicating that he wasn't rolling in cash, as he would assume Jake was. Had he communicated his feelings to Ellie? I wondered. I guessed he had, and that that would have done him no favours in her eyes.

As to what it was about her previous experience that had so impressed Jake, I have no idea. My time was limited, so I wasn't able to check thoroughly, but there didn't appear to be any references in her file.

With Ellie still busy feeding Fern upstairs, I decide to ring him about the Disclosure and Barring Service check, which as her employer he's able to request. He's mentioned nothing since I first asked him. Ellie has been here two weeks now. She's amiable, eager to please, but still I need to know as much about her as I can.

When his mobile goes unanswered, I call him on his office number and am surprised when his phone is picked up by a female. 'PCs Plus Peripherals,' she trills. 'Janine speaking. How can I help you?'

'Hi, Janine,' I manage pleasantly, despite the knot of suspicion tightening inside me. 'I'm Megan, Jake's wife. I'm sorry, I don't think I know you.'

'Oh, lovely to speak to you,' she gushes. 'I'm Jake's new personal assistant. Do you want to talk to him?'

'Please,' I confirm, wondering why else she would think I would be ringing.

'Bear with me,' she says. 'I only started a couple of days ago, so I'm still learning the ropes. I hope I don't cut you off.'

I wait while the phone clicks and goes silent. Another click and more silence, then finally Jake answers. As he will know it's me calling, I dispense with the pleasantries. 'You have a personal assistant now then?' I say, sure that he'll pick up on my sarcasm. 'You're going up in the world.'

'Obviously,' he replies flatly.

'I assume she's there with you in your cosy little office, so I won't keep you,' I add, hoping he'll glean from my facetiousness that I'm ready to fight back. 'I wondered about the DBS check,' I hurry on. 'You said you'd run one.'

'I did. It was fine,' he answers with a sigh, which upsets me. He clearly doesn't think this is important. It is, for obvious reasons. Ellie's been fine with the children, but without references, we still know nothing about her.

'Yes, but it's not fine, is it, Jake?' I disagree. 'It will have been a basic check, which only shows unspent convictions, cautions and the like. We need to do an enhanced check, which will show any roles she's barred from.'

'You're going a bit over the top, aren't you?' he responds, his tone weary. 'She's been with us for two weeks. There haven't been any problems, have there?'

'I don't know, Jake. I'm not looking over her shoulder every two minutes, am I? She's a childminder. She minds children, *our* children, when I'm not there. This is why we need to be certain of her background.'

He emits another despairing sigh. 'Okay, whatever. I'll get it sorted. Is there anything else? I have work to do.'

I note the impatient edge to his voice. 'Could you bring some printer cartridges back with you, please? I have to print off some plans for my meeting this evening,' I say, before ending the call. I feel irritated. Janine will have overheard our cool conversation, and I'm guessing that will be another gullible young woman feeling sorry for him.

Doubting very much that he'll follow up the enhanced DBS

check, even whether he actually did the basic check, I make a firm mental note to do something about it myself.

He arrives home an hour later than I expected him. Sighing in despair of us being able to function on any level, I hurry down the stairs, straightening my shirt collar as I go and hoping I look as confident as I need to be for my meeting with Michael and Carly Simons. He might have told me he was going to be late. He knows I have the plans to print off. But then I didn't give him a chance to, did I? I feel a pang of guilt, then immediately dismiss it as I follow him into the kitchen area to see Ellie's gaze roving over him. Jake glances at her, but only briefly. Still, my stomach drops, a tight knot forming in my throat I can't seem to swallow. It's obvious he's making a great show of *not* looking at her. It hurts. I expect no more of him, not now, but still there's a tiny part of me that clings to the hope that even if he doesn't love me, he'll find some compassion within him to stop all this.

'You're late.' I glance at him and check my watch.

'Evening,' Jake answers, rolling his eyes in Ellie's direction. He's clearly making a point for her benefit. I swallow and ignore it.

'Did you bring the printer cartridges?'

'What printer cartridges?' He glances back from where he's gone to make coffee.

My heart sinks as I realise he's forgotten them. Despite my promise to myself to remain in control of my emotions, I'm upset, sure he's doing this on purpose, and I snap at him, accusing him of dismissing my business as unimportant.

'Don't be ridiculous, Meg.' He sighs, looking embarrassed – again for Ellie's benefit, I've no doubt. 'I don't think that at all.'

Seeing Ellie looking between us like a startled deer, my cheeks burn with humiliation and I turn away. 'Just remember which side your bread is buttered, Jake,' I mutter. I can't help myself. The cartridges are right there on the shop floor. It wouldn't have hurt him to pick them up. He wouldn't *have* a shop floor if not for me.

He offers to go back out, but I tell him not to bother. 'I'll email him the plans. We can print them there.'

'Him?' Jake enquires, a wary edge to his tone.

'Miguel,' I answer, using Michael's professional name, emphasising that it's a professional appointment. That what I do *is* important.

'Right. Give him my regards.' Jake's tone is nothing but scathing.

'I'll make sure to,' I respond. I don't intend to get into an argument about Michael in front of Ellie.

'I could go,' she offers, obviously on a mission to save poor Jake from his bitchy wife's wrath. 'I have Fern to feed, but it shouldn't take me too long to get there and back.'

'Thanks,' Jake answers, as I cross the hall to the lounge to collect my phone. 'I wouldn't worry about it, though. She's obviously keen to get off to *Miguel*.'

I note his scornful enunciation of the name, as does Ellie. Is he playing the wounded husband waiting it out in the hope of impressing her? I wonder. I swallow my hurt and, on the pretext of checking my phone, watch them through the partition wall. Little did I realise when I designed the property how useful walls made of glass would be. Ellie's expression is one of pity, I notice, as she looks at Jake. Jake, for his part, is playing dejected perfectly as he goes off to play dutiful father and check on the children.

'Shall I bring your coffee when I come up to feed Fern,' she offers, her eyes trailing sympathetically after him. She can see no wrong in him, can she? She thinks the cracks in our marriage are because *I* treat *him* badly. She thinks I'm volatile, emotionally unstable, which is exactly as he wants it. She wouldn't realise, of course, that because I suspect Jake's been feeding me tablets, it suits my purposes for him to believe that I am.

Straightening my shoulders, I head for the hall and the front door, glancing at Ellie as I go. She's definitely besotted, working hard to please him. But of course she can't help herself. Once, I would have done anything for him. I did. And now I'm trapped in this glass house with him like a butterfly in a bell jar. I can't allow him to crush me. I have to stay strong. 'I believe Jake has an appointment with a buyer later,' I tell her. 'Can you make sure he doesn't let Ollie spend too much time glued to his screen before his bedtime.'

Ellie assures me she will. But will she? I wonder. Or will she assume I'm being neurotic? I think she'll do as I ask. She'll be aware that too much screen time won't help Ollie go easily off to sleep. She's good with him. I've been wondering whether I did the right thing hiring her. For now, though, I feel safer with her here, and I realise I do need her.

I'm on my way to Michael's when I realise that I've left my handbag behind. I debate whether to go back for it. A glance at the petrol gauge to find I'm low on fuel decides me. Sighing, I pull over to call Michael and tell him I'm running late, and then turn around and head back to the house.

All is silent as I go in. With my antennae on red alert, I go quietly up the stairs. Our bedroom door is closed, and I pause to listen outside it. Hearing no sound from inside, I head towards Ollie's room. Jake's voice reaches me as I listen, and breathing a sigh of relief, I carry on to the nursery. The door is open, and as I glance inside, my heart almost stops beating. What in God's name is Ellie doing? I watch horrified as she lowers Fern so clumsily into her cot, she almost cracks her head on the frame. I'm about to go in there and berate her, but manage to stop myself. I don't want her to think I'm spying on her. I certainly don't want Jake to think I'm spying on him. Fetching my bag, I leave again as quietly as I arrived.

FORTY-SIX

I'm unsurprised when I come home to find Jake and Ellie having a cosy tête-à-tête out on the patio. Jake clearly wasn't expecting me back so early. I left Miguel fine-tuning the details with Carly Simons, who now seems keen to go ahead with the commission, thank goodness. I wanted to get back to check on Fern, having witnessed Ellie's carelessness with her. I'm glad now that I did – in time to see what Jake's up to while my back is turned.

I loiter inside the patio doors, watching as he surveys Ellie thoughtfully over his wine glass.

'Was it the bloke I saw outside your building who made you feel like life wasn't worth living?' he asks her, his voice filled with concern – and my breath stalls. Did Ellie reach a point where she contemplated ending her life? Obviously she did. And Jake knows about it. She clearly confided in him, possibly about her boyfriend's tendency to jealousy too. Jake probably warned her off him – subtly, of course, he was always that. He must have gathered a considerable amount of information about her, meaning he knows that she's vulnerable and will easily fall for someone who seems to care. *Bastard*.

Ellie assures him that no, it wasn't Zach, and then looks away.

Jake studies her pensively. 'You don't want to talk about it, I get it,' he says understandingly. 'Just remember I have a shoulder, should you ever feel you need one.'

'I know.' She glances at him with an appreciative smile. 'Likewise.'

They fall silent for a while. Then, 'It's peaceful, isn't it?' Ellie murmurs. 'Sitting here watching the water.'

When Jake tells her that's why he likes to spend time out there, because it gives him some quiet time, my heart jolts. He's such a smooth liar. In reality, he sits out there trying to salve his conscience.

'I should go,' Ellie says after a while. 'It took me ages to get Fern down, but she'll be due for her next feed soon and I have to make up some bottles.'

'Thanks, Ellie. For everything.' Jake catches her hand as she stands. 'About Megan,' he adds, 'try not to judge her. She doesn't mean to be the way she is. She's just... over-organised, I guess you'd call it.'

My stomach lurches. Why would he tell her that? But it's obvious why. He's painting me as the controlling one, playing on her sympathy. Is he really going to make a move on her? Would he use her so ruthlessly to crush me? I need to stop this. I need to stop *him*. But how? I can't tell her outright that she's in danger without explaining why. And if I sack her, isn't Jake just likely to pursue her anyway, probably even bringing her back here? I have to open her eyes. If she judges me in the process, so be it. He's trying to drive me out of my mind, pushing me as far as he can to the edge. Ellie won't see it. All she can see is a caring, beleaguered man. I need to help her see his true colours. He once said to me – in the heat of an argument about that first infidelity – that every action or cause has an effect. He was talking about my father, blaming his refusal to back his business.

As if my father had taken him by the hand and led him to find a woman to have consolation sex with. I felt guilty. *I* backed him. I must truly have been out of my mind then.

My heart thudding so loudly I'm sure they will hear it, I back away, heading quickly to the stairs and hurrying up them. Nausea and fear churning inside me, I watch from the landing as Ellie comes through the patio doors. As she walks across the hall, I notice how much make-up she's wearing. It's obvious it's for him. What do I do? I'm not her mother. I can't tell her to go and scrub it off. Keeping a rein on my emotions, which are precariously close to exploding, I descend the stairs.

'Fern's awake,' I tell her, startling her.

She looks up sharply, her expression shocked, as it would be since she didn't know I was here. 'Sorry,' she mumbles. 'I was going to get her feed ready. I'll go up and fetch her.'

I narrow my eyes as she hurries towards me. 'Have you been in my room?' I ask.

'I, um...' Her cheeks flush furiously. 'Yes, I—'

'Using my make-up?' I know she has. The chances of us both having the exact shade of lipstick are slim.

Her gaze hits the floor, and furious inside – with her naïvety, with Jake – I leave her to squirm for a moment. Then, 'Suits you. You might do better to remember less is more, though,' I say, walking calmly past her.

Tears prick my eyes as I head to the kitchen. I blink them back hard. I'm not sure why I didn't fly at her. Perhaps because I need to choose my battles. When she goes, I want it to be of her own volition, but it has to be once she has lost her rose-tinted illusions about Jake. I will find a way to reveal his darkness. I will *not* let him do this.

FORTY-SEVEN

Days later, we argue again. Jake minds that I have an evening appointment. I wish I was doing what he imagines I am. As attractive as Michael is, though, I can't use him. I don't have the despicable morals Jake does.

Ellie is waiting in the wings as he heads agitatedly up the stairs, as she always seems to be. 'Everything okay?' she asks him, looking him over worriedly.

'As okay as it ever is,' Jake replies sharply, then immediately apologises for snapping at her. I'm torn between flabbergasted and amused when he compliments her, telling her she looks nice, even commenting on the perfume she's wearing. *It's for her boyfriend's benefit, not yours*, I would love to tell him, though I'm actually not sure it is. I continue to eavesdrop as she goes on, telling him how her boyfriend is a bit moody because he hasn't seen much of her lately. I was right, young Zachary is jealous. Will she cite his jealousy as a reason to end their relationship, I wonder, thereby making herself more available to a man she imagines cares for her?

My heart jars when I hear Jake's concerned response. 'Don't

settle for second best, Ellie,' he says softly. 'You're worth more than that. You just don't believe you are.'

So much more. You're invaluable to a man who's using you to help him get rid of his wife. Anger unfurls inside me and I stride across the hall.

As Ellie catches sight of me glaring up at her, her face floods with guilt. Tearing my gaze away from her, I shoot Jake a furious glance. 'I know what you're doing, Jake Harington,' I warn him again, hoping he'll heed it. 'I know *why*. It won't work, do you hear me? It won't.'

As I spin around to walk away, nausea swirls suddenly inside me, pinpricks of white light forming at the backs of my eyes. Panic grips me and I scramble through my mind, trying to imagine what I might have eaten or drunk that Jake might have had access to. Nothing that Ollie or Ellie wouldn't also have eaten or drunk comes to mind – apart from my wine. There's an open bottle in the fridge. But I've had none since last night. *My tea.* I had a cup earlier, and left it unattended in the kitchen.

The nausea grows worse, rising sourly inside me, and even knowing I have an impending migraine and that I won't be able to see clearly to drive, I consider leaving. Yes, and if I crash the car, won't that suit him? As my head pounds, I mount the stairs instead, seeking the safety of my bed, longing to crawl under the duvet and stay there until the nightmare is over. But it won't be, will it? It will never be over. We made our bed, Jake and I. Now we have to lie in it.

Jake mutters a curse as I reach him. Does he think he might be pushing me a bit too obviously? I wonder. I eye him contemptuously, careless of whether Ellie sees my expression. 'You're so transparent it's laughable,' I hiss, then fly on to the bedroom. Once inside, I lock the door behind me. Pointlessly. Jake won't try to follow me. It seems to me our arguments lately are mostly orchestrated to be overheard.

Feeling tired to my bones, unattractive and old next to Ellie, whose unlined, delicate face is undeniably pretty, I'm debating whether to go back out when I hear Ollie on the landing. He's asking why we're arguing. My heart jars, then freezes as I hear him mention Phoebe's name. With Jake reassuring him, and Ellie out there looking on, I guess my presence will be surplus to requirements even to my own son. After a second, I hear Jake suggest they go and fire up Ollie's Nintendo. I understand why he would, to take Ollie's mind off all of this. The fact that he warns him not to tell me, though, hurts terribly. He's encouraging Ollie to keep secrets from me, knowing that if I intervene it will only upset him.

Wincing as jagged white teeth snap at my peripheral vision, I draw the blackout blinds at the windows, prise my shoes off and lie gingerly on the bed. The pitch black of the bedroom envelops me, and soon I find myself drifting, ebbing and flowing. Floating...

Ollie's in the pool. I don't want him in the pool. Sharp slivers of sunlight bounce off the water, blinding me as I look across it. Where is he? I shield my eyes, squint hard. 'Ollie?' I hear him: innocent child's laughter reaching me from the other end of the pool. The deep end. 'Ollie!'

I plunge into the water, swim towards him, but now the ebb and flow is growing stronger, large waves like erupting lava crashing down on me. I can't see him. I swim harder, try to stay afloat, but I'm weighed down by a thick winter coat. 'Ollie.' At last I spot him. His arms and legs flailing, his small body tiring, tossed like a cork on the water.

He's going under. She's dragging him under. 'Ollie!

'An eye for an eye,' the sea whispers.

No! The skies open and the heavens above me collide furiously. God's wrath raining down on me.

'No!' Jerking upright, sweat soaking my body, I gasp for breath, look frantically around as I hear it again. Thunder. No, not thunder. My heart thrashes against my chest. A door. One of the bedroom doors? Flicking on the bedside lamp, I wince against the bright light and scramble off the bed. Footsteps, I hear them, clacking down the marble stairs. Ellie's footsteps. But wasn't she going out to meet her boyfriend? I glance at the bedside clock to find that hours have passed. How? The tablets. He *did* slip them into my tea. He must have done.

I wait, giving her a minute to go down, then pad silently to the landing and head for the stairs. Seeing Jake crossing the hall towards the lounge, I step quickly back. Where's Ellie? On the patio, I've no doubt. Fear and anger tightening inside me, I go silently down, reaching the lounge just in time to see Jake chivalrously pulling out a patio chair for her.

Seating himself opposite, he sweeps an appreciative gaze over her. 'How's your boyfriend?' he asks. 'Zach, isn't it?'

'That's right.' She gives him a smile. 'He's fine. He has an early start tomorrow, so he didn't mind that we only had a couple of drinks.'

'Sounds like he might have minded?' Jake comments, passing her a drink.

'No, he wouldn't,' she assures him. 'He's all right.'

I note Jake arching an eyebrow in her direction, as if he doubts what she's saying.

She glances tentatively at him. 'Can I ask you something, Jake?'

'Certainly.' He nods obligingly. 'I'll do my best to answer.'

'The wardrobe in the spare room, I can't open it,' she says – and my stomach lurches. 'It's not a big deal,' she adds quickly. 'I was thinking I could store one or two things in there for when I stay over. I just wondered why it was locked.'

Jake furrows his brow, as if clueless. 'I didn't realise it was,' he lies. 'Megan said it was faulty,' he goes on – but now I'm hardly listening.

Why does she want to get into the wardrobe? My head swims, a fresh bout of nausea clenching my insides, and I turn away. Then stop when I hear her say, 'She seems very angry with you.'

'She does, doesn't she?' Jake answers ruefully. 'Although I'm not sure it's me she's angry with. She, er...' He pauses. My heart falters. 'There's someone else.'

Liar! I turn back, staggered. Is he really *still* going to do this? Does he not realise from what she's just said that he needs to get her out of his life before everything comes crashing down around us?

'I'm sorry. I shouldn't have said anything.' He emits an expansive sigh. 'It puts you in an impossible situation. I'm sure we'll work things out.'

'It's okay,' she gushes sympathetically – and I want to shake her. *For God's sake, open your eyes!*

'You won't mention that I said anything, will you?' Jake glances at her worriedly, play-acting. He's bloody play-acting. And if she had any intuition, she would know he was. But she does, doesn't she? She's intrigued by the fact that she can't access the wardrobe. She's guessed something isn't right, and my full-of-himself husband can't seem to see it. This has to stop. *He* has to stop. I step forward.

FORTY-EIGHT

I don't look at Jake as he comes into the lounge. I don't speak. Assuming he won't want this particular argument to escalate in front of Ellie, I guess he will follow me as I lead the way upstairs, where we might have a little privacy. Once in our bedroom, I go across to the window wall and look out at the lush open countryside and woodland that surrounds us. We can see the Malvern Hills from here, majestic, foreboding sometimes, deep, smoky purple when the sky darkens. The hills were ominous on the night that will haunt me for the rest of my life, the sky above them charcoal grey. I've wondered since if it was a warning.

'We have to talk,' Jake says, coming in behind me and closing the door.

Can we talk without arguing? I very much doubt it. A chill runs through me and I wrap my arms tightly around myself and turn to face him. 'About?' I eye him interestedly, wondering whether, in light of all that's just been said outside, all he knows I must have overheard, he will back down, confess and beg my forgiveness. Unlikely. He really does hate me. It becomes more obvious with each passing day.

'This,' he answers with a disconsolate shrug. 'The perpetual arguing. I've done my best, Megan. It's just not working, is it?'

I baulk, incredulous. 'You're unbelievable.' A near-hysterical laugh escapes me. 'We're where we are because of *you*. We're trapped in this prison because of what *you* did. And now you're doing it all over again. What is *wrong* with you?'

He drags a hand over his neck, turns his gaze to the ceiling. When he looks back at me, his eyes are filled with a mixture of desperation and anger. 'I am not doing *anything*,' he grates. 'Why won't you believe me?'

'Ha! Of course you're not. It's all in my feeble mind, isn't it, Jake? Just like it was before.'

His gaze flickers down again.

I stare hard at him as he massages his forehead wearily. 'You know what you did,' I remind him, though I'm sure I have no need to.

'To protect *you*.' He looks back at me, his eyes anguished. 'I did it for *you*. I *care* about you. I care about the children – more than my life – but I can't go on like this. The children can't. *You* certainly can't. You're unpredictable. Irrational. I'm scared for you, Megan.' He searches my eyes, his look so earnest I could almost believe him. I resist the urge to openly accuse him of poisoning me. I'm frightened. Frightened of the denial that will spill from his mouth. Of the truth I will see in his eyes.

'So what do you suggest we do, Jake? Put a For Sale board up? Split up?' I eye him scornfully. 'It's not really an option, is it? Because then I would have to trust you, and I *can't*, can I? You broke my trust.' I bang a hand against my chest. 'You broke *me*.'

'I didn't, Megan.' He heaves out a sigh of exasperation. 'I've told you over and over, but you won't believe—'

'She was naked!' I hiss, anger uncoiling like a viper inside me. 'Lying in *our* bed.'

'And *I* was downstairs,' he insists, as he has from that

godforsaken day to this. 'She'd been drinking. She'd split up with her boyfriend.'

Just like Ellie's about to. I laugh bitterly.

'She was also upset about how you were treating her,' he goes on, actually sounding righteous. 'Bloody upset. We talked. I helped her upstairs, and then I went back down to carry on unpacking removal boxes in your absence. I had no idea—'

'*Stop.*' I spin back to the window.

'I think we have to face up to things,' he says quietly. 'I think we should go to the police.'

I feel the blood drain from my body. Stunned, I turn back to him. 'Don't be ridiculous.'

He tugs in a breath. 'I'm serious, Megan. Deadly. We can't go on like this. It's no life for either of us.'

I scan his face in disbelief. His gaze doesn't waver. 'This is about Michael, isn't it?' My voice quavers. 'You're trying to blame me for what happened, yet you were sleeping with her. Fucking her in my bed while I was working my guts out trying to complete the building works on this house. I was pregnant! Did you not consider for one minute what that would do to me?'

'I wasn't doing anything of the sort! For pity's *sake.*' He rakes a hand furiously through his hair. 'This has nothing to do with Michael. I don't give a shit about Michael, when you got involved with him, whether you're still involved with him. We have to *stop* this. We have to inform the—'

'No! You *can't.* I won't let you.' I move shakily towards him.

Jake backs away. 'You have to face up to what you've done, Megan,' he says flatly. 'We both do.'

My stomach turns over. 'I didn't mean to! You *know* I didn't.' Panic spirals inside me and I try again to recall what happened in those crucial lost seconds when blind anger possessed me. I can't. I never can, no matter how hard I try. Jake reminds me, though. Frequently. 'You drove me to it. I don't deserve to—'

'And *she* didn't deserve what happened to her, did she?' His tone is scathing. He fixes me with a reproachful glare and then turns away.

I stay where I am, petrified, dry-eyed with shock and fear. After a moment, my emotions frozen solid inside me, I take a stumbling step towards the bathroom, then fly in that direction, bolting the door behind me. My blood pumping, my head feeling as if it might explode, I reach for my tablets. It's as I'm popping them from the blister pack that icy realisation seeps through me. He's succeeding, isn't he? *I'm doing exactly what he wants me to do.*

FORTY-NINE

Jake went off to work without a word. He hasn't answered my text asking him to give me some time before doing anything he might regret. I'm growing terrified. I need to formulate a way to stop him. After telling Ellie I intend to pick Ollie up this afternoon, I wait for her to leave and then follow her, my aim to gather information I might be able to use against her, anything that will make Jake turn against her. Only then will she get a glimpse of who he really is. And then I have to convince her to leave, to get as far away from him as possible. From both of us.

Parking a little way down the road, I watch her as she comes out of the school gates, chatting to Fern as she pushes her in front of her. As she approaches her car, I pull out my phone and text her. If she denies I warned her, the text will prove otherwise. *I think you were the last one in after your chat with Jake by the pool last night. You forgot to lock the patio doors. Can you make absolutely sure you do so in future. I think I mentioned that Ollie's not a strong swimmer. We don't want him wandering out there, do we?*

I continue to follow her as she drives away in the opposite direction to the house. Forty minutes later, once she's parked up in the town centre, I follow on foot at a discreet distance and watch as she goes into a walk-in hair salon. She's clearly decided that with me picking Ollie up from school, she'll have time to indulge herself. I have no doubt that's for Jake's benefit, as is her sudden penchant for cosmetics. I feel sorry for her, but with her life at stake as well as my own, I have no room for sympathy.

Feeling jittery inside, uncertain whether it has anything to do with the tablets, whether Jake might have found a way to feed them to me, I go back to my car, take several slow breaths, and then drive straight to PCs Plus Peripherals. Jake's new assistant looks alarmed as I stride into his office without knocking. I don't say anything, simply look at Jake, whose expression is also somewhat startled. Guessing he has no choice but to see me, he turns his gaze towards Janine. 'Could you give us a minute, Janine?' he asks with that smile of his, the smile that says he's a man with a cross to bear, which would be me.

'Yes, of course. No problem.' Her eyes flick worriedly between us. 'Can I get either of you a coffee?' She loiters, annoyingly.

Jake meets my impatient gaze. 'No, thanks,' he says, his smile now becoming awkward.

'Right.' She looks uncertainly between us again. 'I'll just, um, check some stock then.' She heads for the door, then stops and turns back. 'Don't forget you have to leave for your meeting with the property agent about the new store purchase shortly, Jake. You said to remind you.'

Is she providing him with an excuse to extract himself? Or is Jake really intending to expand into a new store? If so, he will need funding. Was he hoping to be rid of me by now, in which case all that's mine would be his? Perhaps I should inform him that I intend to make a new will leaving everything in trust for my children. That might foil his plans.

'Right. Thanks.' His smile is definitely now on the tight side.

Finally, after collecting her bag – which she'll obviously need to check the stock – she leaves. I watch her go. She's a pretty young thing, long-lashed, deer-like eyes and a slim figure. She's obviously easily fazed and not overconfident. Jake's sort exactly.

Once the door closes, I refrain from commenting – on her or Jake's apparent new store purchase. I have no intention of getting into an argument with him here. 'I've left a letter with my solicitor.' I strengthen my resolve and get straight to the point.

I have his attention. He pales in an instant.

'It's to be opened should anything happen to me,' I continue, working to keep any emotion from my voice. 'Obviously, if something *were* to happen to me, I won't be around to care what you do, but just so you know, it implicates you.' I study him impassively for a moment as he assimilates, and then turn for the door.

'Megan, wait.' He's around his desk, coming after me as I cross the shop floor. 'We need to talk,' he says, a panicky edge to his voice as he catches up with me.

'We already did, Jake,' I remind him. 'The outcome wasn't satisfactory.' I stride on, my head high, my heart fracturing inside me. I loved him once with every part of me. Now I have to be free of him, unless he agrees to play by my rules.

FIFTY

Having driven around for a while, I park up opposite the PCs Plus car park and stay in my car to make the phone call I need to. Janine picks up, answering efficiently. 'PCs Plus Peripherals, Janine speaking. How can I help you?'

'Janine, hi. It's Megan.'

'Oh,' she says, sounding rather prickly. 'I'm afraid Jake's not here at the moment. He's viewing some properties after his meeting. He said he would be quite late getting back. Do you want me to leave him a message?'

I know he's not there. I watched him leave. It was some time after this supposed meeting, which meant she was being protective of him, something that greatly peeves me. 'No, no need,' I assure her. 'It was you I wanted to speak to.'

Another 'Oh.' A less assured one this time.

'I owe you an apology,' I press on. 'I'm afraid Jake neglected to do a DBS check I asked him to and I was rather annoyed when I came in. I'm sure he's busy, but it was extremely important. I shouldn't have been so off with you, though.'

'No problem,' she says, relaxing a little. 'I get it. He is really busy, which is obviously why it slipped his mind. I'm not sure what a DBS check is – I'm quite new to computers – but I'll make sure to remind him about it.'

'Thanks, Janine. Actually,' I tack on quickly, before the naïve girl puts the phone down, 'you could probably help me, which would save you bothering him.'

'Of course,' she responds helpfully. 'If I can.'

'The DBS check relates to a former employee of Jake's, Ellie Taylor, who now works for both of us, minding our children. We just need to run the check to make sure we've ticked all the boxes,' I lie, mentally crossing my fingers. 'You wouldn't be able to provide me with the address of the nursery she supplied for her references, would you? I think I wrote the details down wrong. Ellie's taking my son straight from school to his after-school activities. She has the baby with her, so I don't really want to distract her while she's driving.'

'I'll take a look,' she says, clearly the willing sort and definitely naïve. Also sacked, probably, if she relates our conversation to Jake.

I wait while she goes through the files, asking me to bear with her. She soon comes up trumps. I thank her profusely, telling her she's a super-efficient star, and then call the nursery.

'Good afternoon,' I say. 'It's Chloe Wright here from the Office for Standards in Education, Children's Services and Skills. I wonder if you could help me. I'm trying to verify some information regarding a former employee, Ellie Taylor. It's just box-ticking,' I add reassuringly, 'to ascertain I have the facts right regarding your next Ofsted inspection.'

Minutes later, I have what I want, the words 'Ofsted inspection' having ensured they weren't shy in offering up the details I requested about when and why she left. It seems Ellie received an urgent call while at work and left the nursery, in so doing leaving a child unsupervised who was then involved in an accident. The nursery manager was quick to lay the blame squarely at her feet, claiming that she hadn't asked someone to cover for her and citing her negligence as the cause.

Trepidation twists my stomach, my thoughts going to my own children. I've seen no evidence of Ellie being negligent. If anything, she's caring and... But I *have*. My mind shoots to the time she placed Fern so clumsily in her cot she could easily have injured her. Trying to reserve judgement, I go online, hoping to find more. My heart lurches when I come across a newspaper article: *Nursery Assistant Accused of Neglecting Child Cleared of Brother's Death*. The headline screams at me and I scan the words feverishly:

> *Nursery nurse Ellie Taylor, formerly of 23 Acorn Road, Worcester, has been released from custody after being questioned about the circumstances surrounding the death of her brother, Theo Taylor, aged six years, who died from pressure on the brain due to a subdural haematoma. Daily News has been able to establish that Theo's parents have now been charged with cruelty and ill treatment of a child, neglect and failure to protect.*
>
> *DN previously reported that Ellie Taylor had been questioned regarding an incident at the nursery she was employed at in which a child sustained serious injury. DN learned that Miss Taylor had left the child unattended to answer an urgent call from her home address. No charges were subsequently brought.*

A tumult of emotion churns inside me. Confusion as to why I didn't know all of this. Fear for my children. I also feel a deep compassion for Ellie. She was obviously suspected of being involved in her brother's death. What must she have gone through? What did she herself endure as a child? I have no way of establishing the facts without talking to her, or to Jake, who quite probably knows all of this – hence his realisation that she would crave the attention of someone who seemed to care. A new layer of guilt settles heavily on me at my treatment of her. But I didn't bring her into our nightmare. Jake did. And now, with him preying mercilessly on her vulnerabilities, I have to find a way of extracting her from it. I have to make sure she walks away and never looks back. First, though, I have to establish that what I've just read is true. What was the urgent call she received that caused her to leave a child without adequate supervision?

FIFTY-ONE

As I have some time on my hands before collecting Ollie, I decide to drive to the address in the article to see for myself what kind of environment Ellie was brought up in. I arrive to find the property in the middle of a social housing estate, red-brick buildings mostly, uninspiring in their uniformity. Many homeowners obviously take pride in expressing their individuality with brightly painted doors and beautifully maintained gardens. Other houses are run-down. Number 23, though, stands out amongst them all. With scrub and tall weeds covering the lawn, which clearly hasn't been cut in years, and paint that isn't so much peeling as shedding from the front door, it looks sadly neglected.

Might her parents still live here? I'm not sure what compels me, but I park up and climb out. As I approach the house, I note spray-canned graffiti, half scrubbed out, on the front door. I don't have to squint too hard to work out the words *CHILD KILLER* scrawled in ugly black letters. I'm about to turn away when I catch a movement at the window, the half-drawn curtain twitching, a face appearing.

A stony-faced middle-aged woman peers out at me,

scowling in obvious agitation, and I decide that this was a bad idea. I'm halfway back along the path when the door opens behind me. 'Can I help you?' a voice asks. The woman at the window, I assume, turning to face her.

'I'm not sure. I—' I stop as she emits a dry, hacking cough, a result of her smoking habit, no doubt. I note the cigarette she has firmly wedged between two nicotine-stained fingers.

'Well?' Her coughing fit over, she folds her arms across her chest – the cigarette still between her fingers – and regards me suspiciously.

I offer her a polite smile. 'I was hoping to find out a little about Ellie Taylor,' I say. 'She—'

'She doesn't live here,' the woman says bluntly and makes to close the door.

'I know.' I step forward. 'She works for me.'

The woman falters.

'She minds my children,' I hurry on, as she eyes me narrowly. 'I was trying to find out a little about her previous employment, but the nursery she worked at wasn't very forthcoming.'

She takes a long draw on her cigarette. 'I'm not surprised.' She exhales slowly.

I try not to breathe as a thick plume of smoke billows around me. 'I thought you might provide some background information on her,' I push on. 'That is, assuming you're her mother.'

She studies me hesitantly for a second. Then, 'You'd better come in,' she says.

Once I'm inside, she nudges the door closed and takes another draw on her cigarette. The hall is small, and the tobacco fumes that permeate the walls, mixed with the smell of alcohol that seems to ooze from her pores, cause my stomach to roil.

'Your husband didn't share the information I gave him with

you then?' she enquires, and my heart turns over. *Jake?* He's been *here?*

'No,' I say, too quickly. 'He, um... It obviously slipped his mind.' I manufacture a short smile. 'We're both so terribly busy.'

Her smile is knowing, languorous as she looks me over, a glint of something in her eyes, gloating almost. She's enjoying this, sizing me up, gaining pleasure from the problem she perceives in my marriage. 'I'm sure you are,' she drawls.

I don't miss her facetiousness and I find myself actively disliking the woman.

'I suppose you're here for the same reason?' she asks, raising her eyebrows enquiringly. 'I'll tell you what I told him.'

I'm still reeling from the knowledge that Jake visited her, obviously to gain information about Ellie he might use to manipulate her. But isn't that what I'm doing too? No. I dismiss another stab of guilt I absolutely shouldn't be feeling. I'm here to arm myself with any information I might need to stop him.

The woman appears to debate, then, 'Ellie wasn't responsible for her brother's death,' she discloses, and I feel a surge of relief. 'Not directly. Her father was.'

She pauses, stubs her cigarette out in an overflowing ashtray on the hall table and reaches to wipe a tear from her eye.

I wait, sensing that she won't react well to my questioning her.

'My ex-husband is an alcoholic,' she informs me bitterly, after a pause. 'If he hadn't been drunk that day, Ellie would never have left the nursery. That child would never have been injured and my little boy would never have died. I'll never forget the terrified look on his face before he fell.' She falters, emitting a shuddery breath. 'He called her. My little Theo, he called Ellie. That's why she came. She *shouldn't* have.'

She looks away, dabs at her cheek, and then takes a fresh cigarette out of a packet. I stare at her, appalled. Where was *she*, his mother? Here, clearly, if she witnessed what happened.

Why didn't she stop it? How drunk was *she* on the day her child's life was stolen away? And how did a boy just six years old manage to call his sister? He must have been terrified.

'The fact is, though,' another pause while she lights up and inhales, 'Ellie lied, to implicate me. She blamed me for not protecting her and Theo from him. God knows, I tried.'

I wait again, working to keep my thoughts from my face while she blows out a lungful of smoke.

'The thing is, Ellie is unstable, unreliable and impulsive. She wasn't directly responsible for what happened to dear little Theo, but she wasn't blameless. She shouldn't have charged in here, provoking her father, challenging him, Theo caught in the middle of it. He would never have fallen down those stairs if not for her. I'm telling you this for your own good *and* hers. You should be wary of her. I would.'

She looks towards the stairs and my blood runs cold as I see Ollie standing there. It might have been him. And it would have been me who was responsible. I designed the house that has had nothing but bad aura since the day we moved in. I need to find a way out of it. I *have* to find a way to get Ellie away from Jake; to get myself and my children away from him too.

FIFTY-TWO

I'm taken aback when Ollie races towards me across the playground. 'Hey.' I smile, delighted that he seems pleased to see me. 'How did it go today?'

'Good,' he says enthusiastically. 'I got a star for reading out loud.'

'Really?' I'm doubly delighted. I worry about my boy's confidence. He's never been extrovert, but he's been more withdrawn than is healthy since Phoebe disappeared so suddenly from his life.

'Uh-huh.' He nods. 'My teacher said my vocabili...' He trails off, clearly struggling with the word.

'Vo-cab-u-lary.' I sound it out for him.

'Vo-cab-u-lary,' he repeats. 'She said it was very good.'

'Well done you.' My heart swelling with love for him, I crouch down and pull him into a hug. 'What book did you read from?'

He frowns nervously. '*Pokémon Adventures*,' he murmurs, dropping his gaze.

Which presumably Ellie allowed him to take to school in his rucksack, and now my boy is feeling guilty. Angry with myself for making him feel that way, I reach to lift his chin. 'It's obviously helping with your reading skills. I'm proud of you.' I look into his eyes, making sure he knows I mean it.

Seeing relief sweep his face, I realise that I've become the bad guy in his eyes, and I make a promise to myself to spend more time with him. My heart twists excruciatingly as I'm reminded of what Jake is trying to do. He wants to rob me of that time. To rob his child of his mother. Recalling that I intended to do that myself, overwhelming guilt crashes through me. At the time, my only thought was that he would be better off without me. I had no faith in myself, no ability to function even at a basic level. Jake had reduced me to that. And now he's working to drive me there again, with no thought of the consequences for his children. Could a man ever be more cruel? I will not allow him to achieve his aim, and I will use whatever means are at my disposal to do so.

Standing, I extend my hand for Ollie. He hesitates for a second, and then grins up at me and grabs hold of it. 'Are we going to the park now?' he asks hopefully.

'We are,' I assure him.

As we walk to the car, I squeeze his small hand in mine, a shudder running through me as I imagine what poor little Theo Taylor must have gone through. I will probably spend all eternity in purgatory for the things I've done, but right now, while I have breath in my body, I have to keep my boy safe.

After an hour at the park, where I push Ollie on the swing, then throw inhibition to the wind and join him on the roundabout and then the see-saw, which Ollie thinks is highly amusing, we head home, chatting about what we might do when the big holiday arrives.

'Can we go to the seaside like we used to?' he asks. I note the uncertainty in his voice and my guilt weighs impossibly heavier. It's as if he knows that his daddy and I can't spend time happily together.

'We can.' I glance at him with a smile. I fully intend to keep my promise. Ollie and I can go alone. We can make our own fun together. Have a life without Jake.

As we approach the house, my heart sinks to the pit of my stomach when I see Jake's car on the drive alongside Ellie's. Anger tightens like a slip knot inside me. Dutiful Janine really was fabricating excuses for him, wasn't she? Why are young women so completely sucked in by him? I wonder bitterly. Because he's good-looking, charismatic, beleaguered, an image he plays to perfection.

Forcing myself to smile for Ollie's sake, I climb out of the car and help him out. As we walk to the front door, I brace myself and push my key into the lock. I'd like to go in quietly, but that's not possible with Ollie excited because his daddy's home early. As I expect, he scoots inside, charging straight across the hall. I follow him. There's no sign of life downstairs.

'Daddy!' Seeing Jake on the landing, Ollie races up to him.

'Hey, little man? How did school go today?' Jake's tone is delighted, perhaps a little too exuberant. Glancing up, I notice he's actually blocking the landing – in case Ollie sees something he shouldn't? My gaze travels over him. Does he realise his shirt collar isn't turned down properly? That his hair has that tousled, just-got-out-of-bed look? Of course he does. My heart folds up inside me.

'Good,' Ollie answers. 'I got a star for reading out loud. My teacher said my vo-cab-u...' he hesitates, 'vo-cab-u-lary is very good.'

'Oh wow.' Jake laughs. 'The boy's a genius.'

I study him carefully. 'You're home early.'

'My meeting finished early. The guy had a family crisis he needed to get back to,' he says, lying, obviously. What happened to the properties he was viewing? I wonder.

'I'm glad we're not the only ones who have family crises,' I respond acerbically. Then, attempting to moderate my tone, I ask him as casually as I can where Ellie is. My heart hardens as he lies to me again, averting his gaze as he tells me she's in the nursery. As he offers to tell her I'm looking for her, I walk away, heading for the kitchen before my face gives me away. Does he realise how close the rage is to exploding inside me? That were it not for Ollie's presence, I would cheerfully kill him?

Minutes later, Ellie appears. Quietly, I notice, coming into the kitchen like a nervous little mouse. I breathe in sharply, smell her perfume. I don't look at her. If I do, I won't be able to hide the disdain I feel for her right now. And to think I was actually feeling sorry for her. Surely she can't imagine I don't know what's been going on? Here. In my *house*. My head reels as an image of Phoebe flashes into my mind, the fear in her eyes, and I have to work to expel the air from my lungs.

'I'm making Ollie a sandwich. He's hungry,' I inform her tightly, making the point that she's obviously been too busy fucking my husband to have prepared any tea for him.

She starts mumbling something about how she was just going to do it.

'Did Fern not have her feed on time?' I snap over her. My hand trembles as I put down the knife I'm scared I can't trust myself with.

I feel my anger rising as she babbles on about how Fern has been a bit snuffly – anger and terror. Because now that Jake has moved things on, possibly even murmuring the words she will have longed to hear, she's snared like a fly in his web and I have no hope of making her see he's a predator. 'Might that be something to do with the obnoxious fumes she's inhaled at the hair salon, do you think?'

As she flails for excuses, my eyes stray to her hair, which is now close in colour to my own. *Really?* Does she think she can slip so easily into my shoes? She has no idea what it's like to be standing where I am. All she sees is a woman who has everything, including the perfect man, whom she treats abysmally. I swallow my hurt. 'The colour suits you,' I say calmly.

She squirms uncomfortably and I turn away to pick up the sandwich I've made. I'm sure she flinches as I walk towards her. Is it obvious in my eyes, I wonder, that I have an almost overwhelming urge to slap her? 'Nice perfume,' I comment, holding her gaze.

'J'Adore.' She provides the name of the fragrance she's drenched herself in. Does she really think I'm as naïve as she is? That I can't smell him all over her?

'I think you might have overdone it a little. You might want to use it more sparingly next time,' I suggest, making a monumental effort not to do what Jake undoubtedly expects me to do. I can't lose it. This time, I have to keep a careful rein on my emotions.

She says nothing, but I note the swallow sliding down her slender neck, her eyes darting to Jake as he comes into the kitchen. She's hoping for support. I think she will find it sadly lacking.

He glances briefly at her and then towards me as I walk across the kitchen to throw the sandwich I've made pointedly into the bin. 'I thought you were making that for Ollie,' he says, looking mystified.

Pointing out that I don't need to now that Ellie's finally deigned to make an appearance, I go back across the kitchen to hand her the plate. 'You might need to empty the dishwasher before you put that in.' I eye her scathingly. She needs to know that I know. Or at least suspect that I do. 'And then perhaps you'd like to wash the crystal glasses, once you've fed Ollie, of course. They'll need to be hand-washed, as per my instructions.'

She's baffled, clearly, since I haven't given her any.

'I left you a note on the kitchen island.' I nod towards the note I hastily scrawled only a few minutes ago. 'Do you think you could at least attempt some of your chores, and make sure my daughter's needs are seen to in future before lounging about by the pool?'

I'm being cruel, deliberately implying that she's neglectful and incompetent. I've no choice. Realising that Jake is cranking things up, I have to do the same. I can't leave – if I could, I would in a heartbeat – but Ellie has to. Destabilising her – gaslighting her as Jake does me, I acknowledge shamefully – and showing him in his true colours when he doesn't come to her defence is the only way left open to me.

She pales considerably and glances at him again.

His gaze, though, is fixed steadily on me. 'I take it the best glasses are making an appearance for an occasion?' he asks, a telltale tic tugging at his cheek.

'A dinner party,' I provide, though he's clearly guessed what I'm doing, and why. The knives are out – and I am aiming for his Achilles heel. If anything will rile him enough to drop his nice-guy persona, this will.

'Right.' He draws in a tight breath. 'And would this dinner party be in honour of anyone in particular?' he enquires, his tone plainly irritated.

'Miguel.' I use Michael's professional name, hold Jake's gaze defiantly for a second and then turn away to head for the lounge.

'I don't bloody well believe this,' he grates, now completely ignoring Ellie to follow me. I try not to feel too sorry for her. She has slept with my husband, after all. 'You're actually inviting him *here*?'

I remind him that it's my home. It will be interesting to see how he reacts with Ellie in earshot.

He breathes in sharply. 'Jesus. *When?*' he growls.

'At the weekend,' I inform him. I'm hoping that Michael will agree to bringing our planned next meeting with Carly Simons forward. I haven't actually asked him yet. 'He flies back to Portugal in a few weeks,' I go on, ignoring the murderous glint I see in Jake's eyes. He's not going to do that either, is he, murder me with his fangirl looking on? I swallow as his face grows darker, wondering whether he actually might.

I look away, wishing fervently I could remember what happened on that day I can never forget. There are moments that are lost to me, moments when I see nothing but deep, dark red. I know, though, that my anger was so raw, so all-consuming, I could have done anything. 'He has some prospective clients he'd like to introduce me to before he goes,' I continue, confident on the outside. Inside I'm shaking. 'We decided it would be a good idea to have them over here. He thinks the house says far more about my work than my portfolio could. I think he's right.'

'Yeah, well, he would be, wouldn't he, him being God's gift to the world of design?' Jake is not pleased.

'He would actually.' I give him a short smile and remind him that this house is based on one of his brother's prestigious award-winning designs.

He laughs in disdain. 'So when's the red carpet arriving?'

'Your jealousy's showing, Jake. It's not a good look.' I wind him up further as I walk away. 'It's hardly Miguel's fault you don't have an artistic bone in your body.' As I glance back, I note Ellie moving hesitantly towards him.

He appears not to want her sympathy. 'I need to see to Ollie,' he mutters, holding up his hand. 'He's hungry. Do you think we might postpone washing the bloody crystal glasses in Miguel's honour and get him some food?'

I note Ellie's bewildered expression and feel a smidgen of sympathy for her. She will be assuming he's jealous of my association with another man. She's right. She won't realise, though, that it's for all the wrong reasons. That he's also frightened, wondering whether I've confided in Michael about the albatross that hangs around our necks. I haven't. Nor will I ever. It feels good to see the uncertainty in Jake's eyes, though. Empowering.

FIFTY-THREE

I watch as Jake goes agitatedly upstairs, then wander back to the kitchen, where Ellie is flitting about like a nervous little bird, trying to rescue the situation and get Ollie's tea. As I go to the fridge for more wine, she jumps and drops the cutlery she's fetching from the drawer. It clangs gratingly to the floor and I feel my nerves fray. Breathing deeply, I go across to examine the tiles, though I don't care about the house any more. It's a show home, that's all. A mausoleum. 'Do be more careful, Ellie.' I give her a despairing glance. 'And do please try to make less noise. We don't want to wake Fern, do we?'

I feel her eyes burning into me as I go back for my wine. She must hate me, would probably like to make an effigy of me and stick pins into it. I don't blame her.

She quickly averts her gaze as I face her, reminding her to uncork the red wine. 'Jake likes to let it breathe,' I tell her. Will she question why she's playing servant to him now he's had sex with her? I wonder. I hope so. Hope to God she's not so infatuated with him she would forgive him anything, as I tried to. 'Oh, and do remember to wash those glasses, won't you? They'll need polishing once they're dry,' I call behind me as I head to the lounge. Surely at some point she'll wake up to the fact that Jake isn't jumping to her rescue.

'Yes, no problem,' she calls back.

Her voice is strained, I note. She's obviously working hard to sound pleasant, but she's quietly fuming. I stop in the hall on the pretext of tweaking my new white lily arrangement. I'm concerned as I notice her extracting not one, but two bottles of red wine from the rack. I wander on to seat myself on the sofa opposite the hall, where I surreptitiously watch her while checking my phone. I don't see her with the wine as she crosses the hall to the stairs a minute later. She possibly has it secreted in the hand further away from me. A quick check of the wine rack once she's gone up soon confirms my suspicions. No doubt she feels the need to drown her sorrows following Jake's disinterest after their intimacy. Despite the fact that it's my husband she's slept with, I feel her hurt and humiliation. I'm also wary. With alcoholics as parents, how much will she drink? I need to know my children are safe with her.

I hear her go to the spare room, no doubt to hide the wine, and then on to Ollie's room. Seconds later, I hear Ollie skidding excitedly to the landing, and with the marble stairs in mind, I fly towards them.

Clearly also jarred into action, Jake races along the landing after him, his voice edged with panic as he warns him to slow down.

We exchange glances once he's escorted Ollie down. It breaks another part of my heart as I realise that for the first time in a long time, we are emotionally connected, both of us concerned and scared for this child we made together. It lasts a mere heartbeat before the guarded disillusionment returns to Jake's eyes and he looks away. I feel it like a stone in my chest: the hurt, the rejection.

Following him to the kitchen, I watch with melancholic nostalgia as he swings his boy up onto a stool at the bar, chatting naturally to him in a way he hasn't done in a long time with me. We were broken before Phoebe, I realise that now, because of me, because of my feelings of inadequacy – because, though I said I had, though I wanted to and thought I had, I could never truly forgive him for his 'drunken mistake' before our marriage. After Phoebe, we were beyond repair.

Going after Jake as he heads back to the lounge, I hear Ellie coming along the landing. She stops, and my hurt turns to blistering anger as I sense her hovering, waiting like an ever-present ghost. Just like Phoebe, she's always there.

'You realise she left the patio doors open, don't you?' I ask Jake. I need *him* to be angry. I need him to be angry with *her*. When she's disillusioned enough, she will leave and, if she has any sense, have no further contact with him.

'What the hell are you talking about, Megan?' Jake asks, clearly irritated.

'I made myself quite clear, Jake. She left the patio doors open.'

As I continue, forcing the point home that she's allowed Ollie access to the pool, his expression grows dangerously dark. 'I even texted her to remind her that Ollie's not a strong swimmer,' I add. 'The first thing he did when he came home was run out to the patio.'

Ellie shifts on the landing, stepping back, but not fast enough.

Jake catches the movement and spins around. 'What the *hell* were you thinking leaving the doors to the pool open, Ellie?' he seethes.

I glance up at Ellie, who shrinks back under his furious gaze. She denies it, as she would. I don't feel good about lying, but I have to drive a wedge between them. She has to walk away from him.

'You should never have hired her. Drinking wine in the

afternoon?' I drop that in for good measure as I turn away. 'She clearly has a problem.'

'Right.' Jake sighs heavily again. 'Tell me, Megan, is there *anything* I can do right in your eyes?'

I grind to a halt and turn back. 'Are you serious?' I scan his face, incredulous. 'You are, aren't you? Because *you* can do no wrong, *can* you, Jake?'

A scornful smile curves his mouth. 'Like Miguel, you mean?'

'Quite unlike Miguel, actually,' I reply tightly. 'At least he gives a damn.'

'Does he?' Jake's expression is cynical. 'Are you sure about that, Megan? Seems to me his caring nature only appears when he wants something.'

'What's that supposed to mean?' I feel tears prick my eyes. I know exactly what he means. He thinks Miguel's made of the same stuff as him. He's wrong.

He shrugs. 'Nothing. I just think you're living in hope, that's all.'

'Drop dead.' I whirl around, swallowing hard.

'You'd like that, wouldn't you?' he throws after me. 'Sorry, my love, I'm not about to oblige.'

'Me neither,' I yell back. 'Whatever you're trying to do here, Jake, you won't win, I promise you that.'

He follows me to the lounge. 'I have absolutely no idea what you're talking about. It seems to me that it's you who's trying to score points.'

It really is a game to him, isn't it? I look at him with a mixture of bewilderment and terror. 'I'm not trying to score points, Jake,' I tell him shakily. 'It's really not worth the effort, is it?'

'So you're inviting him here for what reason exactly?' he asks, his face rigid with anger. 'Because if it's solely to humiliate me, you might want to have a rethink. We're in this together. Allowing him to get too close is—'

'No we are *not*,' I shout. '*You* made your bed, Jake,' I say, reminding him that this is all because of him, because of what he did. 'Now you can bloody well *lie* in it.'

He looks me over disdainfully. 'While you lie in someone else's.'

'What utter *rubbish*,' I spit. '*You're* the cause of all of this, Jake. You know what you did.'

'Every second of every day,' he assures me tersely. 'Do you know what *you* did, though, Megan? Because it seems to me that you have no conscience whatsoever.'

I don't reply, going to the coffee table to retrieve my wine glass instead. Does he honestly imagine that I don't live with it every second of every day? I swig the wine back. It haunts my dreams, jerking me awake if I dare close my eyes. He *knows* this.

'Do you care, Megan?' he goes on. 'About anything? About Ollie? About Fern? Because it seems to me that—'

'For pity's sake!' I scream at him. I can't bear this. I *can't*. 'Can you just *stop?*'

'Why don't *you* stop drinking that stuff and then maybe we could have a sensible conversation.' He storms across to me. I know as he swipes the glass from my hand that it's me he wants to strike out at. For a second I see my own shock reflected in his eyes, and then he looks sharply away, dropping down to pick up the shattered glass from the floor.

'This has to stop,' he mutters as I stare down at him, my heart pumping with fear. Then, 'Shit,' he hisses, wincing and shaking his hand.

I see the blood, rich red droplets trickling steadily from the wound as he straightens up. I step towards him, some misguided instinct compelling me, but he backs away, as if wary of me.

I watch in stunned disbelief as he heads towards the hall,

cradling his bloodied hand. *She's* there, hovering, her face horrified. Ollie, my boy, he's heard it all. My heart plummets to the depth of my soul as he tears himself away from Ellie and charges across to lock his arms around Jake's waist.

Jake tries to reassure him, telling him he dropped a glass, lying out of necessity, not to protect me, but to protect his son. Glancing at Ellie, he nods towards the stairs. 'Could you?'

Ellie obliges, moving to steer Ollie away. Of course she does. I'm beginning to hate her as much as I'm sure she hates me, but I'm grateful to her for that. 'Your hand,' she murmurs.

'It's fine.' I see him smile at her and I turn away, wrapping my arms around myself, trying to keep the hurt in, to stop my body trembling. 'It was just an argument about nothing.'

Nothing. Apart from what he's gained financially, that's all I'm worth to him, isn't it? The woman he picked up in the pub, she meant nothing. Phoebe meant nothing. When will Ellie realise that that's all she's worth to him too?

FIFTY-FOUR

Jake

Furious with myself for getting into an argument with Megan when Ollie was just yards away, and also with Megan, whose behaviour seems to be becoming terrifyingly unpredictable, I go to the downstairs bathroom in search of the first aid kit. Extracting it from the cabinet, I curse under my breath as I drop it, the contents spilling into the sink. '*Shit*,' I mutter out loud as I hear her yelling at Ellie.

After scooping the stuff up, I swill the gash on my hand and wrap a bandage haphazardly around it. As I tighten it with my teeth, I think about the sheer selfish stupidity of what I've done. Ellie made that fatal first move, her lips brushing mine so enticingly it was almost impossible to resist. I tried, I really did. *Not hard enough, you total shit.*

I knew she would only get hurt. I should have turned and walked away. Instead, I went into that bedroom with her. Why did I do it? Use her so callously? She's vulnerable. I *know* this. I knew she was attracted to me – though Christ knows why when what she must see is a man too weak to walk away from a relationship that is destroying his kids – and I took advantage of that fact, knowing full well there could be no future for us, knowing too that Ellie might imagine there was. I've been a complete bastard, yet still she looks at me with hope in her eyes. How do I tell her there *is* no hope? That there can never be – because I'm trapped in this nightmare for all of fucking eternity? A nightmare made worse by Megan's mission to get back at me. I'd like to tell myself I don't care that she's been having an affair throughout our sham of a marriage, but how can I not when the man she's chosen to have it with is my own brother? It's my fault. I broke her trust. The price I've paid for my drunken stupidity years ago has been high. For Phoebe, it was higher.

As I go upstairs, I see Megan storming from Ollie's room, Ellie emerging behind her looking bewildered. 'What the hell's going on *now*?' I ask in despair. Can she not just lay off the girl?

Megan stalks past me. 'Ask *her*.' She flicks her head in Ellie's direction. 'I really have no idea why you ever brought her here. She's utterly incompetent.'

I glance cautiously at Ellie as I ask what she's supposed to have done.

Megan whirls around, glowering at both of us. 'She left our daughter lying on her *stomach*.'

That jolts me. Fern has asthma. Surely Ellie would know better than to do that.

'I *didn't*,' she protests, desperation in her eyes. 'She was lying on her back. I was going to get her water and I found you two—'

'*And* she's encouraging Ollie to spend far too much time playing computer games.' Megan talks over her.

'He wanted to go to his room,' Ellie argues. 'I was just keeping him company.'

'He shouldn't be constantly cooped up there,' Megan counters. 'He should be interacting with people. Anyone with half a brain would know that, let alone someone who's supposed to be trained in childcare.'

As she takes the stairs down way too fast, I try hard to ignore the déjà vu that sweeps violently through me. I suspect it will do no good to point out that Ollie likes playing Pokémon, that all the kids play it, but I do anyway.

To which Megan responds by saying that this is why children are struggling with their social skills. 'You wouldn't concern yourself with that, though, would you, Jake?' She whirls around at the foot of the stairs to eye me accusingly. 'You're far too busy with other things, *aren't* you?'

She knows. I swallow and look away, tell her I think she's getting things out of proportion. She almost goes apoplectic, going on again about behavioural problems relating to gaming being classified as a mental health condition.

'Don't you think you should be limiting his screen time instead of encouraging him? That *she* should?' she asks, glaring up to where Ellie still stands on the landing.

I breathe in hard. 'Fern's all right, though, I take it,' I call angrily after her as she walks on, 'since you're apparently not concerned enough to be in there with her?'

Her stride falters. 'You need to get rid of her,' she mutters.

'Right.' I nod. 'And should I do this before or after she's looked after *your* daughter while you hold your dinner party in honour of the great Miguel?' I ask, and let it hang.

She strides on without a word.

Cursing in frustration, I glance at the ceiling. How long can we go on like this, slowly killing each other?

'Jake?' Ellie moves towards me, stopping me as I head for the nursery. 'I didn't leave her on her tummy, I promise you I didn't. She must have rolled over, or else—'

'From her back onto her front?' I eye her sceptically. 'She's not even six months old yet.' I don't claim to be an expert in the milestones babies reach, but I know it's too early for her to be doing that.

'But I *didn't*,' Ellie insists. 'Megan must have—'

Fearing what Megan's reaction will be if she sees us talking intimately, I move away from her, telling her I can't do this now. I'm hurting her, I can see it in her eyes, but I have no idea what to do. For Ellie's own good, I should convince her to leave before this whole poisonous mess ruins her life too. 'I need to see to Fern,' I mutter. 'We'll talk later.'

She stares at me tearfully, and realising how crushed she is, I swallow hard and turn away.

'What did she mean?' she asks behind me. 'When you were arguing downstairs,' she goes on, scrutinising me carefully as I turn back. 'She said, "You know what you did". What *did* you do, Jake? What did *she* do that you think she has no conscience about? Is this something to do with Phoebe?'

'Phoebe?' I reel inwardly. 'No,' I answer quickly. 'Why would you think that?'

She holds my gaze, her own both angry and cautious, and I feel my chest constrict with fear and guilt. What does she know? *Nothing*, I try to convince myself. She can't possibly. When Phoebe was reported missing, one of the first things the police did was check for activity on her bank account. Her card had been used. The CCTV footage at the railway cash dispenser revealed someone who looked like her, someone dressed in her clothes, withdrawing cash. The card was used again later, way after she'd gone from here. Megan spoke to Phoebe's mother, explained to her that there'd been a new boyfriend on the scene. Her mother was distraught. 'Did you meet him?' she asked tearfully.

Megan shook her head. 'I only met him once. His name was Sean. We didn't really know anything about him, other than that he was probably married.'

No one has heard from Phoebe since then. Ellie doesn't know anything. She can't.

'It has nothing to do with our previous au pair,' I say firmly. 'She was talking about what happened after Fern was born.' Keeping my eyes locked on Ellie's, I lie through my teeth, repeating how Megan struggled to cope, explaining how I wasn't there for her.

Ellie scowls, unconvinced, and my chest hammers out a warning. I take a breath, try to get my rioting thoughts in order. 'I'm sorry that things seem so complicated, that you're caught up in the middle of it, but please try to understand.' I grope for a way to justify why I've treated her so badly. 'Megan's postnatal depression was severe. So severe she wanted to take her own life. I can't just turn my back on her, or on the children. I have to—'

'Jake!' Megan shouts from downstairs. 'Could you please see to Fern instead of leaving me to do everything. I'm getting her feed!'

I knead my forehead, feeling sick to the depths of my soul. How did this all happen? I have to try and explain things to Ellie. But I can't do that here. 'Can we talk later?' I ask, hoping she'll agree, that I can try to make amends in some way, though I have no idea how.

She studies me pensively for another second and then answers with a small nod. I feel her watching me as I carry on to the nursery.

Fern is an innocent in all of this. In the absence of a mother whose guilt stops her bonding with her, she needs to feel wanted and secure. She needs to feel loved. As I ease her from her cot, hold her in my arms and look into her startling blue eyes, I see the guardedness there that tells me she doesn't feel any of those things.

I smile down at her. 'Hi, sweetheart. What's all this fuss about, hey? Come on, little munchkin, let's make it all better, shall we?' I tell her throatily. I wonder if she sees the uncertainty in my eyes. Whether she senses it.

After a moment, I decide to take her downstairs. Tastefully decorated and bright and airy though the nursery is, she's as much a prisoner as I am stuck in here.

Bending to kiss her forehead, I gather her up. As I step out onto the landing, I stop, surprised to see Megan listening at the spare room door. As I move towards her, she presses a finger to her lips and raises a hand, stopping me. I frown. What the hell is she doing? I take another step, then falter as she looks from the door back to me, her eyes wide with fear. I squint in confusion as she flies for the stairs, then watch in bewilderment as she heads straight to the front door, grabbing her bag on the way.

Wondering what's got into her, I hesitate outside the spare room. I'm debating whether to knock and go in when my phone alerts me to a text.

I fumble it from my pocket, read Megan's message – *She's asked her boyfriend to come here. She wants him to open the wardrobe!* – and my heart slams into my chest.

As I try to think what to do, another text arrives: *I told you to get rid of it. Why won't you listen to me. I can't do this any more. I just can't.*

With Fern still in my arms, I attempt to reply and end up dropping the bloody phone.

Dammit. I bend to retrieve it and the spare room door swings open. 'Sorry.' I meet Ellie's wary gaze as I straighten up. 'Dropped my phone,' I explain with an awkward smile. 'Megan's gone out.'

Ellie looks puzzled. 'She didn't mention anything to me.'

I glance down. 'No. She, er, had to see someone, apparently.' I add another lie to the lie, telling her there's a problem with the alarm at the Birmingham shop and that I need to go and take a look. 'Could you...?' I nod down at Fern.

She obliges, though somewhat reluctantly. No surprise there, given how I've treated her.

'Thanks, Ellie.' I smile appreciatively. 'I might be gone a while,' I warn her, and remind her to set the alarm. With no idea what Megan's up to, I don't like the idea of Ellie being here on her own.

Leaning in to kiss Fern's cheek, I scan Ellie's eyes, wishing I could apologise, make all of this stop. I can't. There's no way to. With no idea what Megan's planning, though, I have to stop her.

FIFTY-FIVE

Killing the engine once we're on the drive, I glance at Megan in the passenger seat. She's shaken to the core, her body tense, her hands clenched so tightly in her lap I can see the whites of her knuckles. 'I'll follow you in,' I say, my voice still hoarse with shock. 'I need to check the damage to my bumper.'

She nods. She hasn't spoken a word all the way back, clearly also deeply shocked. Even under the security light I can see her complexion is as pale as death. 'Will you be okay?' I ask, with no idea why, where we'll go from here. I've never been so scared in my life.

Again she nods, and reaches for her door as if on autopilot. I watch her until I'm sure she's through the front door, then climb out and go around to the front of the car. Surveying the bumper, I expel the air that's been trapped in my lungs since seeing what I know I'll never be able to unsee until the day I die. If not for Ollie – Fern, too – I would wish that that day could be today.

The damage isn't major, but it's obvious. Swallowing back the sick taste in my throat, I climb back in, press my fob to open the garage door and park the car inside. For now, it's the best I can do. *Keep calm.* Going back outside, I run trembling fingers through my hair, pull in several deep breaths, then follow Megan to the house.

Stepping into the hall, I look sharply up as Ellie descends the stairs. She smiles tentatively, and I feel like weeping. 'Her car broke down,' I tell her. 'I passed her on the main road.'

'Lucky you spotted her,' she answers. 'She's in the bedroom,' she adds awkwardly. 'I'm just going to make her a hot drink.'

'Thanks, Ellie.' I offer her a small smile. 'I'll be going in a bit later tomorrow. We limped the car to a garage. I'll need to make some calls and then I'll drive her out to fetch it. Will you stay?' I ask as she heads for the kitchen. 'Please, despite everything? Let me make it up to you?' I can't have her driving down that road on her own, not tonight.

'For now,' she answers, reluctantly I gather from her averted gaze. 'Ollie and Fern need me.'

'Thanks.' I emit a tired sigh. 'We should talk,' I add, wishing I could say more. *Like what? We've blown your world apart, but I'm there for you.* Jesus, this is insane. All of it. 'Do you think we could meet up later tomorrow,' I ask, 'assuming you have no—' I stop, my heart lurching as there's a sharp rap on the door behind me.

Nerves clench my stomach as I turn to answer it. I don't need the dark silhouettes through the opaque glass to tell me who's outside.

'Mr Harington?' one of the officers asks.

'That's right,' I work to keep my tone even and my gaze on hers. 'Can I help you, Officer?'

'DS Jacobs.' The woman shows me her identification. 'And this is PC Amir. We're trying to locate an Ellie Taylor. Are you able to confirm that you know her?'

My heart bangs so loudly I'm certain she can hear it. 'She's our childminder,' I answer. 'Is there a problem?'

'Do you think we might have a word with her?' she asks.

'I, er...' I frown in concern. 'Yes. I'll just go and—'

'Jake?' Ellie murmurs behind me, her voice small and scared, and I'm hard pushed not to stop here and now, to blurt out the whole ugly mess. But it won't stop it, will it? It's happened. I would give my soul to undo it, but I can't.

'You'd better come in.' Sucking in a sharp breath, I stand aside.

Ellie's eyes are pools of sheer terror as the officers step inside. 'I'm Detective Sergeant Hannah Jacobs,' the plain-clothes officer shows her her ID, 'and this is PC Arshi Amir. And you are?'

'Ellie,' Ellie murmurs. 'Ellie Taylor.'

The detective's smile is sympathetic. 'Is there somewhere we could sit down, Ellie? she asks.

Ellie doesn't move, palpable fear rooting her to the spot. 'Could you please just tell me why you're here?' she asks tremulously.

The two officers swap glances. 'We found this address programmed into Zachary Kendall's satnav,' DS Jacobs informs her. 'It's also listed as a contact address for you. Are you aware that you're named as Mr Kendall's primary contact in case of an emergency?

'Emergency?' The blood drains visibly from Ellie's face.

'I'm afraid I have some very bad news,' the detective goes on cautiously. 'I'm sorry to tell you that Mr Kendall was involved in a fatal road traffic accident late this evening.'

Ellie looks as if someone's just punched her. Instinctively, I move towards her, though I would be the last person in the world she would want near her if she knew.

'No!' She recoils, pushing me away. 'He can't be! I've spoken to him. Tonight. He...' She trails off, staring at them in complete shock. 'No,' she whispers. 'Please no.'

'Ellie?' She's shaking, trembling all over. Guilt lodged like a stone in my chest, I reach for her again. 'It's okay.' I ease her to me, try to reassure her. 'It's okay.'

She chokes out a sob, her look one of bewildered disbelief. 'How?' she breathes.

DS Jacobs looks her over guardedly. 'A post-mortem examination will need to be completed to establish probable cause of death,' she answers, 'but we believe he suffered traumatic brain and spinal cord injury. These types of injuries usually occur due to the vehicle rolling over.'

I feel a shudder run through Ellie and ease her closer. My mouth is dry, sweat breaking out over my body as my mind plays it back: Megan appearing as I round the bend on the unlit country road, just standing there in the middle of nowhere like an apparition from a nightmare, her arms wrapped tightly around her torso as she stares out across the fields. I swerve to avoid her, skidding to a stop a yard in front of her, my neck jarring as the front end of the car strikes the metal railings of a farmyard fence. As I race towards her, petrol fumes searing the back of my throat, realisation hits me like a freight train. Her car is parked diagonally across the road. My emotions reel, my only thought to get to her, find out what in God's name has happened. But I know. With sickening clarity, I know. Her expression when I reach her, grasping hold of her shoulders and spinning her around to face me, confirms it. Her eyes sparkle with the same mania I've seen once before, her pupils so dilated they obliterate her irises. 'What have you done?' I ask, my voice a harsh croak.

'It was an accident,' she whispers, lowering her gaze to the mess of mangled metal that was once a PT Cruiser lying in the field below the road.

As I scramble down the embankment, I know that no one could have survived the impact. Zachary is still strapped in, hanging upside down, his head wedged against the roof at an impossible angle, his eyes wide, unseeing. Lifeless.

There was nothing to be done, I tell myself now; nothing I *could* have done but the only thing I knew how to: rescue the situation. Obliterate any visible tyre marks that weren't his, get Megan out of there. Somehow she got back behind the wheel, drove to PCs Plus car park, me close behind her. How could I have done that, walked away? How can I live with it? Any of it?

I have to, I remind myself. Because if this comes out, everything does. 'How did he come to roll over?' I ask the detective, guilt now wedged like a shard of glass in my throat. 'Was there another vehicle involved?'

'As far as we can ascertain at present, no,' the other officer supplies. 'It appears to be due to driver negligence. The deceased...' She glances watchfully at Ellie. 'Mr Kendall was travelling at speed and careered off the road at a particularly hazardous hairpin bend. His vehicle is some years old. It's possible it wasn't regularly serviced.'

'Jesus.' I swallow back the panic climbing my windpipe. 'Had he been drinking, do you think?'

'I'm afraid we won't know that until the post-mortem...'

'Ellie?' I tighten my grip around her as she reels.

I'm trying to support her when Megan descends the stairs. Her face is pale to the point of grey as she looks from me to Ellie, then to the officers. 'What's going on?' she asks, her voice thick with fear. 'Why are the police here?'

'Ellie's boyfriend.' I try to catch her gaze, willing her to keep quiet. 'He's been involved in—' I stop, sure that Ellie is about to pass out.

'He was coming here,' she murmurs.

Shit. I sweep her into my arms as she crumples. 'She needs to lie down!' Carrying her across the hall, I lock eyes with my wife. I don't care what she sees in mine. Pure unadulterated anger burns deep inside me. This has to end. I have to find a way to make it.

FIFTY-SIX

At first I couldn't believe that she was actually going through with the dinner party, which she'd clearly postponed rather than cancelled, as I'd thought she would. But then I decided that if I was going to blow this thing apart, expose the lies we'd told, the lie we lived, make sure the damn house she'd built with 'Miguel' came crashing down around her ears, then it might be an opportune time. It was going to be one hell of a show. We might as well have an audience.

As I drive home, weary from gut-wrenching worry and lack of sleep over the last few weeks, I steel myself. I will have to face the consequences. I deserve to. Even those, though, will be better than the hellish life I've been living. Not living. Existing, that's all I've been doing. I'm tired of being manipulated, jaded to my very bones. And Megan is a master at manipulation. She's even being nice to Ellie. Since the night Ellie learned of Zachary's death and her world disintegrated, Megan has looked after her as she would a sister, insisting she stay in the spare room, making sure she rests. Acting as if she cares. She doesn't care. She's keeping Ellie close because she has to. She doesn't give a shit about anyone but number one. Oh, and *Miguel*. She cares what he thinks, greatly. It's time he had his eyes opened to what the woman who professes to be married to a bastard is really like.

She'll bring me down with her, I don't doubt that for a second. That isn't what stopped me doing what I should have done before now. It was concern for Ollie, for Fern too, once she was born. They would have no one else. Megan's father is a hard-nosed bastard. There's no way I could contemplate Ollie being brought up by him. Nausea and anger so fresh I can taste it churns my gut as I recall his glibness as he withdrew promised funding for PCs Plus days before our wedding. 'It's just not a viable proposition, Jake,' he said, splaying his hands as I sat in the guest chair in his office, a chair deliberately lower than the studded leather one he lorded it in, making me feel smaller than I already did. 'You have no business plan. You're buying in too much stock, trying to run before you can walk. Come back to me in six months. Maybe we can discuss it then.'

As he smiled dismissively and picked up his phone, I had to resist an urge to tell him where to stuff his funding. I had buyers lined up on a promise from my soon-to-be father-in-law. He knew it. He wanted to prove I was a failure. It worked. In doing what I did once I left that office, I played right into his hands. Afterwards, I felt like the biggest failure that ever walked the earth. He didn't want his daughter to marry me. It was that simple. What I did that night after getting drunk out of my skull was my fault, no one else's. No one forced me. It was all on me. I regretted it, could hardly remember it when I finally woke from heavy, alcohol-fuelled sleep. Megan has never forgotten it. What puzzled me was how she knew about it – until her old man approached me after the wedding, that was. 'She still married you then?' He eyed me narrowly, then wrapped an arm around my shoulders, squeezing – too tightly. 'Just don't go having it away with any more brainless young blondes, hey?'

The penny dropped then, resoundingly. The misogynistic,

arrogant prick had had me followed. Had he set it up? I didn't know. I did know he expected me to do what I did when he pulled the funding – go to the nearest pub and get paralytic – because I came from *poor stock*. A product of a low-income family, my own father banged up for drunken assault, my mother gone from my life, and who could blame her? No, he didn't want me marrying his daughter.

But I did. Maybe I was as bullish as he was. I loved her, begged her to give me a chance to prove it, told her I didn't mean to hurt her. I've paid for my mistake ever since. Our marriage was shaky from day one. My fault. I accepted it, tried to work at it. But now it has turned into a war zone, because Megan can't forgive me. She judged me based on my history. There have been casualties: Phoebe, and now Ellie. It has to stop.

Parking on the drive, I note that our illustrious guests have arrived. Michael's hired Jaguar XJ is parked in my spot, which pisses me off. Leaving my car where the dent in it is visible – with the garage awaiting spare parts, there was nothing I could do to hurry the repair up – I brace myself and head for the front door.

Stepping into the hall, I falter, my gaze travelling between Michael and Megan, who have clearly just put some space between them and are eyeing each other with ill-concealed amusement. She's pulled out the stops, I note, wearing an expensive-looking silk number that shows off her shoulders and a considerable amount of cleavage. I glance away and my gaze snags on a painting propped against the hall table, placed there for my benefit, I've no doubt. I bury a cynical smile. It's obviously one of Michael's.

My brother won a scholarship for outstanding achievement in his A levels and was able to pursue his dreams. I don't begrudge him that, contrary to what Megan thinks. At the time, I thought bloody good luck to him. I *do* begrudge the amount of time Megan spends with him. She's always banging on about him, telling me what a fabulous flair for design he has, how talented he is. Meeting up with him often. Too often. Can she not see that he's working to impress her because he fancies her? I certainly begrudge him fucking my wife. The model was her, quite clearly. Same shoulders, same breasts. Has she worn that dress tonight to force the point home? I wonder.

My gaze goes thunderously back to Michael as he extends his hand. 'Jake.' He smiles.

I hesitate, then shake it, prepared to play Megan's ridiculous game for a little longer. Making my announcement while the guests are gathered around the pool might wipe the amusement from their faces.

'Michael.' As I eye him steadily, I wonder if he can read the contempt in my eyes. 'Or are we still addressing you as Miguel?' I assume he thinks his adopted name better befits his highly elevated artistic status.

'The latter,' he confirms. I see from his flicker of annoyance that he has noted my contempt. 'I'm well known by that name now, after all.'

'So I gather.' I hold his gaze. 'Busy?'

'Very. The price of fame.' He sighs theatrically.

I smile wryly, my gaze flicking to the painting. 'Not too busy to dabble in your hobby, I see.'

'Well, she does make a rather captivating model.' He smirks.

Anger rises dangerously inside me and I drop my gaze fast.

'Jakey, Jakey.' Michael sighs again expansively and moves to drape an arm over my shoulders. 'Relax, little brother. You're so uptight. It's just a painting.'

I look disdainfully back at him and then furiously at Megan. 'I'm going to get changed,' I grate, turning abruptly away and heading for the stairs.

Ellie stands at the top of them, and I hesitate. I've been spending as much time as I can at work since 'the accident'.

Partly because I can't be in Megan's company, cannot comprehend in any way how she can just carry on. Mostly because I can't look Ellie in the eye. 'Ellie, hi. I didn't see you there.' I look at her now, offer her a smile, feel sick to my soul as I notice how pale she still is. She's lost weight, I notice, and wish there was something I could do to put things right. There is nothing but what I know I have to. 'How are you doing?' I ask her, though the answer is right there in her tortured eyes.

Assuring me she's okay, she smiles tentatively, rearranges Fern in her arms as the little girl frets. She's been crying a lot lately, often during the night. I wonder whether that's because Megan has been trying to look after her. She loves the child, I don't doubt that, but she's so stuffed full of guilt she finds it almost impossible to be natural with her. I guess I shouldn't keep pointing it out, but *I'm* so stuffed full of anger I can't help myself.

'You?' Ellie asks me.

'I've been better,' I answer, and glance back to the hall as I catch a movement. Michael and Megan are strolling towards the lounge and the open patio doors together. I look away, disgusted. Also furious that she could do this right under my nose and in front of the other guests, all associates of hers – or rather Michael's – she feels the need to suck up to.

'Why do you stay with her?' Ellie asks suddenly.

I'm taken by surprise. I wish there was a way to answer that honestly. 'I have no choice,' I say simply. 'Is she okay?' I nod at Fern, changing the subject.

Ellie glances down at her. 'She's fine,' she assures me. 'Jake,' she looks hesitantly back at me, 'I need to ask you something.'

Noting her serious expression, my heart jolts. 'About?'

When she asks me again whether what happened between us meant anything to me, panic twists my gut. Fearing that someone might overhear, meaning Ellie might be dragged into what has to happen tonight, I take hold of her arm and urge her along the landing.

She's unimpressed, as she's bound to be. 'Well?' she demands.

I struggle for a way to answer. If I tell her it did mean something, her next question is going to be *So why treat me like shit?*

'Was it a mistake, Jake?' she asks, her cheeks flushing angrily. 'Something you took because it was on offer? Is that it? Did you use me to relieve your own pent-up frustration?'

'What? No. That's not how it was.' Realising that I've raised my voice, I glance quickly over my shoulder. 'It *did* mean something. Of course it did.'

'But you haven't *mentioned* it.' Tears spring to her eyes. 'You haven't said a single word about it since that day. In fact, you've barely looked at me.'

I close my eyes. I have to say something. There's no future for her with me. There never could be. She needs to know that. 'Because it shouldn't have happened,' I point out bluntly, hating myself for doing this to her.

She looks sharply away. 'I need to get Fern's feed.'

'Ellie, wait.' I stop her as she attempts to move past me. 'I meant I shouldn't have *allowed* it to happen. I knew you would end up getting hurt and I didn't want that. It was the absolute last thing I wanted. And I didn't mean to avoid talking about it. I just didn't know how. Can we talk? Later? When this charade downstairs is over?' We won't talk later. I won't be around, but she doesn't need to know that.

'Is there anything to talk *about*?' She looks me over, her eyes filled with bitter disillusionment. 'I'd hate you to feel—' She stops as we hear Megan's voice in the hall below. 'I should go.' She looks away.

'I'll take her.' I reach for Fern as she wriggles. Ellie is exhausted, clearly. 'You go and grab her feed.'

She hesitates, and then hands her over and walks past me without meeting my gaze.

With my heart like a lead weight in my chest, I carry Fern to the nursery, talking softly to her. 'Hi, little one. How's it going, hey?' I ask her, as if she could answer. In a way, she does, studying me curiously for a second before reaching a hand excitedly towards my face. I catch hold of it, marvelling at the impossible smallness of it.

'You're beautiful, do you know that?' I whisper. I guess maybe I shouldn't. That I might be sending out the message that physical characteristics are more important than other qualities. The fact is, though, she *is* beautiful. 'Perfect,' I add throatily.

I kiss her tiny fingers and carry her over to the window. The sky is darkening, tumultuous clouds gathering, reflecting my mood. I'm offering up a silent prayer when I hear the door open behind me. I'm not asking for forgiveness. Somehow I can't see God granting me that. I'm simply apologising – for what's happened, for what's to come.

Sensing Ellie approaching, I glance at her and then away. 'She's sleeping with him, isn't she?' I don't know why I'm asking her. I already know. It's not fair on her – nothing I've done has been fair on her – but I need someone else to confirm it. I need to know I'm not going out of my mind.

She doesn't answer. I don't blame her. How can she?

I swallow hard, glance back to Fern, look deep into her wide blue eyes, crystal clear with the innocence of childhood. 'Do you think she looks like me?' I ask, finally acknowledging it out loud. She is beautiful, just like her mother, but she isn't mine.

FIFTY-SEVEN

I watch Megan with wry amusement as she shoots daggers of pure venom at the woman Michael is deep in conversation with, expounding his own virtues. The woman, I gather, is the hotshot in the fashion industry Megan is hoping to secure a refurbishment contract with. *Careful, my lovely, you're in danger of blowing it.* I shake my head and move away, feeling actually hurt as I realise how jealous she is. Looks like the novelty's wearing off for Michael. Such a shame when they've always been so close, I think cynically. Even when we were first dating, Megan seemed to get on better with him than she did with me. I put that down to the fact that they had something in common. Michael was running his own interior design business by then, becoming successful. Megan was aspiring to be. I tried to tell myself they had an affinity, that she found something in him she didn't in me, a techie with no clue how to run a business. Did she fancy him then, though? Would she have opted to be with him if he hadn't been determined to work abroad?

Is *Ollie* mine? The thought hits me like a thunderbolt, winding me. I study the painting of her – now mounted in place of another canvas on the main wall – a sour taste in my throat and my own jealousy squirming furiously inside me. When was it painted? Megan's hair was longer a few years back, around the time she had Ollie. Might she...?

Don't. I warn myself not to go there. Of course he's mine. I suck in a breath, try to slow my racing heart. His eyes are Arctic blue, the same blue as Michael's, as mine, but that's as far as any shared familial traits go. He's like me in nature. He's mine. I would have felt it if he wasn't, just as I did with Fern.

I glance again in my brother's direction, force myself not to go over there and wipe the smug smile off his face as he regales his rapt audience with tales of his successful business endeavours. Does he realise that Megan is spitting feathers? I glance at her as she extracts herself from someone who's been trying to get her attention and walks across to me. I can see from her expression that I'm going to be on the receiving end of her frustration.

'Do you think you could make an effort?' she hisses, her smile rigid. 'I'm supposed to be networking. You standing there looking as if you'd rather be somewhere else doesn't give a good impression.'

I smile acerbically in her direction, then fix my gaze back on the painting. 'I was just thinking. I was wondering how I would portray you if I had an artistic bone in my body, which I don't, as you've pointed out. I decided paint wouldn't be the best medium.'

My eyes stray to the figurative sculpture on a plinth next to the painting. It has a hole right through the middle. I was never sure I quite got the artist's statement. I think I do now. '"The figures appear incomplete to describe a condition of emptiness. Hollow humans",' I read, then lean towards her with a cynical smile. 'It captures you perfectly, don't you think?'

Easing away from her, I keep my gaze fixed stonily on hers as I let the figure slide from my hand. *Ouch!* I wince inwardly as it hits the Italian tiles with a resounding crash. That's really going to piss her off.

Megan's eyes flinch, but she doesn't look down at the damage. I have to give her kudos for that. '*Bastard*,' she growls, half under her breath.

Correct. I nod and smile again, and then make suitable apologies – for the benefit of the guests. I gain some satisfaction as I notice Michael ushering the woman he's obviously trying to impress in the direction of the patio. Watching Megan storm towards the stairs brings me no pleasure. I loved her once, tried so hard to regain her trust. Now there's nothing inside me but slow-burning hatred. She's right. I've made my bed, and I will lie in it, but not here, not with her.

I watch her reach the landing and debate whether to go up after her. Fern is awake, I can hear her faintly. With Megan in the mood she's in, I'm not sure I can trust her with our daughter right now. Moving towards the hall, I stop as there's a crash from the dining area. I snap my gaze in that direction to see Ellie drop to her knees with a wad of table napkins in her hand. Red wine spilled, I guess, noting a blood red trail dripping prophetically from the raised dining area down the lounge wall. That will please Megan. Sighing, I walk across as Ellie crawls around attempting to limit the damage. My anger hardens. She shouldn't be doing this. She was hired as a childminder, not a bloody servant. 'Sorry,' I mouth, as she meets my gaze. Her eyes are filled with anger and humiliation and brimming with tears, and it tears me apart. This is my fault. All of it. Why didn't I do what I should have done that fateful day that changed the course of my life for ever? I should have been stronger. Instead I was weak, terrified and pathetic.

I'm about to go up and lend Ellie a hand when Megan shrieks from the landing, 'For God's sake, Ellie, will you stop making eyes at my fucking husband and get up here and see to Fern! She's *crying*.'

FIFTY-EIGHT

'Christ, is she ever going to stop?' I glance at the ceiling in despair and sheer disbelief. Megan's losing it. She's been losing it for a long time. How did we ever think we could keep a lid on this? 'I'll go.' Struggling to contain my agitation, I glance at Ellie, who looks unimpressed. I feel it, the scorn emanating from her. She's right to feel that way. If she knew all there is to know about me, far from attracted, she would be repulsed.

Swallowing back the disdain I feel for myself, I head fast for the stairs. Reaching the landing, I grind to a stop as I hear Fern emit a raucous cry. She doesn't just sound upset, and Christ knows she's been that lately. She sounds terrified. Fear gripping me, I race into the nursery. Megan is standing with her back to the door, holding Fern. Even from here, I can see that the baby is rigid in her arms, her chest wheezing and raw as she sucks air into her lungs and bellows it out. *Jesus.* She's going to fucking well drop her in a minute. My blood pumping with shock and anger, I lurch towards her. 'What the hell are you *doing*?'

She whirls around. 'She won't stop. I can't get her to *stop*.' She stares at me with that manic glint in her eyes that strikes terror right through me.

'Give her to me.' I approach her cautiously, reach carefully for Fern.

Megan holds on to her. 'She doesn't want me.' Her tone edged with bewilderment, she looks down at the distressed child in her arms. 'I can't calm her.' Her face darkens as she looks back at me, something shifting behind her eyes that petrifies me.

'Megan, you need to let go of her.' I try again to take her.

'She doesn't *want* me. She wants fucking Ellie!' she cries, clutching Fern so close to her now that I'm sure she'll break her fragile bones.

'Megan, please let me take her,' I beg, my throat thick with emotion.

She studies me coldly. Then, 'I'm taking her out,' she announces, spinning towards the door.

'No way!' I'm in front of her in a split second.

'I'm going to drive her around.' Megan holds my gaze defiantly.

'You've been drinking!' I shout, careless of who might overhear. 'You'll take that little girl out over my fucking dead body!'

'Ha,' she retorts. 'I wish.'

'Put her down.' I lock my eyes hard on hers.

She doesn't flinch.

'I swear to God if you don't, Megan, I will ring 999 right now.'

'Will you? *Really?*' She laughs scornfully. 'You'll have some explaining to do then, *won't* you, Jake?' Her eyes narrowing to icy slits, she studies me a second longer, then attempts to push past me.

My blood pumps, fury coursing through my veins, my gut twisting as Fern sobs pitifully. This isn't going to happen. There's no way this is happening. I reach to clutch Megan's arm, my fingers digging hard into her flesh. 'Put. Her. Down.'

'You're *hurting* me.'

'Now!'

As she squirms, I squeeze harder, lock my other hand around the back of her neck and steer her towards the cot. Despite coming from *poor stock*, being used as a punchbag by my old man when he felt inclined, bullied by the great *Miguel*, I've never laid a hand on anyone. In fact, after my treatment at *their* hands, I made it my mission not to. I'm ready to now, though. More than. 'Do it,' I spit.

'Bastard.' She repeats her estimation of me tearfully.

'Don't waste your breath, Megan. I know exactly what I am.' Needing her to realise that I'm deadly serious, I give her another shove, and finally she lowers Fern. Clumsily. Too clumsily.

My stomach lurches as her head glances off the side of the cot.

Almost dumping her on the mattress, Megan simply glares down at her and marches off. I glance after her, disbelieving, and then back to Fern. She's not crying. Not moving. 'Fern?' My blood freezing, I place a hand on her tummy. Is she breathing?

Nausea and fear churning inside me, I reach for her and lift her out. '*Fern?*' I repeat, scanning her face urgently. 'Fern!' I shake her. Her eyelids flicker. She cries – and my heart starts beating again.

FIFTY-NINE

Megan

He's betrayed me, over and over. And now he's threatening to betray me all over again. He said he would call the police. He wouldn't *dare*. Terror grips my stomach as I consider that he actually might. He's an accomplished liar. I know this for a fact. Even without the bare-faced lies he told me about Phoebe, I only had to watch him manipulating Ellie to realise how easily he can make people believe his lies, portraying himself as the victim. I won't allow it. I will *not* allow him to paint me as the villain.

Creeping back into the nursery, I stare down at the little girl he loves even thinking she's not his. How can he doubt my feelings for him, believe that it's his brother I want rather than him? For all his seriousness and introspection, it's him I love. Yet he prefers other women over me. He loves the children over me.

Fern is quiet at last. Quite still as she lies in her cot looking like the perfect angel. I'd been frightened when I'd come up earlier to find her lying still. It was me who'd woken her, gently shaking her to make sure she was breathing. I'd been so emotional I'd obviously frightened her. It was no wonder she sobbed. She's settled now, though. Peaceful. 'I'm sorry, sweetheart,' I whisper, trailing the back of my hand over her soft cheek and then leaving the room quietly.

I hear Jake down in the kitchen, talking to Ellie, no doubt trying to gain her sympathy while he's ruined my life. How could he have been so hateful in front of my guests? His smashing of that figurine was symbolic. It was me he wanted to see broken into a thousand pieces. Doesn't he know that I am?

I won't let him do this to me. Though my feelings for Ellie are torn between fear and hatred, I won't let him do this to her either, someone who simply isn't strong enough to challenge him. Perhaps that's her attraction. I don't know. I do know the game has grown very dangerous. My hand going to the bruises on the back of my neck, I draw my phone from my pocket and play back the video I took from the landing after he forced me from the nursery. He could appear to be shaking Fern out of concern, I suppose. Equally, though, put together with his violence towards me – I've made sure to photograph the bruises on both my arm and my neck – it paints a very different picture of him, that of a violent man. After the smashing of the statue so publicly, the loud argument we had as our guests left, I suspect no one would doubt it should I have to use this against him.

Tucking my phone away, I go downstairs, pausing in the hall as I hear Jake and Ellie talking in the kitchen, Jake apologising for his abysmal treatment of her, his voice heart-wrenchingly sad.

'Don't, Jake. I really don't want to hear any more of your self-pitying bullshit,' Ellie warns him when he comes out with the classic *if things had been different*.

I watch as, looking considerably peeved, she struts from the kitchen, and my estimation of her shifts a little. Perhaps she's not so meek after all.

As I head in search of a much-needed drink, Jake appears,

also looking annoyed, presumably because things are not going quite as he planned. 'Why are you still doing this, Megan?' He grinds to a halt when he sees me.

'I have no idea what you're talking about,' I reply flatly. I won't let him see me upset – as if he would care anyway.

'For fuck's sake! I *know*!' He rakes a hand furiously through his hair. 'You *know* I do. Do you really expect me to go on with this bloody sham?'

Folding my arms across my chest, I study him dispassionately. 'You don't have any choice, do you, Jake? Thanks to you, we're destined to be together for ever. Best learn to live with it.'

'Doomed, more like.' He eyes me coldly. 'Does *he* know?' he asks.

I tip my head curiously to one side. 'About what you did?' I'm referring to Phoebe.

'You know damn well what I'm talking about.' He drags his gaze away.

I assume he's talking about his ridiculous notion that Fern isn't his. I study his face. He looks exhausted, haggard. He's hurting. But I am too. There's no way to fix this. No bandage that will stop the bleeding. The wounds we've inflicted on each other, on other people, are too deep.

'I need a drink.' Drawing in a breath, I head for the kitchen.

Jake swings around as I walk past him. 'I've had enough of this,' he mutters.

'So what are you going to do? Leave me?' I ask over my shoulder. 'You won't. You know you can't. Oh, and just for your information, I know about *you*, too.' Having glimpsed Ellie hovering on the landing, as she always is, I decide it's time she had the scales well and truly peeled from her eyes. She needs to walk away from him. For her sake, as well as my own, I need to make sure she does. 'You just can't help yourself, can you? Does it boost your ego, Jake, having poor unfortunate young women idolising you?' I ask him, my tone deliberately belittling. 'I can't quite see the attraction myself. She's improved her look, largely by copying mine, but she's quite a plain little thing, isn't she?'

I note Ellie stepping sharply back and consider I've made my point. Jake doesn't want her. He never has. He's used her. She needs to now realise that.

Jake replies after a beat. 'Beauty's only skin deep, though, isn't it, Megan?' he says caustically. 'Standing next to her, pound for pound, she's way more attractive than you could ever be.'

I really can't help but smile. Does he imagine she would regard that as a compliment? As her footsteps echo along the landing above and then across the nursery, I go to the fridge, extract a bottle of wine, pour a large glass and wait.

Jake soon follows me. 'Where's this going to end, Megan?' he asks, his tone almost conciliatory. '*How* is it?'

I glance at him. 'We could always bury the hatchet,' I suggest. 'Try to work out a way to live together.'

'What, here?' He glances bleakly out of the patio-facing window as thunder rumbles ominously overhead. 'For ever?'

'For ever isn't really that long, though, is it? Life's short, as we both know.'

He draws a hand over his neck, furrows his brow as if contemplating something. I've no idea what. Despite his threats, he knows he doesn't have any other option.

I wander to the island, take a sip of my drink, study him thoughtfully. He really does look exhausted, still handsome, but jaded. I almost feel sorry for him. But I simply can't afford to, not any more. This has to end. 'She's not quite as naïve as you think she is, you know,' I venture.

He looks at me, his expression distracted.

'She doesn't treat Fern that well,' I add, and wait.

He narrows his eyes in confusion. 'How so?'

I take another sip of my wine. 'Do you not wonder why Fern cries so much lately? You might think differently, but the fact that it coincides with Ellie being here can't have escaped your—'

A shrill scream from upstairs interrupts me, and my stomach turns over.

Alarmed, Jake snaps his gaze to me, then races to the hall.

Ice-cold dread pooling in the pit of my stomach, I fumble my phone from my pocket and follow him. Jagged lightning cracks the night sky as I reach the landing, thunder rumbling in its wake like a dark omen.

Approaching the nursery door, he pauses — no more than a brief second, long enough for me to see his shoulders tense. Then he pushes the handle down and thrusts the door open. 'What are you doing?' he asks, his voice hollow.

'She won't wake up,' Ellie cries from across the room. 'I can't make her wake *up*!'

As Jake stumbles forward, I jab 999 into my phone. 'Ambulance,' I murmur, my voice almost failing me, my legs trembling beneath me. 'My baby...'

Taking a step after him, I freeze. She has Fern. She's holding her clumsily, sobbing uncontrollably. Fern's head is flopping backwards. She's *hurting* her! But she's already hurt. My heart falters. I knew she was. As I climbed those stairs, adrenaline and terror driving me, I *knew*. I clutch the door frame as Jake strides across to Ellie, willing myself to go in, unable to make my legs function.

When he reaches her, he falters, and my heart almost stops beating. 'Give her to me,' he says gruffly, his voice filled with palpable horror.

Ellie only clutches her closer.

I move tremblingly forward, then stop, torn in half as I hear Ollie on the landing.

'Mummy,' he says tremulously, 'I'm frightened.'

My throat closes, and I waver, then whirl around to stop him coming in.

'I said *give* her to me!' Jake yells.

I gather Ollie to me, feel his small body trembling.

'*No.*' I hear Jake behind me, his voice that of a broken man. 'What did you do to her?'

'Nothing. I was j-just holding her,' Ellie stutters. 'Megan was in here. Earlier. She—'

'What the *fuck* did you *do* to her?' he screams.

My heart wrenches unbearably as he emits a primal cry that seems to come from the depths of his soul. Quickly I catch hold of Ollie's shoulders and usher him towards the stairs. 'It's all right, sweetheart. Mummy's here,' I try to reassure him, clutching his hand tightly to help him down. 'Everything will be all right, I promise.'

Lies! Lies! I scream inside. My chest booms as I hear sirens outside. Blue lights rotate, sweeping through the glass walls of the house, and I realise my call was still connected while I stood petrified with fear. Hurrying Ollie to the kitchen, I help him onto a stool at the island. 'Stay here. I won't be long.' I hold his gaze. I know he can see the tears in my eyes, hear Jake's heart-wrenching sobs, and his terrified expression almost breaks me.

Going to the front door, I yank it open as a police officer reaches it. 'Thank God.' My voice cracks and the tears come full force. 'My baby...' I choke the words out. 'She's hurt her. I think she's...' The officer lurches forward to catch me as my head reels and the floor undulates beneath me.

SIXTY

As I come through the door after visiting my baby's tiny grave, where I cried until I retched dry tears and couldn't cry any more, I gaze around our house made of glass. It was supposed to be our dream home. It turned into a nightmare. The fracture lines ripped through it even before the building works were fully completed. My solicitor assures me they'll return a guilty verdict. What satisfaction is there to be gained from that, though? Fern is gone. Nothing can bring her back. How much of this was Ellie's fault? I search my conscience as I stand where she stood on that fateful day she first came into my life, and I know the guilt is all mine. I colluded with Jake to bury our secrets. That's why we are where we are today.

Walking across the hall, I hear my sharp-heeled shoes clack against the marble floor. The noise irritates Jake. I'd like not to care, but I do. I care that his feelings for me are non-existent. There's no hope for us any more. I realised that long before my baby became a casualty. Still, though, I hoped. On the day I discovered him with Phoebe, all hope died. I still can't believe his insistence that there was no intimacy between them. Does he honestly think I'm that gullible? That I would believe she stripped naked and slipped into our bed in the hope of... What? Seducing him? It's preposterous. He knows it is, yet still he lies. Even then, a small part of me still loved him, craved his love in return. I was delusional. We were broken beyond repair that day. Nothing left thereafter but anger, guilt and despair.

Going upstairs, I breathe in sharply as I reach the top. It's impossible, I know it is, yet I hear my baby's plaintive cries echoing along the landing. I'm sure that if I venture into the nursery, the cot will be rocking; that if I go across to it, she will be there, her sparkling blue eyes, so like Jake's, filled with accusation as she looks up at me. As I attempt to go past the room, I falter and turn to the door. 'I'm sorry, sweetheart,' I whisper, pressing my forehead against it. 'So sorry.' I choke back the sob constricting my throat and allow my tears to fall. *What have I done?*

As I stand there, I hear her musical mobile playing hauntingly, beckoning me, and I press the heels of my hands hard to my ears. *It's not there! You're imagining it.* I feel a sharp stab of pain as I recall how Jake tried to convince me while I was carrying Fern that what he was already doing with Phoebe was all in my mind, and try desperately to block it out. I can't block out the ghost of my baby, though. The essence of her. I loved her. I did. I don't know why I couldn't express it. Yet I do know. I didn't deserve the pure, untainted love of an innocent child. Her absolute trust in me. I didn't feel worthy.

I miss her, so much I can't breathe, can't eat, can't sleep. It feels as if part of my heart has died with her. How am I to allow myself to grieve, though, when I was so ready to scar her for life by taking my own? She was barely a week old, so tiny, so fragile, so in need of someone to protect her. Jake found me before the oblivion I craved claimed me. When I woke in the intensive care unit, he was staring down at me, his ice-blue irises drilling into mine, seething with anger, and something else. Fear. 'Why did you *do* it?' he grated, his face inches from mine. He wasn't talking about my attempt on my life, I knew. He was talking about what had happened when my fury exploded. As I studied him, unable to speak with the breathing tube scraping against my larynx, I realised that he truly didn't understand the depth of the hurt he'd caused me.

He came to see me again once I was moved to a ward. 'Okay?' he asked as he arrived at my bedside, his eyes scrutinising me warily.

I looked away. I wasn't okay. I was terrified, angry and lonely, and so ashamed.

He pulled up a chair and took hold of my hand, a frown creasing his brow as he trailed a thumb over my knuckles. 'What's done is done, Megan. We can't change it,' he said, his voice strained, his eyes full of sincerity as they found mine. 'We have to think of our future now, our children's future; be there for each other and move on from this together.'

I stared at him, incredulous. *How?* I wanted to ask him. How did one move on from something like this?

'I can't do this without you, Meg,' he went on emotionally. 'I need you.'

He wasn't lying, I realised. He'd thought about it, hadn't he? He'd realised he needed to be with me, to keep a watch over me, but he didn't care for me. He didn't love me. With the trust between us eroded, he was trapped. As was I. We were glued together, just as I'd hoped we would be when I'd discovered I was pregnant. Such an irony.

The thought sobers me and I work to gain control of my emotions. I made up my mind while lying in the hospital that I had to be stronger. I have to stay strong. In bringing Ellie home, he thought he could drive me to that desolate place of hopelessness again. He was wrong.

Steeling myself, I go to the spare room and push the door open. It reeks of Ellie, the J'Adore she drenched herself in. Walking across to the window, I thrust it open, then go to the wardrobe, where I take a breath and extract the key from my pocket. Ellie was plainly perturbed by the fact that it was locked, hence the call to her boyfriend, obviously made in a fit of pique after Jake's treatment of her. I can't help feeling for her. I felt for her the night young Zachary died, despite being aware of her intimacy with my husband. Knowing she was about to receive the news about the tragic accident, I tried to look after her.

The squeal of brakes as his car veered towards me scrapes through my skull, and I try to shake it off. I know I can't, though. It will always be with me, just as surely as Fern's cries will. Why did I leave him? Why did I stand frozen in the road, my ability to function seeming to have deserted me?

I see Jake looking steadily into my eyes as he asks me if I'm okay to drive. 'You're in shock,' he says as I stare at him, trying to comprehend where I am. 'You'll be okay,' he assures me. I still don't remember climbing into the car, the drive to the PCs Plus car park.

Pulling myself back to the present, I insert the key into the wardrobe and open the doors. A different, yet familiar scent invades my nostrils, making me feel immediately queasy. Taking a shallow breath, I reach to extract my Olivia von Halle slip dress, the dress Phoebe borrowed without asking, the dress she was desperately trying to hide her nakedness with. With its spaghetti straps and low back, it would have suited her. It's certainly a cut above the skimpy, provocative clothing she normally wore, which I have no doubt was to attract Jake's attention.

Her perfume's all over it, the dark stains that bled into the cream silk standing out starkly. Walking across to the bed, I place it there for disposal, then go back to the wardrobe. Running my hand along the top shelf, I retrieve the PCs Plus identity tag she left on the dressing table and gaze at her photo with a mixture of anger and sorrow for all she suffered because of Jake. She was an attractive young woman. With her lustrous dark hair tumbling over her shoulders, she's smiling prettily for the camera. I can see the attraction. I saw it the second Jake brought her here.

Why did he do it? While I was *pregnant*? I guess now it was because he truly did believe Fern wasn't his. Why did he cheat on me that first time? With my father withdrawing the funding he'd promised him, he only had my love to lose then, I suppose, which obviously wasn't worth very much. With Phoebe, he was risking everything: his business – which had been funded by me and which I had majority shares in – his opulent lifestyle, the image that went with that lifestyle. Why do it all over again with Ellie when there was so much more at stake: our future, our lives? It was orchestrated. It had to have been. He thought I was weak. Because I'd made an attempt on my life, he imagined I would do it again. He wanted to destroy me. I will *never* give him that.

SIXTY-ONE

As I push the items I should have disposed of months ago into a bin bag to take to the waste disposal site, I hear Jake come through the front door, back early from work for some reason. He doesn't speak. With Ollie at a childminder's of my own choosing, an older, mumsy-type woman with all the right credentials, he has no reason to. He has nothing to say to me. We have nothing to say to each other. There are no arguments left we haven't had. No more barbed words we can wound each other with.

My heart sinks and hardens all at once. This existence is no existence, but he could at least acknowledge me. He's not the only one who's broken and hurting; stuffed so full of guilt it's impossible to breathe. Tying the handles of the bin bag together, I carry it to the front door. I'm about to inform him that I'll be back soon, but then wonder what the point is. He won't answer.

Yanking the door open, I step outside, then stop. *I can't do this any more.* I inhale sharply, then curse furiously as hot tears of frustration and hopelessness explode to roll down my cheeks. Swallowing hard, I look to the sky, a bright, dazzling summer blue sky. It reminds me so much of Fern's beautiful eyes, I feel another part of me die inside.

I breathe deeply, trying to compose myself, then drop the bag and whirl around to go back inside. I pause at the foot of the stairs to scrub the tears from my face and summon up my courage. I have to talk to him. We have to find a way forward if we're to stay together here in this house.

He's in the bedroom, his back to me, clearly about to go and shower. I hesitate at the open door. He has a good body, toned. As my eyes rove over his torso, I feel a familiar tug in the pit of my stomach. The physical contact between us dwindled once Phoebe had moved into our lives. I could feel the electricity between them immediately. I tried to convince myself I was being neurotic based on my own insecurity. The fact was, though, she was beautiful, unflawed by childbirth or age, fond of walking around in shorts and T-shirts or tight yoga leggings, though I'd never seen her doing yoga. How was I to compete with that?

The first argument Jake and I had after she arrived was when I insisted on keeping the lights off while we made love. I see him now, laughing, but not unkindly, more in bemusement. 'Why?' he wanted to know. 'You've never worried about that before.' He sighed, disbelieving and angry when I told him. 'Christ, what is it with your obsession about my fancying Phoebe?' he asked, sounding completely exasperated. 'I *don't*. She's our childminder, for God's sake. It really is all in your mind.'

Of course that was the catalyst for a full-scale row, all with Phoebe in earshot – the spare room in the old house was closer to the main bedroom. It was *him* who'd damaged my self-esteem, I told him. *Him* who'd made me so body-conscious. The row escalated. We didn't make love that night. Our lovemaking thereafter was sporadic. I felt so bloody lonely.

Bracing myself, I step into the bedroom. I'm surprised when

I see Jake reach for his jeans and sweatshirt. 'Are you not showering?' I ask as he tugs them on.

'Not now, no.' He turns to the wardrobe, and I feel my heart miss a beat.

'Are you going on a work trip?' I look at the open suitcase lying on the bed.

He shakes his head and walks back with several work shirts.

An icy chill of apprehension ripples through me. 'So why are you packing?'

He goes to the chest of drawers, extracting underwear and T-shirts. He doesn't answer.

'Jake!' My heart palpitating like a terrified bird in my chest, I demand his attention.

He slams the drawer shut. Walks back to the bed. Dumps everything in the case. 'I'm leaving,' he says shortly.

My heart stops dead. 'But you can't.' I stare at him, uncomprehending.

'Can't I?' He looks at me, the merest glance, then goes to the bathroom.

My stomach turns over. Nausea rising hotly inside me, sweat prickling my skin, I follow him. 'You know you can't.' My mouth is dry as I watch him collecting his toiletries.

He walks back to where I'm standing at the open door, a challenge in his eyes as he holds mine. 'I think you'll find I can,' he says coldly, and steps forward.

With no choice but to, I move aside, then spin around after him as he goes back to the case. 'I'll call the police,' I warn him, my voice tremulous.

He drops his stuff into the case. 'Do it,' he says, slamming the lid shut and picking the case up.

'I will.' I follow him to the door. 'I swear I will.'

He stops. 'Will you, Megan? I mean, really?' His tone is derisive as he glances back at me. 'Because you know something, I actually don't think you will.'

'You're calling my bluff!' I go after him to the landing. 'Do you think I don't know that? It's a mistake, Jake. I'm warning you, I'll do it! I swear to God I will.'

'I'll take my chances,' he throws back, and carries on down. 'Be careful on those stairs. They're bloody lethal,' he adds acerbically as I race after him to the front door.

'Jake!' I follow him outside. 'Don't you dare leave me! Don't you *dare*.'

He doesn't answer, climbing into his car and slamming the door as I reach it. His look is one of sheer contempt as he reverses, the wheels churning up gravel.

Watching him drive away, my chest pounds. He can't do this. He can't leave me on my own with all of this. He *can't*.

Trembling, shocked to the core, I turn bewildered back to the house – and freeze. It's not there. The bin bag I dropped outside the front door is gone.

Sick panic grips me and I race back inside, flying up the stairs to our bedroom to yank my sock drawer open. It's not there, the bank card I hid. It was tucked in a sock, the sock rolled up with its pair. Might Ellie have found it while snooping? No. Fear crackles through me like ice. *He* has.

SIXTY-TWO

I call him on his mobile. He doesn't answer. My hands shaking so badly I can barely hold the phone, I try his office. My heart thuds manically against my ribcage as I wait for Janine to pick up. She does, eventually. 'PCs Plus Peripherals, Janine speaking. How can I—'

'Janine, hi. It's Megan.' Working to keep my voice even, I stop her. 'Is Jake there? I need to have a quick word with him.'

'Hi, Megan. No, sorry. He's out at one of the other shops, I think. I'm not quite sure when he'll be back. Do you want me to give him a message?'

'No, don't worry,' I reply brightly, and force myself to breathe. 'You couldn't let me have Katherine Tyler's address, could you? Jake asked me to pop something in the post to her, but he forgot to leave her details. Typical.'

'Oh, right.' Janine sounds put out. She's clearly wondering why he wouldn't have asked her, since she's his capable personal assistant. 'Kat's actually in today.' She recovers herself. 'If you hang on, I'll go and fetch her.'

'No, don't bother,' I say quickly. 'I have a taxi here to take me to the cemetery,' I lie, my throat closing as I imagine my baby's tiny body lying in its impossibly small coffin, so lonely, so cold.

'I'll grab it now,' Janine says, her own voice catching, and my guilt weighs so heavily in my chest I don't think I can bear it.

I try Jake again as I drive. After Ellie was released on bail, my solicitor said she would be staying with a friend. She couldn't disclose where, of course, although I asked, imagining Jake might be privy to the information. I saw this Katherine comforting Ellie at Zachary's funeral, though. It occurred to me then that she appeared to be the only close friend Ellie had, and I'm assuming, praying, that this is who she's staying with.

Once I arrive at the address, which appears to be a ground-floor flat in a terraced house, I park a little way down the road and then hesitate before climbing out. Is Ellie likely to want to see me? I think not. I certainly wouldn't if I were her. Checking my watch and noting that it's office closing time, I decide to wait in the car, hoping that Katherine will come straight back from work. I try Jake again as I do. He's still not answering his phone. Doesn't reply to my frantic messages or texts. He has the bin bag. It could only have been him who took it. He obviously discovered the bank card and took that too. A mixture of fury and fear churns inside me. I have to stop him.

At last I see Katherine walking along the road. Quickly I push my door open and climb out. 'Katherine,' I call, hurrying towards her.

She squints in surprise, then, 'You shouldn't be here,' she says, attempting to walk around me.

'Katherine, please...' I move to stop her. 'I'm not here to upset Ellie, I promise you. I just need to talk to her.'

'She won't want to see you,' she states flatly.

'Could you ask her?' I look at her pleadingly. 'Could you tell her I have some information that might help her?'

She eyes me suspiciously. I'm not surprised. Ellie's undoubtedly told her how vile I was to her. 'What information?'

I take a breath. 'I can't share it with you. It may have to be used as evidence. I really do need to talk to Ellie. I'm only here to help her, I swear.'

Katherine gives me a long, searching look and I pray she can see I'm sincere. 'You can ask her yourself,' she says after a moment, and nods past me.

My nerves churn violently as I turn to see Ellie standing outside the house. Her arms are folded across her chest, her expression hard. I guess she'll be hostile. She has every right to be, but I pray she will listen to me.

I brace myself and walk towards her. Far from hostile, she looks wary as I approach her, wary and scared. With her face make-up-free and pale, and her hair scraped into a band, she's back to the timid little mouse she was.

'How are you?' I ask.

It's there then, the burning anger I expected to see in her eyes. She doesn't answer me. She's waiting to see why I would come here, whether it's to lay blame and rub salt into her wounds.

'I need to talk to you, Ellie,' I steel myself to go on. I need to try to convince her I'm not here for my own ends. 'You don't have to answer me if you don't want to, but I hope you'll hear me out.'

She scans my eyes, then, 'It's okay, Kat,' she says, turning to lead the way inside.

I follow her through the door, Katherine close behind us. As we go into the flat, Katherine stops me. 'I'll give you some space,' she says. 'But I'll only be outside in the garden.'

Hearing that as a subtle warning, I nod. It's good that Ellie has her as a friend. She certainly needs one.

Ellie's sitting on the sofa when I turn around. Knotting and unknotting her fingers in her lap, she keeps her gaze fixed firmly down. I sit in the only other chair, opposite her.

'How are you?' I ask again, stupidly. She only drops her

gaze further. 'I really do need to talk to you, Ellie. Whatever you did, you don't deserve to go to prison.' I keep my tone soft, choosing my words carefully. 'To have the rest of your life stolen away from you.'

She meets my gaze briefly, her expression a combination of curiosity and caution.

I press on. 'Jake, though, he does. I believe he was responsible for what happened to Fern. He's killed before.'

SIXTY-THREE

Ellie looks sharply up, then away again. She's reluctant to implicate him. Of course she would be. In her naïvety, she might even believe she's willing to spend the best part of her life in prison to save him. Does she imagine he would do the same for her? That he cares for her? That he will come and see her? She's had so much harsh experience in life, yet none when it comes to relationships and the games people play.

'You saw it, didn't you? Jake's car?' I ask carefully. 'The damage to the bumper?'

This time she holds my gaze. Her eyes, rapidly scanning mine, are awash with conflicting emotion.

'He ran your boyfriend off the road,' I say with a suitable mixture of forcefulness and sympathy. 'It was Jake who was responsible for what happened to Zachary.'

Her pupils grow wide and I wait while she processes, her expression one of shock and doubt. Finally, 'I don't believe you,' she says with a spark of defiance.

'It's true, Ellie,' I go on determinedly. 'I'm not lying to you. I don't know whether it was planned or whether it was a spur-of-the-moment thing. I don't believe it was an accident, though.'

Tears spring to her eyes. 'But I don't understand,' she murmurs, stunned. 'Why would he do something like that?'

'I can't be sure.' I frown in feigned confusion. 'My guess is he was scared Zachary would take you away from him.' It's a lie, obviously, but it's what she wants to hear.

She wipes at the tears spilling down her cheeks.

I press on. 'You have to believe me, Ellie. I would never have told you this, but I'm scared. Truly I am. Not just for myself, but for Ollie.'

'Ollie?' She looks alarmed.

I can see she's concerned. She cares for Ollie. That much is obvious. 'I don't believe you did what you've been accused of,' I say firmly. 'I was confused at first, deeply shocked, as you can imagine, but I don't believe it. I didn't want to think that Jake was responsible. I tried to tell myself he wasn't. I can't lie to myself any more, though.'

Ellie is studying me hard. How can she believe all of this of the man who presented such a caring persona? The man she's in love with. No, she doesn't want to believe it, yet she does. She's sensing this might be a lifeline for her.

'He was jealous,' I plough on, dangling that lifeline, feeding her untruths that, because of her shattered self-esteem, she will want to believe. 'You must have realised how possessive he is. He might do it subtly, but he's a driven man who goes for what he wants, in both business and pleasure. He can't bear to lose his toys, don't you see? He couldn't bear the thought of losing me, even though he didn't love me, even though he'd had numerous affairs.'

She looks dubious.

'He slept with Phoebe.' I force the point home. 'He even kept some of her things. I don't know why he would do that, other than to hurt me.'

She averts her gaze, and I see the wheels going round. She's thinking of that phone call. The fateful last call she had with

Zachary. The call she must have suspected Jake had overheard when she found him outside the spare room.

'Did he spin you the same line he did her?' I crease my brow in sympathy. 'Tell you that I was the one who was cheating? About which, of course, he was devastated. I wasn't, Ellie. You've no reason to believe me, but it's the truth. He didn't believe me either. He thought Fern wasn't his.' I swallow emotionally. 'There was nothing I could say to convince him otherwise.'

She sits in silence for a while, her face deathly pale. Then, 'He told me,' she says. I can see from her distraught expression that she's reluctant to believe it. 'When Miguel came to your dinner party, Jake went upstairs to Fern. He was looking at her really strangely and he asked me if I thought she looked like him.' She glances away again, as if recalling, then snaps her gaze back to me. 'Do you think that's why...?' She stops, her expression one of dawning realisation.

I nod and press my hands to my face. 'I need to show you something.' Drawing in a tremulous breath, I bring my phone from my pocket, select the video of Jake and hand it to her.

She studies it for a long, silent moment.

'You have to help me, Ellie.' I gaze pleadingly at her as she looks up, her face horrified. 'You have to help yourself.'

'How?' She chokes the word out. Her emotions are torn, as obviously they would be.

'I'm not sure. I wondered...' I hesitate. I don't want to accuse her. 'Did you see anything? Or find anything, perhaps? In the house, anything at all that might incriminate him?'

She bows her head. Nods after a second. 'Phoebe's passport,' she admits, her voice small. 'I found it.'

SIXTY-FOUR

I'm disorientated as I drive home. My life has unravelled around me, my baby lost to me before I'd realised how much I loved her. Acrid grief crashes through me as I picture her beautiful blue eyes constantly searching mine, as if looking for confirmation of my feelings. My career, which I need so desperately to maintain my sanity, is in jeopardy. I have no association with Michael now. He betrayed me too, ignoring me when I so needed him not to. He clearly prefers Carly Simons' company to mine. And Jake wanted his freedom so badly he tried to kill me. My heart twists excruciatingly. He looked genuinely horrified when he' thought I was accusing him of feeding me those tablets, but he has been. I know he has. He would say that my moods are erratic without them. He *has* said that, telling me they swing so violently sometimes it terrifies him, that he has no idea what I might do, no idea whether I know what I'm doing.

I recall what he said the day I found him with Phoebe. The hairs rise on my skin as I feel his arms around me, feeling secure in them just for the briefest of moments. Then petrified when he whispers, 'You lost control,' and presses a soft kiss to my forehead.

The sharp blast of a horn jars me, and I realise I'm straying across the road. *Concentrate*, I will myself. *You are strong.* I have to be. Jake hasn't managed to kill me or get me to do the job for him. Now he's using an unspoken threat to try to condemn me. But the game isn't over. I have the video. I've left a statement with the police. I'm confident it will be enough to get them to take action. I would give anything to see Jake's face when they locate him and arrest him. And I'm sure they will. He can run, but he can't hide. If he pushes me, I also have the passport, handled not by me, but by *him*.

But what of Ollie? He didn't smile as I crouched to give him a hug before leaving him at school this morning. He hasn't smiled in a long time. He's bewildered by all that's happened, clearly missing Ellie. I need to be there for him, much more than I have been. He needs a constant in his life, not childminders, or a father who would abandon him. He needs me, his mummy.

As I approach the house, I'm annoyed to find a works vehicle parked in the lane. It's obviously there to carry out some kind of road or water maintenance, judging by the digging equipment and hoses on the back of it. They might have informed me, I think, tense and irritated as I negotiate my way around it; I might have had visitors who needed to access the drive. My chest constricts as I'm reminded of the dreadful dinner party that ended with Fern's short life being snatched away. Jake's the one to blame, without doubt. It would never have happened if not for him. He will get his just punishment; his freedom will be snatched away too. He won't fare well in prison. Child killers don't, I've heard, with punishment meted out by inmates who abhor them. Ellie is guilty of no more than being coerced by him. Her punishment will be to live with her conscience for the rest of her life.

As I reach the end of the drive, I'm shocked to see two police cars parked on the opposite side of the island that houses the water feature. Trepidation twists inside me. Have they already issued a warrant for his arrest? But surely it's too soon. And I told them they wouldn't find him here, that he's left.

Parking my car, I climb out. I'm perplexed to find there's no sign of the actual officers. Grateful that Ollie isn't with me to be further destabilised by all of this, I unlock the front door. Once inside, I head straight for the lounge area. Icy apprehension ripples through me as I realise the patio doors are open. Hesitantly I approach them, and my heart booms out a warning as my eyes fall on Jake. His hands thrust deep into his pockets, he's standing at the side of the pool, staring down into it.

My eyes pivot towards the gaping hole and the excavation under way at the bottom of it, and my heart freezes. *It wasn't me.* I reel and gasp to draw breath. 'It wasn't *me.*' Snatching my gaze away from the broken tiles, the mud and the grey flesh of the limb that protrudes from it, I meet Jake's gaze. There's no glint of malice in his eyes, no hint of triumph. No simmering fury or burning hatred. There's nothing. He looks completely impassive.

'It was him!' I explode.

As I stumble backwards, an officer begins reading me my rights. 'Megan Harington, I am legally obliged to inform you that I am arresting you for the murder of Phoebe Anderson. You do not have to say anything, but—'

'I didn't *do* this. He did.' I point tremblingly at Jake, take another step back, only to realise a second officer is standing behind me.

Jake tips his head to one side, regards me coolly. 'I wasn't here when the pool was filled in, though, was I, Megan?' he points out. 'I was at a conference in Bristol.'

Liar. My blood turns to ice in my veins and I look at him in stunned disbelief. He wasn't here when the concrete was poured. He *was* here when the foundations went in, when the soil was being churned. *He* churned it.

Panic spiralling inside me, I struggle in vain to pull away as my arms are drawn behind me, cold metal snapping over my wrists. 'He's *lying,*' I cry.

'You do not have to say anything,' the officer goes on, 'but it may harm your defence if you do not mention when questioned something which you later rely on in court. Anything you do say—'

'He's lying! How did he know where she was? Ask him that. How did you *know?*' I glance feverishly from the officer to Jake.

His gaze doesn't falter. 'This is the house you built, Megan,' he replies smoothly. 'You oversaw the entire process. It didn't take me long to work out what you'd done, once I found the identity tag you were trying to dispose of, along with the dress with Phoebe's blood all over it.'

'He's lying!' I scream the words.

Jake surveys me coldly. 'It's over, Megan,' he says, his tone dispassionate. 'I've told them everything. About your obsession with Phoebe, your insane accusations about me having an affair with her. You killed her, Megan. For Christ's sake, own up to what you did and give her mother some closure.'

'I didn't mean to,' I murmur, terror twisting inside me. 'I d-don't remember what I did, but I didn't mean it. I swear I didn't.' I look imploringly at the police officer. 'Jake?' I appeal shakily to him. His eyes are as hard as steel.

Nausea burns my throat and I look away, my gaze travelling to where the deep end of the pool should be. Phoebe is there. She's always there, the ghost of her treading silently in my footsteps. She whispers through my dreams. I see her when I'm wide awake, watching me. Across the playground, across a busy street, she stands there silent, accusing, whispering, *Set me free.*

I see her now, her startled face as she spots me in the bedroom doorway. She blunders out of the bed, her eyes darting wildly around as she scrambles for her clothes. I watch as she struggles into my Olivia von Halle dress. She's perfect, I acknowledge. More perfect than I could ever be, before or after pregnancy. Even stricken with fear at what I might do, her face is beautiful, sensual lips that beg to be kissed, eyes the colour of bittersweet chocolate peering through a tangle of glistening raven hair. 'Nothing happened. Jake wasn't with me,' she whispers fearfully as, keeping her back to the door frame, she slides past me. That's the lie that sparks the blind fury that consumes me.

I don't remember catching up with her on the landing. There's nothing until Jake's voice reaches me. He's standing in front of me, gently opening my curled fingers, removing the tendrils of raven hair that lie in the palm of my hand. He scans my eyes, his own flecked with fear, circles his arms around me and whispers, 'You lost control.'

He kisses my forehead, eases me close. I look over his shoulder. Phoebe lies at the foot of the stairs, her beautiful hair splayed about her, her lifeblood flowering beneath her, staining the tiles crimson.

He loves me. He wants to be with me. Phoebe is whispering right beside me. But she can't be. It's all in my mind. Isn't it?

'Anything you do say may be given in evidence,' the officer finishes, and I flinch. 'You need to come with us, Megan,' she adds. Her tone is soft, sympathetic almost.

'It's not true.' I blink in confusion. 'Jake buried her. I have her passport. Ellie found it.'

I pause, look at Jake. He shakes his head. Clearly he thinks it isn't enough, compared to what he has. 'He killed Fern,' I say. I feel the tear that slides down my cheek. 'I have video evidence. He *killed* her. He killed my baby.'

SIXTY-FIVE

Jake

This wasn't supposed to happen. I didn't want this. Any of it. I didn't want to use Phoebe. It was the last thing I wanted to do. Megan just wasn't there. She wasn't there for me, or for Ollie. She wasn't there because she was with my brother. Did she imagine I didn't know? Of course she didn't. I bury a cynical laugh. It was some ridiculous tit-for-tat game and I desperately didn't want to play it. I'd tried to make it work, to make it up to her, but she had never forgiven me for the hurt and humiliation I'd caused her before we'd married. She changed, became wary of me. There was nothing I could say or do to make her see that it had been a horrible, drunken mistake; that I wasn't comparing her to some perfect, seductive woman I'd found too irresistible not to have sex with right before our wedding. I couldn't even remember what the bloody hell the woman looked like. I'd told her this until I was bone weary with the effort of trying to convince her. She didn't believe me. She simply refused to. In the end, when I realised it was futile, I just wanted her to go, to disappear with fucking *Miguel* and leave me alone. Why couldn't she have just done that?

I swallow back the sour taste in my throat, my chest heavy with guilt as I see Phoebe in my mind's eye, whole and beautiful in the flesh, sitting astride me. The look of ecstasy on her face in that sweet moment that I imagined would sustain me in a barren marriage. The shock as I tried to get her to stop screaming to Megan that it was her I loved, her I wanted to be with. The horror as she flailed down the stairs. Brief puzzlement as she landed. And then, for an instant, sheer unadulterated terror before the light faded from her eyes. Why couldn't she just have kept quiet? I didn't want to leave my marriage for her. I still hoped. I desperately didn't want to leave Ollie.

She tore my shirt. As we made our way to the bedroom, lust driving us, she yanked it open. There was a button missing. I noticed it when I went back to the spare room to shove Phoebe's things in the wardrobe and peel the shirt from my body. It was wet through with mud and I pushed it into the waste disposal. I scoured the bedroom for that button. Searched the patio and every corner and crevice of the house. I never found it. Will the police? I glance back to the deep hole in the ground as they lead me away and pray that they won't. All I ever wanted, the reason I stayed in a marriage that was bleeding me emotionally dry, was to be there for my son. To be the father I never had. Without me, Ollie will have no one.

As I'm guided into one of the police cars, I can feel Megan's eyes burning into me from where she sits in the back of the other. I don't look at her, dragging a hand over my eyes instead, trying to block out another graphic image: Phoebe, her lifeless eyes wide open and accusing. I begged her forgiveness as I reached to close them. The soil raining down on her, slowly obliterating her face, is an image I will never forget, one I don't deserve to. Megan's eyes, I see those too, wild, frenzied as she flew from the bedroom, following Phoebe to the landing.

She understood when I told there were no circumstances under which we could go to the police. *We have to think of the children*, I told her, placing a hand on her stomach, though it pained me then to acknowledge that the child she was carrying might not be mine. *We have to be here for them.*

Perhaps we should have remembered the adage 'People in glass houses shouldn't throw stones'; certainly not at each other, I think cynically as I'm driven away; certainly not within the walls that have become their self-imposed prison. The facade was bound to fracture eventually.

SIXTY-SIX

Megan

As I'm not yet charged with anything relating to Phoebe's death and I've given my evidence, I'm able to watch the rest of Jake's trial. He looks shell-shocked. I'm not sure he's able to believe that it was Ellie who damned him. Her statement confirming how shocked he'd been realising that dear Fern wasn't his, combined with my own account of what happened both during our marriage and around Fern's death had been enough for the police to charge him. He's currently being questioned about his relationship with Ellie. It will be interesting to watch him try to lie his way out of his involvement with her, as he tried to lie his way out of his involvement with Phoebe.

'Were you aware of Miss Taylor's history, Mr Harington?' The defence barrister, a deceptively pleasant-faced woman with sharp grey eyes, gazes compassionately at him as she waits for him to respond. I've noticed she has a proclivity for subtle displays of emotion: a deeply furrowed brow as she processes some disturbing piece of information, her eyes filling at some particularly painful detail. I imagine she's a mother. And as a businesswoman in what is still largely a man's world, I also imagine she's using her guiles to get the jury onside. I can't help but admire her.

'At first, no.' Jake closes his eyes briefly. The circles beneath them have grown darker with each day of the trial.

'But you learned later that there were some worrying issues in regard to her employment at...' the barrister pauses, glancing down at her notes, 'Kiddie Cave Day Care?'

Jake answers with a tired nod. His complexion is as pale as alabaster, and with his unshaven face, which adds to his look of a man who's physically and emotionally exhausted, I have no doubt he's working to gain the sympathy of the jury.

'Could you answer out loud for the benefit of the court, Mr Harington?' she asks him.

'We did,' Jake obliges. 'That is, my wife did.'

I glance at Ellie, who's clearly taken aback by that revelation. Her eyes, which have been glued to Jake since he took the stand, are filled with bewildered disbelief.

'And are you able to share with the court what your wife learned, Mr Harington?'

Jake takes a shaky breath. 'We discovered that she, that Ellie...' He falters, pressing his thumb and forefinger to his forehead.

'Do you need a moment, Mr Harington?' the defence barrister asks.

'Mr Harington?' The judge turns to him, his look impassive.

Jake shakes his head. 'No. Thanks. I'm fine,' he says, and wipes a hand over his face.

'Your wife learned that Miss Taylor was responsible for an injury to a child, did she not?' the barrister goes on after a suitable pause.

'Objection,' the prosecution interjects. 'Inflammatory, Your Honour. Miss Taylor is not on trial here.'

'Sustained.' The judge casts the defence an admonishing glance.

The woman concedes the point with a polite nod. 'I'll rephrase, Your Honour,' she says, her mouth curving into a small conciliatory smile. 'Mr Harington, did you learn that Miss Taylor had left a child unattended?'

'Yes,' Jake answers.

'And did that child sustain a serious injury while unattended?'

'I gather so, yes,' he confirms.

The woman's brow knits into a confused frown. 'Yet still you continued to employ her?'

Jake hesitates before answering. 'We weighed the facts. My wife asked her about it.'

I glance again at Ellie. Her expression is now one of shock. I didn't ask her about it. I felt for her when I learned about the circumstances surrounding her brother's death. I truly did. I felt for her when she arrived at my house. She was young, naïve, unworldly – quite obviously already starstruck. She would never have imagined that Jake had a hidden agenda.

'And?' The woman urges Jake on.

He frowns, as if uncertain of the question.

'Can you tell the court what conclusion you reached based on the conversation Mrs Harington had with Miss Taylor?'

Jake nods. 'Ellie had apparently received a call regarding a family emergency and had to leave at short notice,' he provides.

'The emergency being an injury to her brother, Theo Taylor?' the barrister asks. 'A subdural haematoma that resulted in the child's unfortunate death.'

'Objection.' The prosecution lawyer is on his feet in an instant. 'Irrelevant, Your Honour.' The glance he shoots the defence is scathing. 'The question does not relate to the issues in the trial.'

'Sustained. Miss Simmons, please stick to the pertinent

facts.' The judge eyes the defence barrister despairingly, then turns to the jury with a sigh. 'The jury should disregard the improper question,' he instructs them.

'Your Honour.' Miss Simmons smiles in acquiescence. She's quietly confident, though, that her point has been made. 'Could you continue, Mr Harington?' She turns back to Jake. 'You were telling us why you deemed it safe to continue to employ Miss Taylor.'

'We believed her,' he says simply. 'She said the incident at the nursery was an accident. When she told us about her brother...' he pauses to glance at Ellie with a mixture of pity, concern and confusion. *Nice touch, Jake*, 'we decided to give her a chance.'

'Would you say you're a caring man, Mr Harington; that you care about Ellie Taylor?'

Again Jake hesitates. 'Yes,' he answers with another tight intake of breath.

'Mr Harington, your wife has told the court you had an affair with Miss Taylor. Is that true?'

'I...' Jake falters once more. 'Yes,' he says at length. His expression one of deep remorse, he drops his gaze.

'And would you agree that when Miss Taylor realised it was just that, an affair, and that you didn't want to be with her, that you were choosing your family over her, she decided to destroy that family?'

'Objection.' The prosecution barrister looks fit to implode. 'Your Honour, this calls for speculation. For the benefit of the jury, I would also like to emphasise that Miss Taylor is *not* the accused.'

The objection is sustained, but I doubt it will help Jake. Miss Simmons is doing her best to show him as a compassionate man; a man who's honest enough to admit his flaws. In reminding the jury that Fern's death was caused by the same injury that killed Ellie's brother, she's introducing a strong element of doubt. The video, though, I think will dispel that doubt adequately enough to drive the last nail into his coffin.

'No more questions, Your Honour.' Miss Simmons smiles again. She waits while Jake is escorted back to the dock. Then, 'Your Honour, if it pleases the court, the defence would like to call Mr Michael Harington.'

Michael? My heart catapults against my ribcage. *But how?* More to the point, *why* is he here? My gaze shoots to the prosecution lawyer, who looks as stunned as I am. 'I object, Your Honour,' he says, with a tight intake of breath, 'most strongly. No advance notice was served regarding this witness.'

'I think you'll find it was, Mr Barrows.' Miss Simmons glances towards him as he scrambles through his paperwork, and then to the judge. 'May we approach, Your Honour?'

Even sitting, I feel I might pass out as they quietly converse. When Michael comes into the courtroom, I feel the blood drain from my body.

I stop breathing when, after he's been sworn in and has stated his name, Miss Simmons asks her first question. 'Mr Harington, you were present at the dinner party organised by Mrs Megan Harington on the night of Fern Harington's unfortunate death, is that correct?'

'It is,' Michael answers.

She nods. 'And can you tell the court where you were at approximately nine thirty p.m.?'

'Yes.' He takes a deep breath. 'I was on the landing. I was showing a prospective client the layout of the property. The house was based on one of my designs.'

'And can you tell the court, to the best of your recollection, what you witnessed while on the landing?'

Michael's gaze flicks to Jake. 'We witnessed, that is, my client and I—'

'Objection,' the prosecution interjects. 'Calls for speculation. The witness cannot speak for someone else.'

'Sustained. Please bear witness only to you own observations, Mr Harington.'

Michael answers with a small nod. 'I observed Jake and Megan arguing,' he replies, and dread pools in the pit of my stomach. 'Jake appeared distressed.'

'Can you tell the court, in your opinion, why he appeared distressed?'

'I can. Fern was crying,' Michael obliges.

'Also distressed,' Miss Simmons asks quickly, 'in your opinion?'

'Very.' He takes another sharp breath.

'And Jake Harington was distressed for the child, was he not?'

I glance desperately at the prosecution barrister. He half rises as if about to interrupt, and then sinks down again.

'In my opinion, yes,' Michael confirms. 'Megan was insisting on taking Fern out. She said she was going to drive her around – to stop her crying, I assumed. Jake was adamant she wasn't going to because she'd been drinking. He said, and I quote, "You'll take that little girl out over my fucking dead body."'

Miss Simmons looks deeply perturbed. 'What was Megan Harington's response to that, Mr Harington?'

Please don't. I will him to look in my direction. To acknowledge me. To please not do this to me.

'She laughed,' he replies tightly. 'She said, "I wish."'

There's a deathly hush and I sense people's gazes angling sharply towards me. I don't dare move. Can't breathe. He's won. Michael has just helped Jake slot into place the last piece that will destroy me.

'And can you tell the court what happened next, Mr Harington?' Miss Simmons goes on, determinedly extracting every last detail with which to seal my fate.

Michael kneads his forehead. In that moment, he looks so

like his brother it's uncanny. Yet I thought he was different. That he truly cared for me. He didn't. He doesn't.

'Jake wanted Megan to give Fern to him,' he responds. He looks reluctant, but he has no choice, does he? I suppose he thinks blood is thicker than water. 'She wouldn't,' he goes on.

'And did Jake try to take the child from his wife?'

'No.' Michael shakes his head. 'Megan was holding onto her very tightly. Eventually he persuaded her to put her in her cot. Unfortunately...' he falters. His gaze when he finally looks at me is full of regret, 'she banged Fern's head on the rim of the cot as she did.'

The court is so quiet that for an agonising moment you might have heard the beat of a bird's wing.

'I moved away from the door as Megan stormed out. I wasn't sure what to do, to be honest.'

'And are you able to tell the court what happened next, Mr Harington? Take your time.'

Michael hesitates before answering. 'I went back to the nursery door,' he continues, his throat hoarse. 'Jake had picked Fern up. I could tell from his expression that he was scared for her, terrified actually. Fern appeared very still. He spoke to her. He sounded anguished. Eventually he shook her in his arms. She stirred. Cried a little. I've never seen him so relieved in his life.'

He's missed out how Jake persuaded me to put her in the cot. Fear settles like an icicle inside me as I realise it will make no difference. Everyone in that room will believe it was me who killed my child. Me who is guilty. I think I believe it too. In keeping her prisoner in our gilded cage made of glass, didn't I seal both our fates?

EPILOGUE

TWELVE MONTHS LATER

Ellie

Watching the last of the packing boxes being loaded onto the removal van, I feel an overwhelming sense of sadness. I could have lived here, but for the ghosts. The glass was fractured. I knew it as soon as I walked into the house.

As I turn away, I'm joined by Jake. 'Ready?' he asks me, smiling sadly.

I nod and reach for his hand.

He drops his gaze, trails his thumb over the back of my hand. After a second, he looks back at me, his expression one of cautious uncertainty. 'I didn't hurt Phoebe,' he says earnestly. 'Megan's claim that I allowed her to believe that she killed Phoebe, that I was gaslighting her,' he pauses, a look of confused bewilderment crossing his face, 'it's not true. You know that, don't you? I would never do something like that to a woman, let alone...'

As he trails off, clearly too emotional to speak the words, I squeeze his hand firmly. 'Of course I do,' I assure him. 'I have eyes, Jake. I saw what was happening. I *know* you. I love you.'

Relief floods his features. 'Me too,' he says, his voice gruff. Squeezing my hand back, he gives me another small smile, and together we walk towards his car where Ollie waits. I think Jake will be as glad as I am to see the back of the house. Of Megan, too. I didn't think the police would believe me when I told them about her, how she suffered from massive mood swings, how I'd worried that she was losing control. But once they'd looked into her medical history, learning of her depressive episode, which resulted in her suicide attempt, her GP's concern that she seemed unable to bond with her baby, they accepted that I was telling the truth. Michael confirming that he'd witnessed Megan's irrational behaviour, her banging Fern's head against the cot, cleared Jake, thank goodness. When I'd told the police how devastated Jake was when he acknowledged that Fern wasn't his, I was trying to make them see that he'd loved and cared for her despite his doubts. That he was a good man. It had backfired when Megan told her lies, swearing that he was the last one to see Fern alive. Her lies had been exposed, though. In regard to Phoebe, too. Jake was nowhere near the house when the pool had been filled in – he had witnesses to prove it. When the house had been searched forensically, they'd found a strand of Phoebe's hair, secreted in an envelope and pushed to the back of the top shelf in the locked wardrobe. Microscopic evidence had shown it had been forcibly removed. Megan's DNA on the envelope – DNA that she'd accused Jake of planting there – had finally convinced the police to charge her. She'd obviously killed Phoebe in a fit of jealous rage. They had no doubt concluded that she was a very sick individual.

Jake was heartbroken. He admitted that he'd cared for Megan, probably always would, that he'd felt so responsible for her that he could never have contemplated leaving her. I understood that. He was fundamentally a caring man. He would never have done what Megan had also accused him of. She'd said he hated her, that he was trying to drive her out of her mind. What rubbish. Jake isn't capable of hating anyone. He certainly didn't hate her. Aside from the fact that he'd done everything in his power to keep their marriage together, put up with so much hatred and vitriol hurled at him, one only had to see his anguished expression, the tears he'd wiped from his cheeks as she'd made her ridiculous accusations, to realise that. She was undoubtedly unhinged but not because of anything Jake had done. She still has the ordeal of the summing up and sentencing to come. She was charged with diminished responsibility manslaughter, which can carry up to a twenty-four-year custodial sentence. That's going to be hard on Jake, on little Ollie, but I will be there for them. I'd made sure to provide the police with any information they needed, confirming how scared Jake was for Megan – *of* her at times. How I overheard him on several occasions asking her if she'd had any word from Phoebe. I'd told him about the bank card I'd found. When I handed it to him and he read Phoebe's name on it, he was almost overwhelmed. 'We'd best hand it to the police,' he said, taking a ragged breath.

I studied him as he ran a hand over his face, clearly upset – for Megan. 'But you've handled it now,' I pointed out – his fingerprints would be all over it.

I didn't mention the shirt button. I'm not sure why, but something compels me to keep it. It's a reminder, I think, of how one tiny thread when pulled can unravel everything.

I know he mourns the loss of Fern, but in a way I think I've done him a favour by taking the source of his torture away. I didn't mean to. I squeezed her small body too close, too tightly. I just wanted to comfort her. I wish I could tell him, unburden myself of my guilt. It won't help him, though. This is a chapter in my life, Jake's life, best put behind us. At least now the ghosts will be buried and Jake and I can move on together.

I place my free hand on my growing tummy as we drive

away. I won't be so careless with my baby. I won't be employing a childminder. I intend to stay at home with her, to be a good wife to Jake. He's grateful, I think, for his freedom. Freedom to be with me. We work well together. I'm confident he will have no need to stray.

A LETTER FROM SHERYL

Dear Reader,

Thank you so much for choosing to read *We All Keep Secrets*. I really hope you enjoy reading it as much as I enjoyed writing it. If you would like to keep up to date with my new releases, please do sign up at the link below, where you can grab my FREE short story, 'The Ceremony'.

www.bookouture.com/sheryl-browne

I think we're all aware of how fragile trust is, something that is easily broken within a relationship by secrets and lies. The longer a secret is kept, the bigger the lie grows, until the consequences might be catastrophic. *We All Keep Secrets* – rarely do we reveal everything about ourselves or all that we might think or feel about the person we share a relationship with. A single untruth or betrayal can whittle away at that relationship, eventually eroding all trust. More than that, though, lies can eat away at the self-esteem of the person on the receiving end of them. Perhaps they should walk away. So often, though, a person will try to change themselves, pushing themselves to look better, be better, in order to win back the attention or approval of the person who's lied or perhaps cheated on them. She, or he, becomes the giver, the 'liar' becomes the taker, and we have the classic symptoms of a co-dependent relationship.

We All Keep Secrets looks at such a situation, a toxic relationship damaged at the outset by betrayal; at the person on the receiving end of the lie and the shame of the person who told it. They're a dysfunctional couple. They should call it a day and walk away. What happens if they can't, though, if the betrayal that might have been fixed with forgiveness and understanding never is, growing eventually into a much bigger, darker secret that forces them into co-dependency and sucks in the people around them. How far will they go to keep that secret? Who is the giver? Who is the taker? Who's guilty? I'll leave you, the reader, to judge.

As I pen this last section of the book, I would like to thank those people around me who are always there to offer support, those people who believed in me even when I didn't quite believe in myself. To all of you, thank you.

If you have enjoyed the book, I would love it if you could share your thoughts and write a brief review. Reviews mean the world to an author and will help a book find its wings. I would also love to hear from you via social media or my website.

Happy reading, all!

Sheryl x

www.sherylbrowne.com

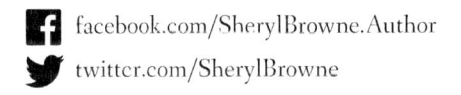

facebook.com/SherylBrowne.Author
twitter.com/SherylBrowne

ACKNOWLEDGEMENTS

As always, heartfelt thanks to the fabulous team at Bookouture, whose support of their authors is amazing. Special thanks to Helen Jenner and her wonderful editorial team, who work so hard to make my books shine. Huge thanks also to the fantastic publicity team. Thanks, guys, I think it's safe to say I could not do this without all of you. To the other authors at Bookouture, thank you for being such a super-supportive group of people.

I owe a huge debt of gratitude to all the fantastically hard-working bloggers and reviewers who have taken time to read and review my books and shout them out to the world. It's truly so appreciated. Thanks to all of you, *We All Have Secrets* is my fourteenth psychological thriller with Bookouture. Unbelievable!

Final thanks to every single reader out there for buying and reading my books. Knowing you have enjoyed my stories and care enough about the characters to want to share them with other readers is the best incentive ever for me to keep writing.

Printed in Great Britain
by Amazon